Men in Blue

Congratulations on Being Single!!

♡ Jessie + Mom

Men in Blue

Devyn Quinn
Myla Jackson
Delta Dupree

APHRODISIA

KENSINGTON BOOKS
http://www.kensingtonbooks.com

APHRODISIA BOOKS are published by

Kensington Publishing Corp.
119 West 40th Street
New York, NY 10018

All Kensington Titles, Imprints, and Distributed Lines are available at special quantity discounts for bulk purchases for sales promotions, premiums, fund-raising, and educational or institutional use.

Special book excerpts or customized printings can also be created to fit specific needs. For details, write or phone the office of the Kensington special sales manager: Kensington Publishing Corp., 119 West 40th Street, New York, NY 10018, attn: Special Sales Department, Phone: 1-800-221-2647.

ISBN-13: 978-0-7582-3797-2
ISBN-10: 0-7582-3797-9

First Kensington Trade Paperback Printing: August 2009

10 9 8 7 6 5 4 3 2 1

Printed in the United States of America

Contents

THE HARD WAY

Devyn Quinn

1

A warm female body pressed against his, jostling Drew Hardage out of the lethargic daze that usually followed a long night of lovemaking. Another languorous rub followed, chasing away fatigue as familiar sensations began seeping through every inch of his body.

Full awareness trickled back into his sleep-hazed brain when Drew opened his eyes. The spill of glossy platinum strands across the snow white pillowcase and the naughty smile of curving red lips met his bleary gaze. Even with her hair tangled and her makeup smeared, she was still a beauty. Looking at her never failed to summon the tug of need deep in his loins.

His reaction surprised him, catching him off guard. He blinked, close to spellbound, hardly able to believe this gorgeous creature had allowed him to join her in bed.

His companion rubbed against him again, fluid and graceful. The brush of naked skin on naked almost caused his heart to skip a beat. Familiar warmth surged beneath his skin, flooding through his body. Heat pooled in his groin, hardening his penis into a viable length a woman could work with. His primal appetite rumbled, voicing a blatantly sexual demand.

Drew's jaw tightened as his brain filled with a menagerie of erotic images—the visual pleasure of holding her hips as he thrust into her, taking him deep inside her clenching sex.

Body stiffening against the rush of desire trilling through his veins, he curled one fist tight, taking a deep breath to catch his emotions before they slithered out of his grip. As always, he had to be aware of every move he made, every word he said. One wrong move could cost him more than the nude woman beside him.

One wrong move could cost him his life.

Not that he wanted to think about that now.

Tucking the thought back into a dark corner in his mind, Drew preferred to concentrate on the matter at hand: satisfying his partner. "Looks like you are awake and ready to play."

Mischief glinted in the depths of eyes as clear and sparkling as a Caribbean lagoon. "You're damn right I am." Her words came out deep and throaty, her voice a sensual mix of whiskey burn and vodka smooth. In anger her voice could wound like a whip through flesh. Aroused, it could drop a man to his knees, make him beg to hear her heated whispers of passion.

Having achieved the desired effect, Mara Luce stretched against him, sensuously nudging one of her smooth, slender legs between his. Toes painted with a brazen shade of red polish brushed against his ankle. Her simple caress was all it took to keep the necessary sparks alive. His senses suffered another electrifying jolt, especially to that part of his anatomy she'd already worshipped eagerly with her mouth, her hands, and, most important of all, her tight, welcoming sex.

Lifting his weight on an elbow, he couldn't resist leaning over her for a quick kiss. "Now this is the way I wish I could wake up every day of the week." His lips brushed her cheek. "It would make getting out of bed a hell of a lot easier."

Mara turned her head slightly, whispering into his mouth. "Don't you mean it would be harder to get out of bed?" she teased. One warm palm settled possessively on his bare chest. Fingers curving just a little, her perfectly manicured nails dug into his skin. The female aggressor in her permeated through his senses.

Pulling back a little, Drew smiled. Like a wildcat in heat Mara never failed to score his skin in a deeper, fiercer way during sex. She didn't just make love to a man. She owned him. No scars meant no commitment on her part. By the scars across his back, ass, and thighs, Drew considered himself a committed man. He took it all in the line of duty. "If I could stay like this all day, babe, I sure as hell would."

Placated, Mara straightened her fingers, playfully circling one flat male nipple. "Just checking," she purred.

They were both naked except for the sheets tangled around them as they lazed in the afterglow of mind-twisting sex. Mara's breasts rose and fell, tempting him to bury his face in the deep cleft between them. Rose-shaded nipples beckoned to be caressed, touched, and tasted. The smooth curve of her belly disappeared beneath the sheet covering her hips. No matter. He'd soon get another chance to take his pleasure. Her body was an oasis many men sought, but few were allowed to explore. To be granted an embrace in her arms was to be handed the keys to the gates of heaven.

Drew had his key, and was more than ready to use it. But first he had work to do.

Sliding a hand up her abdomen, he cupped one full breast. "So what do you think about being able to wake up together every day?"

Mara's breath caught, a brief rush of air passing over her lips. Her breast pressed harder into his palm. She wasn't drawing away, and that was good. "I think it sounds wonderful . . ." she started to say. Heavy lidded eyes briefly shuttered, closing him out.

Drew leaned closer, angling his body so he could look down at her sensual mouth. He teased the pink tip with a little more insistence. "But you're scared of leaving Zinetti," he prompted. Not a question, but a statement to prod her into acknowledging why she hadn't yet given her answer to his proposal.

Hearing the name of her boss, a shiver whisked through Mara's body even as her mouth twisted down in revulsion. Eyes still closed, her breath rattled tremulously. "Witness protection," she whispered as if saying the words aloud would somehow condemn her. She shook her head. "We wouldn't have a chance. He'd kill us both just for thinking it."

Making a subtle power play, Drew leaned in closer, lowering his face to hers. Having put in almost a year of undercover work, he wanted out. His nerves were beginning to wear thin from the constant stress of keeping his guard up. To walk in sunlight again as an officer of the law and not the hooligan he'd been posing as for nine months. He just had to convince Mara it was time to get out of the life—and make her want to go with him. Every bit of evidence he'd gathered would be doubly damning with her knowledge to back up the investigation.

Drew brushed her lips with his, whispering words only she could hear. "We can get out, Mara. I can arrange it all with the feds. All you have to do is say the word and we're gone. Once we're in protective custody, Zinetti won't be able to lay a hand on us." Though there was no way the hotel room could be wired with any outside listening devices—they were very careful about choosing places to meet—he wasn't willing to take any chances. He was too damn close to freedom to blow it now.

Mara opened her eyes and shook her head. "I—I can't. Even the law can't keep Zinetti away. You know that. Anyone who tries to walk away gets a guaranteed death sentence, just like

Bruce." Another shiver tore through her. "I'm not going to die like a dog in the street, Drew. Staying with the family means staying alive."

The impact behind her words sent a hot tremor though him. Realizing she was slipping away, Drew narrowed his gaze. Just when he thought he had her in the palm of his hand, she managed to slip right through his fingers.

He had to give Mara credit. Though she'd allowed him to slide between her sheets, she wasn't the kind of woman who'd let a man jerk her around. From the beginning she'd made the rules, kept him on a short leash.

When Drew had first set eyes on his present bedmate, he hadn't been expecting a mob accountant to be so damn good looking. Frankly, he'd been expecting some young tootsie when the old mob boss had introduced his "girlfriend." What he hadn't envisioned was a charming, mature woman of thirty-one with a gorgeous smile and engaging personality.

Mara Luce. Clement Zinetti's right-hand woman. A woman who knew and saw more violence than any civilized female needed to. But more than having a pretty face and luscious body, Mara had brains. A lot of brains. Holding a master's degree in business, her ability with numbers was uncanny—especially when put to the task of hiding the gangster's copious assets from the government. One of the many reasons Uncle Sam had such a tough time curtailing the illegal pursuits of Boston's local mafioso was that all his activities appeared to be perfectly legitimate. Zinetti paid his taxes and his public businesses were above board. It was all smoke and mirrors, though, and Mara Luce was the master conjurer who worked the illusions behind the scenes.

Drew knew Mara had a point when it came to wanting to stay put. Bruce "the Bruiser" Nordstrom, a two-time felon, thug, and general no-good bastard, had been the last man to try and get out of Zinetti's organization. He hadn't gotten very far, very fast. An ax liberally applied had ended Bruce's intentions to become the state attorney general's star witness to rest forever. To rub it in, the killers had dumped Bruce's remains along the highway in plastic baggies. A lot of plastic baggies. It had taken months to pick up the stoolie and put him back together again. His head and hands were never recovered.

No one had ever been fingered for the crime. Not enough evidence. Somehow Zinetti had found out about Bruce's intentions and stopped the traitor dead in his tracks. Literally.

A slight tic pulled Drew's mouth into a frown. He'd known Bruce Nordstrom. They'd grown up in the same neighborhood.

There but for the grace of God go I, he thought grimly.

With Bruce's murder still fresh on her mind, Mara would never agree to bolt. Drew had to convince her the only way he knew how. He had to appeal to the one weakness that would break down her stubborn façade. Her heart. And with Mara it was hard to lie, play the games of seduction.

Before she could say another word, Drew kissed the curve of her jaw, near her ear, moving his lips softly along her cheek. "We're not going to make the same mistakes Bruce made. I promise. You just have to trust me, Mara. Say yes and I'll handle everything."

Mara's breathing accelerated even more. Not entirely convinced, she pressed her hands to his chest, looking at him with a mixture of suspicion and longing. By the look in her eyes, she walked the line between agreeing and backing away completely.

"Don't play me, Drew," she warned, clearly desperate to change the subject while she still had some control over it. "We have a good thing going here."

Drew took control, capturing her wrists and pinning them down against the mattress before rolling on top of her. His hips sank between her spread thighs, his cock settling against the soft nest of her belly. Slender and sleekly muscled, Mara was a lot of dynamite wrapped in a little package. She couldn't have weighed a hundred pounds soaking wet, yet she had all the necessary firepower to take on a man twice her size.

Supporting his weight on his elbows, he looked down at her. "It can be better, Mara. I promise."

Mara flinched and trembled, twisting her wrists against his grip. "I told you I don't want to talk about it," she started to say. Her protest broke off into silence. Instinctive fear of the hell-storm of violence such a move would unleash broke over her, drenching her in nervous perspiration.

Her musky scent only served to arouse Drew further. Right now his mind wasn't on getting her to agree. He was more concerned with the throb of need between his legs. If seducing Mara was what it would take to get her to walk away from her life in organized crime, then he'd do whatever it took.

The biggest problem he had to face was making sure his own heart didn't get caught up in the game as well. Hard to do, but he would manage. Somehow.

"Just trust me, babe." Uncurling his fingers, Drew allowed her to free her hands. Getting her to the point of discussion was a small victory within itself. "You know I would never let you get hurt."

Frowning, her eyes closed briefly. A single tear slipped down her cheek. But only one. She blinked the rest away. But the seeds of doubt were still rooted deep enough to have influence. "I've been lied to before, Drew. How do I know I can trust you?" she asked slowly.

It was the question that always came up, putting up a wall Drew hadn't yet managed to scale.

Unable to climb over it, he'd already figured this time he'd have to go right through it like a battering ram, knock it down to so much rubble. Hard as nails, Mara Luce wasn't the kind of woman who wasted tears. The fact he'd gotten a few out of her was proof her feelings for him ran a lot deeper than she was willing to let on.

The truth—and trouble—was she couldn't trust him. Their entire relationship reeked, tangled in the web of lies undercover work entailed. There was no time to think about the morality of seducing a mob boss's moll. He'd deal with the fallout when the time came. For the moment he'd have to settle for the pat answer, the easy answer. The answer that would get Mara to do what he needed her to do: turn state's evidence against one of Boston's most notorious gangland chiefs.

Like a frightened animal, Mara needed reassurance, a strong and steady hand to lead her through the mine field. "Have I ever given you any reason not to trust me?" he asked, spinning her words around on her with the ease of a practiced liar.

The hush between them was deep and consuming. Minutes ticked away. Despite the deceptions on Drew's part, they were connected as lovers. No matter what the future might hold, he'd already committed to protecting Mara. *Even if she hates me once the whole truth comes out.*

Her answer arrived with hesitation. "It's not you I don't trust." She spoke slowly, working her way through her internal reservations. "It's me. I'm not sure about my commitment to you, babe. When I leave the family, I have to know what I'm walking into is rock solid." She reached up, caressing his cheek with slender fingers. "You make it all seem so easy, but I still have to look out for me, you know? Nobody else ever has."

Drew kept his wince private. At least she was being honest. Mara clearly wasn't ready to make the vital decision. She still didn't see any future for herself in witness protection. Somehow, he had to convince her that his pledge was unyielding, that he'd take her every step of the way.

He nodded. "I understand. You think I'm not good enough."

A crease of concern wrinkled her forehead. She stroked one

forearm with a placating pet. "It's not that. You know I'm crazy about you, Drew." A short laugh escaped. "You're the best I've ever had." She stroked harder. "And all I want."

Drew snorted irritably. Swatting her hand away, he reached out, catching her chin. "Fucking me is one thing, babe. But trusting me is another." He gave a little squeeze. "Do you think I like having to sneak around Zinetti to see you?"

Goosebumps racing across her bare skin, Mara shook her head. The conversation was definitely getting to her. She clearly didn't like it, but also didn't know how to break away from the ties binding her to organized crime.

"He pulls all the strings and we dance to his tune, Mara," he answered quietly. "Think about it."

More hesitation crept into her gaze. Her features folded under the strain of carrying the burden of skepticism and pain. She started to make the usual excuses. "I owe him too much—"

Drew shrugged, tweaking the tip of one erect nipple. "Well, I don't owe him a goddamn thing." He gave the nub a little twist, reminding her who had control. "Neither do you. You have a right to a life where you don't have to sneak around like a thief."

Mara arched on the mattress, a silent plea for more. "We're not sneaking," she said softly. "We're just being careful."

Visually locking her into place, Drew lowered his head. Her response to his touch revved up his internal engine all over again. Right now there was too much talk and not enough action.

"Shut up," he growled low under his breath. Seconds later his mouth claimed hers.

Right now, words were useless. He'd have to do the convincing with his body, let their lovemaking speak for itself.

2

Mara's lips were pliable but ravenous to consume as well as be consumed. Arms sliding around his body, she arched under him, desperate to take everything he had to give.

Drew had to admit he could never get enough of her. Mara's musky sweet taste, the warm depths of her mouth, of the electric shocks racing across his bare skin every single time her fingernails scraped his skin. He drank it all in like a man determined to immerse himself in every rapturous vice the world offered.

In this case, all his vices came from a single source. Keeping heart and head separated was turning into an impossible feat to manage.

Love was an indulgence he couldn't afford.

Lust, however, was perfectly acceptable.

When he'd first begun this assignment he'd never imagined the way to bring Clement Zinetti down would be through a woman. Fortune had smiled at the right time, giving him a perfect entrance into Mara's realm. A gangster's accountant needed an able bodyguard when handling millions of dollars. The path from bodyguard to clandestine boyfriend hadn't been hard to walk. Mara ate beefcake the way a kid ate candy. It helped that she liked her guys big and brawny. It turned her on more to be abused, a quirk Drew found he enjoyed more than a little.

Mara Luce liked rough sex, liked a man to handle her like he intended to do a little damage. Even as she clenched her nails into the muscles across his back, her swollen nipples brushed against his chest, ripe and ready for the slow sweet torment of a male mouth.

"No more talk," she grated. "Just fuck me. Hard."

It was just what Drew planned to do. The heat of sexual need burned through his body like battery acid.

Sliding lower, he closed his lips around one hard tip, suckling deeply. The little tip still tasted like the sugary body powder she always sprinkled on before sex. He sucked harder, flicking with his tongue. A series of small tremors shimmied through her.

Mara swallowed hard. "God, everything you do feels so right."

Drew lifted his head long enough to answer. "I try to give you what you want," he said. "All I'm asking is that you think about getting out while the getting's good, honey. Yeah, it's true you live nice and make a lot of money. But money isn't everything when everything that man does threatens your life and freedom. You get snared by the feds, and you'll see the inside of a prison, too." He took a deep breath, hammering in another lie to get her to take the bait. "I've been there, babe, and getting raped with a broom handle isn't pleasant to endure."

Mara's fingers flexed. Damn, her nails were cat-claw sharp. "I know, I know. Just give me a little more time." He felt the tension in his fingers as she gripped him. "We'll go. Soon."

Inwardly Drew grinned to himself, but nodded deadpan. "Promise?"

"I promise." The fire of lust was burning hot behind her crystal blue gaze.

Drew's eyebrows lifted suggestively. Without saying another word, he licked the tip of her other nipple. The soft moan of pleasure she gave drowned out all of the little voices in his head cautioning him not to get too emotionally involved with her. She still believed him to be on the wrong side of the law, an ex-con with a felony sheet and a willingness to stab a man in the back if it would get him one step ahead.

For now, though, he wasn't thinking of the time when he'd have to leave her, when there would be no more stolen nights in her arms. For now he intended to take everything she had to give.

Mara moaned and gyrated her hips. "Drew, make me feel it." She made another small sound that could have been a moan, her whole body pliant and eager for his commanding touch. "You know I love what you do to me."

Drew laughed, low in the back of his throat. "I know what you need, honey." He kissed a hot path down her rib cage, lazily lapping his tongue against her skin. Heart hammering double time in his chest, he had to force himself to slow down. The urge to take her right then and there was hard to rein in. Harder yet was to keep from taking off like a rocket before he'd even gotten a chance to slide into her buttery depths.

Sliding lower, Drew positioned himself between her legs, gaining access to her most intimate places. He stroked the silky skin of her inner thighs as she lifted and spread her legs. Her skin quivered with expectation and need, anticipating the pleasure he could deliver.

Drew reached out, the tip of his finger skimming through the folds of her soft, damp labia. Her hairless mons was already wet with the juices of desire. Her natural scents mingled with the spritz of a cinnamon-scented body spray she'd used earlier. That smell was all it took to make his erection surge against his abdomen. Ripples of wonderful sensations gathered inside his core, threatening to explode in a wave of release.

Mara whimpered as his finger sank deeper between her lips and came in contact with her clit. Her body tensed, her mouth pursing with pleasure.

"I feel how much you need me; you're so wet," Drew whispered, tracing her labia with the tips of his fingers. "Been thinking about my cock, about how you like it rammed up your cunt?"

Mara nodded. "Uh-huh." Licking the tip of one index finger, she traced the tip of one nipple, then tugged it hard. "Make me come, Drew. Control me, any way you want."

He grinned. Mara Luce was a woman who knew what she wanted, and he was more than willing to oblige her.

Internal mercury shooting straight toward the danger zone, Drew didn't have to be told twice. Mara enjoyed having her body manipulated. She liked to watch, too. Dirty girl. A woman who actually enjoyed the many pleasures of nasty sex, there was nothing she wouldn't try. In the name of satisfying the beast called lust, he'd done things to Mara he wouldn't dare confess to the ears of any priest.

Pressing two fingers together, he slid them into her sex. Strong inner muscles gripped his fingers.

Mara angled her hips, a silent plea to go deeper. "More," she ordered through a breathless moan.

Drew delivered, dragging his fingers out, then sliding back in with a slow steady motion. Each penetration of her gripping sex made his skin tingle with an overwhelming feeling of yearning.

Unable to ignore the needs of her body, Mara lifted herself up so she could watch him. She moved her hips in a slow rhythm to match his penetrating digits.

Drew smiled, his hungry gaze skimming the length of her nude body. "Come for me, babe. Let me see you enjoy it."

Face flushing red, Mara nodded and bit back a soft moan. Arms on either side of her body, palms pressed flat against the mattress, she cried out when Drew unexpectedly forced his fingers all the way up to the knuckle.

Mara closed her thighs without dislodging his hand. A little gasp of pleasure fluttered over her lips even as an all-over flush began to creep across her pale skin. Arching her back and gasping with pleasure, she rammed her hips against his fist. A shudder tore through her and the clutch of vaginal muscles tightened. Another moan slipped from her throat, low, deep, and long.

Mara's lids fluttered shut a moment. "God, that was good." Perspiration coated her skin with a fine gloss. With her milky skin and mass of platinum locks she looked like an angel tumbled down from heaven. She smiled. "Now give me what I really need."

Drew repositioned himself on his knees. His gut throbbed with urgent need. Grabbing her hips, he flipped her over onto her stomach, then lifted her up. Her bare ass was all his for the taking.

Drew smiled at the sweet, taut curves. He placed a palm on one exposed cheek and squeezed. "You've been a very naughty girl, Mara."

She wiggled her rear. "How naughty?"

Drew aimed his hand, bringing the flat of his palm down across her rear. A cracking sound filled the hotel room. "Bad enough to deserve an ass paddling until you mind me right." Another slap followed, then another and another until her pale flesh glowed with a nice rosy tint.

Mara moaned, but didn't try to escape. In her mind, being punished for enjoying illicit sex absolved her of all wrongdoing. She justified her cheating with a little flagellation. The victim was never guilty. "I want more," she managed to force out between gasps.

With each slap Drew delivered, his own body responded

with a surge of pure red-hot lust. The urge to grab her hips and rub his erection between her blazing cheeks until he came was almost too much to resist.

Control rising dangerously to the point of explosion, he took a deep breath, holding off. The piece of ass he was about to get was ten thousand times better.

"You're going to get it now, babe." Positioning himself at a more comfortable angle, Drew guided the swollen crown of his cock toward her dripping slit. Her outer lips felt like warm silk. Making her wait for it, he slid in slowly. The tight, wet heat of her sex clasped around him.

Heart missing a beat, he guided one hand around her body, delving between her thighs for the soft rise of her clit. Her breath came in ragged bursts as he began to manipulate the small hooded organ with long strokes.

Mara responded instantly, pushing back against him to take him as deep as physically possible. "God, I love feeling every inch of you inside me."

Seated to the balls, Drew shuddered. The throb and ripple of her around him threatened to send him over the edge.

Drew deliberately drew out to the tip, then pumped his full length back in. The slide of hard flesh penetrating wet flesh caused his entire body to tremble with delight. He quickened his pace, banging her hard.

But it wasn't enough for Mara. She turned her head, catching a glimpse of them together in the mirror over the bureau. A little smile widened her lips. "Fuck me right, Drew," she urged.

The heat of her need spurred Drew on. Withdrawing from her creamy depth, he spread apart her ass cheeks. Her little puckered anus beckoned like a bull's-eye. Settling the cherry-ripe crown of his penis against the target, Drew pressed for entry. The sexual juices wetting his shaft eased his penetration into forbidden territory.

Mara moaned out a few unintelligible words. Her thighs

shook as she concentrated on allowing her anal muscles to relax. "Make me take it, baby." Her voice was brisk, terse. "Make me mind you."

Chest rising and falling, Drew felt like he'd stepped into an incinerator. It seemed to take only seconds before he was sheathed all the way inside. Heated muscles claimed him in a deeper, more intimate way.

Just as they had so many nights before, their bodies quickly fell into a synchronicity, a rhythm perfectly mirroring each other's movements. His body pounded Mara's even as she welcomed each punishing thrust. Only this time there was a renewed determination behind his intense pummeling.

A string of thoughts ran through his head. *This time I'll make her see things my way*, he decided. *This time I will get her to say yes.*

Reaching out, Drew wound his fingers into her hair.

Yanking Mara up on her knees, he pressed his free hand against her Venus mound, gripping her tightly even as his middle fingers penetrated her creaming sex. Speared front and back, she was helpless. His lips were barely an inch away from her left ear.

"I'm not playing any more games with you," he grated. "I want out of the business and I want you to come with me." To emphasize his words, he ground his hips harder against her ass.

Caught by surprise, Mara groaned in violent protest and squirmed helplessly against him. "I told you. I'm not ready to cut and run."

Drew hardened his resolve. It was time to use the one card he'd been withholding during their sexual games, the play that would force her to hold her own and call his bluff. "Tell me you're ready to let this go." Fingers and cock delved deeper, claiming and conquering. "No other man fucks you the way I do."

Mara's hands shot around behind her, catching his hips and

digging her nails into flesh deep enough to wound. She shivered hard. "You know I need what you give me."

Drew winced against her punishing grip, biting down on the soft curve between her shoulder and neck. A chilly sweat formed at the base of his spine. Icicles stabbed his insides. It was a test of wills, a play of who could take the most pain and walk away intact. "Come with me, dammit. Leave with me or I swear to God I'm walking away."

Mara writhed against him, her body shuddering when the first tremor of climax thundered through her. "Don't walk away," she cried out, grinding her hips against his to take in every last bit of his surging heat. Her core of pure molten lava devoured him. Fingernails sinking deeper into his punishing hips, she shoved him straight into the abyss of sheer bliss.

Gripping her so forcefully that he bruised her skin, Drew climaxed hard. Hot semen jetted, filling her to the brim.

They fell to the mattress together, the exhaustion of their intense lovemaking driving them down with one last, exquisite shudder between their bodies.

3

Crawling in the door of his apartment early Sunday morning, Drew only wanted to sleep. The previous night with Mara had worn him down to a nub. Talk about energetic. For such a tiny woman, she was insatiable.

His apartment was bare bones living. A bed was the only stick of furniture in the whole place. Except for his clothing and other small personal items, no one would be able to identify it as occupied. He wasn't living there, just existing. He usually used the place to shower and change before heading back out on the streets. He never ate there and the nights he slept in were few and far between. It wasn't his home and he wasn't there to get comfortable.

The idea of home had long faded from his mind. He was a drone, a soldier in the war against the criminal element. Becoming a criminal meant living like one. He'd forgotten how decent people acted. Crime had consumed him, and each day he spent working undercover tore out another piece of his soul and tossed it away. He hung out with the baddest of the bad, men who didn't deserve another free day in the society they preyed on like a disease.

Only Mara kept him human, kept him from slipping. She was his narcotic, the drug that kept him stable and focused on the job.

Mara. God. What he wouldn't give to be back in bed with her now, pulling her curvy body close to his, inhaling her unique scent. Each time they were together it got harder and harder to drag himself out of her arms. Fear of needing her gave him the willpower to get up and leave.

He wasn't looking for a commitment. Of any kind.

When he'd joined the force, Drew had made the decision to remain a single man. Too many of his buddies were going through problems with their women. The long nights and late hours, the unknown danger around every corner were hell on a relationship. For sexual relief, Drew usually cruised the bars where cop groupies hung out, picking up women who had a thing for getting it on with a man who had a badge. He thought it might be the handcuffs. Chicks dug the handcuffs.

He frowned. Sex. Yeah. He had plenty of that. And it hadn't taken long for meaningless, empty sex to wear thin.

Before going undercover, he'd mostly avoided women. He hadn't given any female a serious second glance in a long time. Then came Mara Luce, a woman wrong for him on so many levels. The memory of her exotic, sultry taste whirled through his brain with hurricane-force intensity. Arousal pooled deep inside his groin.

Cursing viciously under his breath, Drew closed his eyes and took several deep breaths. *And that only makes me want her more.* He spent entirely too much time thinking about Mara, creating dream scenarios of what their lives might have been like if they'd met under different circumstances. Just thinking about not having her again tied him in knots.

Building castles in the air wasn't something he usually did.

Once she's in the program, she'll be gone. Untouchable. Untraceable. Nothing more than a nice memory to keep him warm through those long, lonely nights a cop on patrol faced.

But that wasn't what he wanted. Not at all.

Too bad he didn't have any other choice. No point in questioning fate. Just accept it and move on. Not looking back would probably help.

Taking off his clothes and tossing them on the floor next to the bed, Drew stretched out, already close to falling into a doze. He thought he'd made progress with Mara and that was good. She actually seemed to be considering walking out on the mob boss. She was still scared of the idea. No doubt there. But she was thinking about trying to make an escape from the criminal elements consuming her life.

I'm close.

As his eyes slipped shut, he believed he could see a light at the end of the tunnel, actually envision the day when he could go back to living the life of an honest man. He hated the deceit, hated the lies. Both elements had a long reach, stretching all the way back to his childhood.

Hours passed in silence, but his brief foray into bliss wasn't destined to last. The bleat of a cell phone broke through his leaden slumber.

Drew groaned and rolled over to reach for his cell phone, tangled somewhere in a pocket of his pants. He was on call twenty-four hours a day, seven days a week, the price of working in the realm of criminals. Any time Zinetti had a job for him, his phone buzzed.

Flipping it open, Drew checked the text message that had arrived in his in-box. His heart nearly stalled mid beat.

007 was all it said.

Acid immediately welled up from the pit of his gut.

Drew swallowed thickly. "Oh, shit. Not now, damn it. Not

now." Blinking hard to clear his fuzzy vision, he fumbled with the tiny pad of the phone, texting back: W&W? Shorthand for when and where?

A second text arrived about a minute later, an address in a part of town that was largely abandoned. Midnight, sharp.

Drew checked the time, a quarter after five. On the edge of exhaustion, he'd slept the entire day away. The sun would soon be sinking in the west, bringing with it the cloak of night, and the shadows his kind needed to operate effectively.

"Fucking fantastic," he muttered.

Tossing the phone back onto the floor, Drew dropped back onto the lumpy mattress that never failed to put a twinge right in the small of his back. This was a message he'd never received during this entire operation, one he'd dreaded because it meant he'd be taking a step up in the gangster's family business.

007.

Drew had just been handed his license to kill.

4

The location of the hit was one of the many semi-abandoned old cargo warehouses in South Boston. Fog thickened the damp August night, bestowing everything with a surreal quality. Everyone moving on the face of the earth appeared to be ghosts occupying a phantom dimension.

Pulling into a dimly lit space numbered 133-67, Drew saw a cadre of cars, all black sedans, the color of the vehicles blending into the murky shadows. Cold prickles condensed at the base of his spine and he shivered. This place was definitely enough to give anyone the creeps.

Because of the high level of security and surveillance modern technology allowed, it was safest to meet in the dead of night. All the vehicles and men had already been swept for tracking or listening devices, all cell phones turned off, and any possible tails dodged in traffic.

Killing the engine and lights, Drew wondered who the unlucky bastard might be. Once the order went out there would be no reprieve. Everything about the Mob's operation ran like a well-oiled machine, humming right along at maximum efficiency.

Though he'd been summoned many times before, tonight was the first time Drew had been called to one of these kinds of meetings. Serious business was about to go down. *Guaranteed.*

Upon his arrival, a man got out of one of the cars and walked over to his. Drew recognized Jimmy Mancuso, one of Zinetti's right-hand men. No one got to Zinetti until they went through Jimmy. Small and wiry, Jimmy looked like a good wind would knock him down. That idea deceived. Jimmy Mancuso was never unarmed and was lethal with any weapon he put his hands on.

Walking at a brisk pace, Jimmy made a signal with his hand. "Get out."

Drew opened the door and got out. "I'm here." The heat from his breath showed in the chilly air. He shivered again, glad for the jacket he'd put on. The leather was nowhere near as nice as the long trench coat Mancuso wore, but it was warm and that's what counted.

Clearly annoyed, Mancuso looked him up and down. "You're late," he growled by way of greeting.

Drew shrugged and gave an excuse close to the truth. "I got lost." He looked around, taking in the all-but-empty warehouse. "First time I've ever been here."

Lighting a cigarette, Mancuso sneered through a rush of smoke. "What's the matter, princess? Doesn't your goddamned GPS system work?"

Drew shrugged. "Don't use them," he said.

Mancuso made a scoffing sound deep in his throat. "Don't know why the boss is even bothering with a monkey like you. Bashers don't handle this kind of serious shit." The words rolled past his lips as though they tasted like lemons in his mouth.

Drew would agree to that. Murder was serious shit.

"I got here as soon as I could," he said.

Mancuso's grunt indicated that he didn't care what Drew had to say. He turned on his heel and started to walk toward one of the larger sedans. "Just get your ass moving," he snapped, quickening his steps to stay ahead.

Drew nodded amiably and set into motion behind the pipsqueak. "Right." He briefly entertained the image of bringing one of his fists down on the little bastard's skull. Standing over six feet and built like a brick latrine, Drew knew he was perfectly capable of snapping Mancuso in half without breaking a sweat. One thing he didn't mind at all as a cop was beating up the bad guys.

Someday I'll get to kick that little rat's ass.

He couldn't help smiling to himself as they walked. He currently functioned in the organization as the muscle. Recently Zinetti had moved him into working backup to the guys who ran security. Security was what other people who owned businesses paid to make sure their stores were safe. Refuse to pay and a basher would step in and mess things up a little, a crude but effective form of extortion.

Drew had racked up a lot of felonious damage when storeowners squawked about paying up. Getting to know the business moved him into a higher level of responsibility, allowing him to familiarize himself with the men who were farther up the food chain in Zinetti's organization.

Getting the coded text message could only mean one thing. He was about to be taking another step up the corporate ladder.

Mancuso clearly wasn't happy about it, either.

Two more men stood beside the luxury sedan Zinetti waited in. Drew recognized Jimmy's brother, Zach, and yet another far-flung Mancuso cousin, Joey Salvatore. Both had been trigger men on past jobs and were ruthless and efficient in the delivery of death.

Joey greeted him with a slap on one shoulder. "Thought you died, man."

Drew shrugged. "No such luck."

Zach Mancuso wasn't so friendly. "You pansies going to chat all night?"

"I'm just showing up like I was told," Drew said briskly, reminding everyone he hadn't just appeared on a whim.

Jimmy Mancuso swore under his breath. "We're already running late," he prodded in a nasty tone. "Get on with it."

Zach Mancuso made a familiar gesture, using his index finger and thumb. "You loaded?"

Drew nodded, playing it cool. He owned more guns than any sane man had a right to. "Yeah." He patted his holstered weapon, a nice 9mm Glock. "Definitely."

Zach nodded. "Keep it handy."

Jimmy Mancuso didn't seem pleased. "I don't know that you even need to be here."

Drew sighed. "Give me a break, okay? I'm just here because I was called." He took a step away, ready to walk. "You don't want me here, say the word and I'll split, man. Your call." It wasn't Jimmy's call and Drew knew it. Jimmy had a boss, too.

Since day one, Jimmy Mancuso had done everything and then some to bust his chops. Drew hadn't taken Mancuso's bait because he needed to work his way inside, gain their trust by hook or crook. He'd been a good soldier. No reason to knock his dick in the dirt now.

"The boss is waiting," Zach reminded his brother.

Jimmy Mancuso's beady gaze narrowed. He jerked a thumb toward the car. "Get inside and listen up."

One of the guards opened the car door. Drew caught his breath as he slid inside the dimly lit interior, in the front passenger seat.

Clement Zinetti sat behind the wheel. The dashboard display cast an eerie green glow on the old man's sanguine features. He looked like a pale corpse recently exhumed from an unquiet grave. A cigar clamped between his thin lips filled the limited space with thick smoke. The men standing outside the tinted windows appeared to be little more than ethereal phantoms, guarding their liege, the angel of death.

Pressure, he thought. *I think I might be cracking up.* Too bad he didn't have time for a full-scale meltdown.

Without quite looking his way, Zinetti spoke. "You're late," he said by way of greeting. "You were supposed to be here almost a half hour ago."

Drew absently tugged at the collar of his shirt, not so immaculately pressed but clean. "I got held up."

Still staring straight ahead, Zinetti puffed on his noxious stogie. "Next time I call you, you come faster," he grunted.

"You can count on me." Drew released a silent sigh of relief. He'd been afraid word of his affair with Mara might have leaked back to her boyfriend. If it had, he'd probably be kneeling on the floor about now, hoping a bullet to the back of his head would kill him quickly.

Zinetti unexpectedly dialed in to ignore. He lapsed into silence.

Drew sat, trying not to fidget. At that moment the man sitting beside him didn't appear to be any more menacing than the average stockbroker. He certainly didn't appear to be the most dangerous man in the city. Far from being a coarse, unfinished man who'd spent his life in the pursuit of crime, Clement Zinetti was a product of wealth—heir to an empire the Italians had set to building in the late 1800s.

Far from crumbling, the Sicilian empire in the new world had not only managed to survive, but to thrive. As long as greed and lust existed inside the human soul, men like Zinetti were there to feed the disease, continuing to fatten their bank accounts off the weak, the uneducated, and the addicted. Yes, the American dream had indeed come true for immigrants who operated in the shadows and slums. Drugs. Weapons. Flesh. There was nothing the family didn't deal in to turn a dime.

Contemplating the smoke rising from the tip of his cigar, Zinetti deigned to speak again. "Want one?"

Drew didn't. The smell of the cigar was enough to make him gag and puke. He breathed through his mouth, trying not to inhale deeply. "I gave up the habit," he said cautiously.

Zinetti grunted an acknowledgment. "Hard to quit," he muttered under his breath.

What could Drew say? "It is," he remarked, wondering where the hell this odd conversation might be going. Though smoking was out, he could have used a cup of coffee loaded with cream and sugar. It was a quarter to one in the morning and he needed a pick-me-up. For some reason his ass was dragging and he couldn't seem to get a move on.

Zinetti finally stubbed out his nasty stogie. "How's your mother?"

Jolted by the change in direction, Drew took a quick breath to slow his thudding heart. "She's good, God bless her soul. The nursing home has been really good for her."

Zinetti nodded. "Alzheimer's, right?"

It took a moment for Drew to realize Zinetti was feeling him out, getting the details straight. He needed to make sure who he was dealing with. This wasn't the first time cops had tried to sneak in undercover agents.

A scowl crossed his face. "Yeah. She doesn't know who I am anymore. I'm just some man who comes to see her now." The absolute truth.

Zinetti knew it. "Pity. It's a shame. Lonnie Dee always said good things about her."

Mention of his uncle caused his internal antennae to perk up.

He nodded, cautiously. "Lonnie always looked out for us."

Zinetti fiddled with the cane propped on the seat beside him.

He didn't actually need it to walk. He just liked carrying the heavy, gold-crowned stick. In his younger days he'd been known to beat the hell out of his victims with it. "Lonnie was a good man. One of the best."

Guts clenching, Drew's internal apprehension ratcheted up ten more notches. Throat aching, he swallowed thickly. "Yeah, we all loved him." He echoed the sentiment as enthusiastically as he could. Given that Lonnie DeForest was trouble with a capital T, it was hard to chime in with any real emotion.

It was strange to be sitting there sharing confidences with the man he was supposed to be putting behind bars, but Zinetti's personal knowledge of his family was one of the reasons Drew had been plucked from the ranks of the Boston State Police by the feds. He'd been picked because "Lonnie Dee" was Lance DeForest, Drew's uncle on his mother's side. He had an automatic in with the New England Mafia unofficially known as the Beacon Hill Gang.

Drew knew the history of his family's dabbling in crime backward and forward. After all, his uncle Lance had been the stuff of legend when he was growing up in the Southside projects. Everyone knew Lonnie Dee was one of Zinetti's best triggermen before being sent to prison for assassinating the owner of a gun store who refused to move some stolen weapons. While the FBI had managed to gather enough evidence to convict Drew's uncle of the slaying, they'd been unsuccessful in getting Lonnie Dee to roll over and name the man who'd smuggled in the guns, the one who'd ordered the killing.

Drew glanced toward the ceiling, suddenly wishing he were somewhere else. Anywhere else but here. Right now, he'd give his left nut to be back in bed with Mara, banging away at that oh-so-tight pussy of hers.

Instead he was stuck here, rehashing a past he'd rather forget. Growing up and going into law enforcement hadn't gotten him very far. He was still walking the same old streets, only this time everyone believed he was doing so on the wrong side of the law. No one had expected any of the Hardage boys to make good. Both his brothers had done prison time, too.

Whoop-de-fucking-do.

What Zinetti had was old news. No big secret, nothing he'd hidden. He came up poor and he came from crooks. His father . . . well, he never knew the man who'd knocked up his mother and walked out before Drew turned a year old. His uncle Lonnie Dee had always been the one who helped put food on the table and made sure he had clothes to wear when he went to school. His mother knew the money her older brother dutifully handed over was stained with blood, but she'd had the sense to turn her head and keep her mouth shut. After all, she had three growing boys to feed and wages as a waitress only went so far.

Grimacing at the memories he'd rather not revisit, Drew shoved them out of his mind. It was probably better that Lonnie Dee hadn't lived to learn he'd become a cop. Part of the family pride was you made a wide berth around the law. Never a stoolie, Lonnie had died honorably in prison, stabbed by another inmate over a candy bar.

Zinetti gave him a tap on the arm. "You know," he began in a conversational tone, "when you first came to work for me, I had my doubts about you."

Uh-ho. Hot point.

Drew mentally shook off the unwelcome touch. "Oh, yeah?" The conversation was about to take another turn. He decided to play dumb. Looking like a big lug with a brain the size of a marble helped. "Because I'm a felon?" Part of his undercover identity had entailed a stretch behind bars.

Zinetti didn't blink. "Because you were a cop," he smirked.

Drew struggled to keep his face blank. Of course, Zinetti knew about his time on the force. Zinetti also knew Drew had been kicked off for shaking down pimps and dealers, and assaulting the ex-partner who'd threatened to rat out his paycheck-enhancing activities.

At least that was the cover story the FBI had built around his identity when he'd agreed to go undercover. It had taken months to set up the scenario and see it through, prison time and all. His official file as an officer also read as a rap sheet.

Only his boss, Captain Lewis Abbot, and the federal agents working in the Organized Crime Division knew the truth. Officially he wasn't even on any state payroll, though he did have a numbered account with a tidy sum stashed away, part of the bonus he'd been paid to sign on and give away a few years of his life to criminal activities. To his colleagues and the world at large, Drew Hardage was dirty. He had the perfect pedigree to join the Mob.

Irritation twisted inside him.

"What do you want? A fucking resume?" Drew smacked his chest with the flat of his palm. "I've never been anything but straight with you. What you see is what you get." And though he didn't want to say the words, he knew he had to hammer trust home.

Zinetti acknowledged Drew's outburst with a single nod. "So maybe the acorn didn't fall that far from the family tree."

Drew's stomach twisted with disgust. He moistened his lips. "Just like Lonnie Dee, I'm your man."

Making such a statement might not have been the wisest thing to do, but he sensed the mobster was actually waiting for the signal, a demonstration of loyalty proving his allegiance without a doubt. He'd never invoked the name of his dead uncle to get ahead within the organization. Now he felt it was absolutely necessary to prove he was just as ruthless.

Zinetti nodded. "Good. That's just what I wanted to hear."

Suddenly exhausted, Drew slumped down in the seat. He wasn't a crooked ex-cop. He just played one in the name of justice.

Closing his eyes, he rubbed the lids with thumb and forefinger, wishing he could wipe away the tension this operation had piled on his psyche. In creating this new version of Drew he'd almost forgotten who the old version was. Looking inside the lies and deceit, he realized he didn't like the 2.0 model at all.

It has to end soon, he decided. Otherwise he might actually begin to believe the words he'd said to Zinetti.

After a moment his hand dropped. He'd known what the text message meant the moment it had arrived. "You got a job for me?" he asked, voice barely above a whisper.

Their gazes met across the narrow expanse. "You've been wanting to move up," Zinetti growled. "Tonight I'm giving you the chance to make your bones."

5

The trembling started deep inside. Sweat drenched him all over again. Drew tried to control his nerves, but that wasn't happening.

Oh, shit.

The Mob boss had just made him an offer he couldn't refuse.

His mind went into overdrive. How the hell could he get out of pulling the trigger without blowing his cover? More important, how could he stand by while someone was murdered in cold blood? The answer wasn't easy. Being trapped between a rock and a hard place threatened to grind him down to dust.

Drew scrabbled to find his nerve, holding on tightly. "When?" His voice quavered slightly.

Zinetti reached for his stick. "Now." He opened the door. "In the trunk."

Drew fumbled to find the handle and get out of the car. He trotted around the front of Zinetti's car, following his boss toward Zach Mancuso's sedan. The men all gathered around.

"Open it," Zinetti grunted through a puff on his cigar.

Joey Salvatore handled the keys, opening the trunk and revealing its contents.

Looking into the depths, Drew's eyes widened with surprise even as disbelief sizzled through his entire body. He had to blink, not once but twice. He could hardly fathom who was inside.

It's not possible, he tried to tell himself. He blinked again, but his eyes were not lying to his brain.

Wrists bound in front of her, Mara Luce lay in the trunk. She sprawled inside, naked except for a pair of flimsy lace panties. She'd been blindfolded. A piece of duct tape across her mouth kept her from making more than low, muffled sounds.

A wild thought zipped through Drew's mind. *They know about us.* The accompanying image of Jimmy Mancuso blasting a bullet through his brain wasn't a welcome one.

Zinetti banged the car with his cane. "Get her out of there."

Zach and Jimmy Mancuso pulled Mara out of the trunk. Curses and threats punctuated the thugs' efforts to keep her under their control. Kicking and writhing, Mara Luce was doing everything she could to prove she wasn't an easy woman to handle.

It took every ounce of self-restraint Drew possessed to keep from rushing to her aid. Powerless to help her, he could only watch as she struggled to escape their manhandling. Purple splotches covered her pale skin. Bruised and bloodied, she hadn't allowed herself to be taken without a fight.

The Mancuso brothers held on tight, pinning her between them. Her breasts jiggled enticingly, eliciting a few obscene remarks from the men around her. They wouldn't mind having a piece of Mara at all.

Drew inwardly cursed himself for being caught by surprise. The trembling started deep inside him. He tried to control it, but he wasn't able to get a grip on his emotions. "What's going on?"

"Shut up and pay attention," Zinetti snapped.

Feeling more helpless than he'd ever felt in his life, Drew remained rooted to the spot. Right now he barely felt the chill enveloping the warehouse or the wet cling of clothing plastered to his perspiring body. He could easily imagine Jimmy Mancuso slapping Mara around before Zach and Joey tied her up and tossed her in the trunk of their car. As it was, she didn't stand a chance against these sociopaths.

"Here you go, boss," Jimmy Mancuso cracked. "One whore at your service." He gave one of her erect nipples a savage twist. "Bet that makes you cream your panties, eh, Mara?"

An indignant gasp leaked from behind the tape keeping Mara Luce silent. Twisting like a wildcat on crack, she blindly kicked out toward Jimmy Mancuso's crotch, attempting to punt his balls between his shoulder blades. She missed, but not for lack of trying.

Jimmy Mancuso delivered a sound clout to the side of her head. Mara reeled, dropping to her knees.

The men quickly dragged her back to her feet. "Do that again and I'll beat the living shit out of you," Jimmy threatened.

Drew's lungs burned with the need to drag in a breath of air. He blinked, wondering if what he was witnessing was even real. Seeing his lover—naked and tied like a dog—on the receiving end of an execution order wasn't something he'd anticipated when he'd slipped out of her bed and dressed less than a day ago.

Zinetti made a brief motion with his hand. "Let me see her face. I want to look that bitch in the eyes."

The blindfold came off. Mara blinked, trying to gain a sense of her surroundings. Taking a moment to get her bearings, she sucked in a couple of deep breaths.

Looking at her, so vulnerable and alone, made Drew ache

with yearning. He wanted to grab her and kiss her, soothe away all her pain and fear. Goosebumps pimpled her mottled skin. He couldn't fail to notice her nipples were hard little beads.

Drew closed his eyes, remembering how Mara's body had pressed against his, her voluptuous curves compliant against the contours of his sleek frame. As much as he tried to block the images, his mind insisted on replaying the visions of their recent time together. The sensation of sliding his erection into her eager sex was unforgettable.

Mara was a demanding lover, almost desperate in her need to be held tightly, kissed deeply, as though she was trying to fill some strange, aching emptiness inside her soul.

Zinetti leaned on his cane. "Looks like you got caught in the wrong bed," he greeted through a mouthful of smoke.

Forcing himself to stay calm, Drew opened his eyes. When he'd left their hotel room, she'd been lolling in bed, reluctant to get up and dress. She didn't want to go home, back to the empty bed with icy sheets waiting at her apartment. The late night thrill of sneaking out, the illicit trysts, were all a part of the dangerous turn on she relished.

Zinetti reached out, catching her chin in an iron grip. "But it isn't just any man my little honey here has been screwing."

Unable to speak, Mara unsuccessfully tried to turn her head.

Zinetti held on tight, giving her head a little shake. "No, my Mara has to go and spread her legs for the feds." The gangster's words stunned.

Teeth gritting with frustration, Drew could barely think past the roar of blood pounding through his temples. "What are you saying?" he mumbled stupidly. If Zinetti knew Mara was sleeping with a cop, he might already know the identity of the man. Not knowing exactly what was going on was sheer agony.

Grinning, Zinetti's hand dropped. "Word's come down from

the inside the feds are trying to sweet-talk our girl here into turning state's evidence."

Drew's heart fell, hitting the concrete beneath his feet with a thud. Somehow Zinetti had gotten wind of the operation taking place against him. His information was spot on.

The black pressure of impending doom pressed down on him with the force of a two-ton anvil. "You sure about that?" he asked, the words slipping out before he had time to consider the wisdom behind the question.

Zinetti glanced at Drew. "We have a new man on the inside, an agent who needed to supplement his puny federal income." He laughed. "Every man has a price, it's just a matter of finding one with the weak moral links. Whoever said crime doesn't pay never met a fed with a mortgage."

Drew arched a brow. "You sure it's legit?"

"Rock solid." The mob boss eyed Mara, giving her a light slap on the cheek with his open hand. "So who is this secret agent man you've been fucking behind my back?" A harder slap followed, one that reddened her cheek. "Once I get his name, he won't breathe another day."

A rush of nausea distracted Drew. He felt a little woozy, sort of disoriented. Catching his breath, he swallowed hard. Vomiting his guts up now wasn't the thing to do. Somehow he'd just barely dodged being caught with his pants down around his ankles.

He'd known going in that his cover could be blown at any time, and what those consequences might be. He wasn't exactly unprepared for that contingency. What he hadn't been prepared for was the fact Zinetti had a mole operating within the federal agency, someone who could gain access to top-secret operations against organized crime.

Mara's toast, he thought wildly. And if she named him as her lover, it was pretty clear he'd be going down with her.

Muffled words escaped Mara's taped mouth. She was obviously trying to speak.

Drew briefly considered pulling his weapon and taking his best shot. Once that tape came off Mara's pretty little mouth, she might sing a tune he didn't want to hear.

Joey Salvatore savagely ripped the tape off. "Can't hear you, bitch."

Mara Luce's eyes flashed with all the vengeance of hell unleashed. "I said fuck you!" she snapped.

Drew's heart lurched. She was beautiful, defiant, and totally unrepentant. Brave woman. Stupid, but brave.

Zinetti's hand shot out, delivering a hard slap. The crack sliced ominously through the chilly air permeating the warehouse. "Right now your ass is on the line, Mara. There's only one way I might let you walk out alive, and that's if you tell me that federal prick's name."

Mara briefly shot her gaze Drew's way, but her eyes held no overt signs of recognition.

Drew had never told her straight out he was a cop, though by now she'd most likely put two and two together.

Despite the beating she'd taken, Mara obviously hadn't given him up to save her own hide. She was one tough cookie, proving that no one got anything out of her that she didn't want to give. Right now her silence was the only reason Drew was standing upright.

He gave a little shake of his head, sending a silent message her way. *Please, keep cool. I'll get us out of this.* Trouble was he didn't exactly know what he intended to do. Yet.

Drew eased a hand toward his holstered weapon. His fingers itched to tighten around the butt of his automatic. Just in case. He had no compunction about pulling the trigger if it would save Mara's life. His assignment was to bring in a living witness, not get her killed.

Catching his intention, Mara immediately blinked and turned her head away. Her message was clear. She wasn't going to rat him out if she could help it.

Emotion tightened Drew's throat. He wondered if he could have held it together had their positions been reversed. Standing naked and exposed, would he have possessed enough nerve to defy Zinetti?

A blood-chilling shiver raced down his spine. *Focus*, he ordered himself. There was no time to worry about anything except getting Mara safely out of this mess and into federal custody. Getting out wasn't going to be easy, but that didn't mean it was impossible. Once they were safe, he could stop and think about the next step.

An unexpected smile played around the corners of Mara's mouth. Drew's heart skipped a beat. He knew that smile meant something inappropriate was about to come out of her mouth.

His stomach rolled at the idea. If pain was involved, Mara liked it. Too much. An adrenaline junkie, she liked walking that dangerous tightrope. One slip would cost her everything, but she didn't seem to care. In her philosophy, life was meant to be lived on the edge.

Anticipation kicked Drew's heart into a faster rhythm. He wasn't feeling suicidal and wanted to walk away alive. Craving danger was one thing. Letting it jeopardize your life was another.

Mara apparently didn't give a shit. "If you'd have been ten minutes earlier last night," she told her captor, "you'd have seen him for yourself."

Zinetti's face iced over. "Is that right?"

"Yeah, that's right." Mara's tongue came out, swiping at the blood caked at one corner of her mouth. "You could have seen that great big dick of his pounding me into one screaming orgasm after another." Tasting her own blood, she laughed. "Something I never got out of you."

Drew winced. *Ouch*. Talk about rubbing it in at the most inappropriate time. Mara apparently wasn't afraid to die.

Zinetti stepped up to her. The corners of his mouth were stretched into a sort of sardonic grin, as if he couldn't decide to laugh at her or curse her. "I'll bet he has a big cock."

Mara grinned, split lip and all. "More than you'll ever have." Her voice quavered ever so slightly. Despite her bravado, the fear was there.

It was the wrong thing to say.

The mobster scowled, pushing the bulbous head of his cane between her thighs and pressing it upward. It vaguely occurred to Drew the crown of the cane resembled a very large penis.

Zinetti jabbed her. "I don't need a cock to fuck you over, babe," he growled between clenched teeth.

Mara gasped when the pseudo-phallus connected with her tender sex. Still gripping her tightly, Jimmy Mancuso leaned in. "Does that make you wet? I'll bet you like something hard pressing against that pussy of yours."

Zach Mancuso laughed and grabbed his crotch with one hand. "We'll be glad to give it to you any way you want it. You have a lot of dicks here tonight, all thinking about ramming your sweet poon."

Close to vomiting, Drew tightened his jaw against the lurch of his queasy stomach. Bowels tightening into knots, he didn't dare close his eyes again for fear of entertaining the visions of these men violently raping Mara before they killed her.

Zinetti continued pressing between her thighs. "I know other men sniff around, take a piece or two of the tail you hand out," he said, speaking in a slow and deliberate tone. "I could handle it because you're the kind of woman who needs a lot of cock."

Mara bit her lower lip, refusing to say anything.

Zinetti gave her another vicious jab. "But one thing I will not tolerate is you fucking with my living. You know too much, and what you know isn't going into any courtroom. The rules of this business are absolute and sacrosanct."

Without warning, Mara snapped under the pressure. Bravado suddenly deflating like a balloon losing air, she nodded in defeat.

"And nobody gets out," she murmured, repeating the credo every made man—and woman—knew by heart. She visibly shuddered, but quickly got herself back on track. She clearly didn't intend to beg for her life.

Giving her a final nasty prod with his cane, Zinetti leaned in to deliver a quick peck on Mara's forehead. "You do not walk away from the family alive."

Mara's head dropped as despair pressed down on her like a giant, smothering fist. Her order of execution had just been signed and sealed. It was just a matter of time before the delivery kicked in.

Turning away from Mara, Zinetti gestured at Drew. "You and Joey are going to handle this."

Drew swallowed hard, summoning the courage to give the appropriate response. He couldn't let anything get in his way. Not now. Staying alive right now meant playing the good soldier, pretending to do exactly what he was told. It meant being aware of any chance to get Mara out of this mess without letting his emotions take control.

Joey Salvatore eagerly rubbed his hands together, showing anticipation. "Right," he said briskly. "It's done."

Zinetti lit a fresh stogie. "I don't care where you take her or what you do before you off her," the old man said bluntly. "Fuck her, beat her, make her beg. Just make sure whatever's left isn't found."

6

Less than ten minutes later, Zinetti and the Mancuso brothers abandoned the scene of what was intended to be a violent crime.

The boss had made his orders absolutely clear. Drew and Joey were to get rid of Mara, no matter what it took.

Holding one of Mara's arms, Joey Salvatore looked at Drew. "How you want to do this, man?"

Taking a deep breath, Drew reached for his gun. It slid out of the holster with only the barest of whispers. He flicked the safety off with his thumb.

Joey smiled his approval. "Going to do her quick," he noted.

Drew shook his head, leveling his weapon on his partner in crime. "I'm going to take you out, Joey," he said quietly.

Jaw dropping with surprise, Joey Salvatore eyed the gun in disbelief. "What the fuck?" he started to say. Pushing Mara aside, he made a grab for his own gun.

"Look out!" she warned.

Drew didn't hesitate to pull the trigger. He aimed a shot

straight over Joey's left shoulder before jerking the gun over. Eyes narrowing, his hand didn't shake a bit. With the cold calculation of expert training, he knew exactly what he was doing.

The next shot was guaranteed to go right between Joey's eyes. "Try it and I'll put you down," Drew warned.

Joey's hands went up. Sensible man. Smart move. "What's going on, man?" He laughed. "You got the nerves over icing a chick? Come on. She's just a whore. She deserves it."

Unable to hold his temper, Drew clouted Joey across the face. "Shut up." Snagging the gangster's weapon from its holster, he gestured toward the trunk. "Shut up and get inside."

Joey sneered. "What if I don't?"

Drew pushed the barrel of his gun against Joey's head. "I'll blow your fucking brains out right here," he snarled back. "Your choice."

Joey Salvatore made the right decision, climbing into the trunk. "What the hell's gotten into you, man?"

"I have a conscience," Drew snapped, reaching up to shut the trunk.

Mara piped up. "He's got a cell."

Drew paused. "Toss it," he ordered.

Joey tossed his fancy phone.

"And the car keys," she prompted helpfully.

Surrendering his car keys, Joey Salvatore glared. "Bitch."

Drew slammed the trunk down on Salvatore's ugly face. "We have to get out of here," he warned. "This won't buy us much time."

Mara Luce held out her tied hands. "Think you could cut me loose?"

Holstering his weapon, Drew fished for his pocketknife. He sliced through the rope binding her wrists. When she was free, he slid his jacket off his shoulders. "Put this on," he said, handing it over to help cover her nudity.

Mara slipped into the jacket, gratefully pulling its warm

folds around her. "Thanks." She shivered. "I don't think I'll ever be warm again."

Drew hurried her toward his SUV, opening the passenger door and shoving her inside. "We don't have much time." He ran around to the driver's side and slid behind the wheel. "Right now we have to make tracks."

Mara looked scared. "Where are we going?"

Cranking the engine, Drew turned the massive vehicle around and aimed it toward the exit. Outside was a tangle of streets, easy to get lost in. The derelict area wasn't exactly any place he wanted to spend a lot of time in. "I don't know." His words were true. Right now he didn't have a clue.

The only thing he was sure of was that his contacts within the Bureau were now tainted. Communicating with them would most likely tip off Zinetti that he'd taken Mara and ran.

Hitting the gas, Drew took the South side streets as fast as legally possible. At this point he certainly didn't want to attract the attention of any cops out on patrol. He had to find a safe location, hide Mara until he was sure they could come in safely. Until that time, they were on their own.

Mara reached for the controls to crank up the heat. "Guess this means I'm out of the family." Chuckling softly, she cut a glance his way. "You, too."

Now that the tension had eased a bit, Drew couldn't resist smiling. The sound of her voice sent tiny little shivers down his spine. "Yeah, I guess so."

Wanting to get off the streets, Drew pulled into an underground public parking garage. Out of sight would be a good place to lay low while he considered what he had to work with. He hadn't exactly been caught unprepared. He had cash and weapons stashed in his vehicle, along with a few items that would make living on the run a little more comfortable.

"Why didn't you tell me you were a cop?" Mara asked, her tone sounding curiously distant.

Eyes glued to the steering wheel, Drew shrugged. "Announcing you're working undercover usually isn't the way we do things."

"I see." She drew a breath. "And what about sleeping with me? Was that part of the plan?"

This time Drew had to look at her, cutting a quick glance her way. Even disheveled and half naked she still looked beautiful, a delicate porcelain angel whose cracks didn't detract from her allure.

"No," he said honestly. "I had no idea what happened between us would happen."

She cocked her head. "So you weren't sleeping with me to make your case against Zinetti?" she asked.

A sudden rush of fury swept through him. "No. I wasn't sleeping with you to get the evidence on him. It wasn't that way. It wasn't that way at all." The very idea that he'd manipulated her, used her, made him want to vomit.

Mara drilled deeper. "Then what was it?"

Drew's throat tightened. Denying he had feelings for her was clearly impossible, but it was also something he wasn't quite ready to admit. Falling in love wasn't part of the job. "I wasn't using you," he said slowly.

"Then what were you doing?" she asked.

Drew sighed, rubbing tired eyes. "I thought I was doing my job," he murmured. He wasn't really sure why he'd dragged things on so long, kept going back to Mara again and again. In the back of his mind, the truth reared its head. Once she went into witness protection, he'd be left behind. The affair would have to end. At the time, going with her wasn't an option.

Now he wasn't so sure.

Mara shook her head. "You sure had me fooled." She made a breathy sound that might have been a laugh. "I never thought my Prince Charming would be a cop." Although her voice was laced with cynicism, Drew recognized the strain behind her words. Unless she turned state's evidence against Zinetti, gave up all his dirty financial maneuverings, she was just as guilty.

Heart beating rapidly inside his chest, a smile twitched across his lips. He reached out, cupping her bruised cheek. "I can still rescue you," he said, and meant it. Somehow, through all this inane sneaking around and double-crossing, he'd fallen head over heels.

Capturing his hand in hers, Mara kissed the center of his palm. "I've always wanted to be rescued."

The caress of her warm lips against his hand bestowed new life on the ribbon of need curling around his loins.

Exhaling a breath he hadn't been aware he was holding, Drew pulled her toward him, unable to resist the urge to taste her moist lips. After the night's brush with danger, his body seethed with unreleased tension. Unused adrenaline had backed up in his veins, keeping his nerves raw and on edge.

With a soft sigh, Mara's mouth opened under his, her sweet lips parting in supplication. He needed to taste her, drink her in, take everything she was willing to give.

"I want you," he murmured against her mouth. "Now."

Hands gripping his shoulders, her fingernails bit through his shirt, digging into the skin beneath. "I want you inside me, driving as hard and fast as you can," she moaned against his stubbled cheek.

Drew didn't hesitate. Hitching his seat back as far as it would go, he pulled Mara into his lap. Her thighs willingly parted to straddle him. With practiced ease, she settled her hips against his. Enticed by the sultry heat emanating from her sex, his erection strained for release.

Mara's lower body ground against his, a silent plea for more. Her skin was still scented with the earlier musk generated by their lovemaking, a wild earthy scent of pure lust.

Sliding his leather jacket off her shoulders, Drew tossed it aside. He drew in an unsteady breath at the sight of her breasts, rounded mounds of flesh. Her areolae were a delicate shade of rose, enticing to look at. The little tips were bead hard, begging to be sucked.

Sliding his hands around to cup her ass, Drew urged Mara to lift her body. Planting her hands on his shoulders, she guided one tender bud toward his waiting mouth.

Drew's lips closed around her nipple, tongue swirling around the enticing tip.

Mara's breath hung in her throat, becoming a long, breathy moan as she arched against him. There was no mistaking her enjoyment of the sensations.

Drew teased her other nipple, rolling and tugging it with a firm grip. His other hand slipped inside her panties, fingers delving into her crack to caress her puckered little anus. He pressed, a silent signal for her to relax and let him in.

Mara's head dipped back. She pressed her weight against his swelled erection, dry humping him with a most enticing maneuver that involved a shifting of the hips only a woman could manage.

Easing his mouth away from her nipple, Drew caught his breath. The way she rubbed against him threatened to make him come right then and there, something he doubted she would appreciate.

To slow her down, he eased her back against the steering wheel. Her panties were still very much on, but not impossible to work around. The sight of the lacy white material covering her eager sex almost caused heart failure.

Mara looked down, watching with anticipation as Drew slipped a hand back inside her panties. Her legs were already spread over his lap, giving him full access to her creaming depth. "What are you going to do?" she whispered in a sexy, husky voice.

Drew smiled. He was in control and he wasn't giving in until he had her in total submission.

"I want to watch you come." He crooked his middle finger upward, stroking through her damp labia to find the small hooded organ. The glide of her most intimate flesh giving way under the invasion of his finger sent a corresponding caress all the way through his body. Heat curled around his cock like a fist, causing his balls to draw up tighter.

Mara let out a gasp when he made contact with her clit. Her body trembled with short, sharp jolts of pure electric desire.

Drew stroked harder, watching her give herself over to pure pleasure. Eyes closing, she pursed her moist lips enticingly as long, slow moans slipped out of her throat.

She reached up, catching one of her own nipples, giving it a sharp tug. "Oh, damn," she murmured. "That feels so good."

Mesmerized by her reaction to his touch, Drew swallowed thickly. "You want more?" he asked, barely able to make the words coherent. Just watching her take her pleasure from his touch was enough to drive him to the edge.

Raw need drove her answer. "Yes, oh yessss . . . ."

Drew slipped two fingers inside her slit. She was moist, wet, tight around him. His fingers pressed deep as his thumb worked her sensitive clit. Her tremors of orgasm began in small waves, continuing until completely engulfing her in heated convulsions.

Mara cried out, her breasts rising and falling as she caught the glorious wave of pure sensation.

This was the moment when Drew wanted to be inside her.

Fumbling with his pants, he somehow freed his raging erection. His cock rose against his cobbled abdomen, ready for the feast. Tugging her panties to one side, he pressed his feet against the floorboard and lifted his hips against hers. His aim was true. Their bodies came together perfectly, fitting as though made for each other. The friction of their joined bodies was sweeter and hotter than anything he'd ever experienced before.

Threading her fingers through his thick mane, Mara tipped

his head back against the headrest. "What are we doing here?" she breathed in a husky whisper.

Panting, Drew shook his head. "I don't know, babe." His hips jerked upward, impaling her with thrust after delicious thrust. Desire was an inferno inside his soul, threatening complete and total incineration. He didn't care. He had Mara. Risking his life meant nothing. He'd do it again to keep her safe—and in his bed.

Mara tightened her grip, a strange sort of desperation filling her gaze even as her delicious sex worked its magic. "I'm not ready for this to end."

Neither was he.

Drew's hands circled her waist so he could guide the momentum building between them. Hot inner muscles pulsed around his shaft, sending an answering tug deep inside his loins. The friction building between them was becoming close to unbearable.

Holding off ten more minutes would be a miracle.

7

Spending the night in a parking garage in the back of an SUV with a naked woman wasn't the worst way to pass the hours. Especially since those hours were made a lot more comfortable thanks to a sleeping bag and pillow tucked under the backseat. It went without saying they'd had sex in every conceivable position, before folding down the back seats and snuggling up together.

Drew woke up next to Mara, safe and snug in his arms. She lay curled, looking as small and fragile as a sleeping kitten. Every muscle in his body ached, but in a good way. The strain was worth it, because it had satisfied Mara.

A glance at his watch revealed that it was a little before six in the morning. They'd need to get going before the place started filling up with people on their way to work. The less he and Mara were seen around the city, the better.

Getting out of Boston was going to be his prime objective once they hit the streets. It wouldn't take long for Zinetti to figure out he and Joey hadn't reported back with the details of Mara's death. Once the boss figured out both of them were missing, he'd put two and two together. And when he found Joey Salvatore, there would be hell to pay.

Easing himself up slowly so he wouldn't disturb her, Drew smoothed a stray lock of hair off her face. She mumbled in her sleep, his name on her lips. Naked and vulnerable, she trusted him. Wanted to be with him.

That touched him in the most intimate place, causing his throat to swell in a most unexpected way. Even when locked in the grip of slumber she was beautiful. Just looking at her caused his heart to squeeze in that oh-so-familiar manner he'd been trying to ignore for months.

Knowing she wanted him was a powerful aphrodisiac. He had to admit it. Arousal burned anew, low and hot in his groin. A tremble inside shook him to the core. *I think I'm in love.*

This time he didn't cringe when the thought occurred. He didn't flinch because he'd recently come to recognize the truth behind the realization. He was thirty-three years old and for the first time in his life he'd gone head over heels for a woman. A very dangerous woman. Considering both of them were on the lam, it was a pretty amazing feeling.

Drew had worked undercover before, had fucked more than his share of women during that time. He'd never let his heart overrule his head, though. He was on the job and the women he'd spent time with were just objects, a means to get the information he needed to make the case.

Being with Mara Luce was different, way different, on so many levels. It wasn't just the sex. Behind her tough chick exterior was the vulnerable interior of a woman who'd seen her share of bad times. Though she rarely spoke of it, the signs of abuse were there. Growing up inside the guts of organized crime had given her a bird's-eye view of all the bad things men could do to each other.

Drew lightly stroked her bruised cheek. He so desperately

wanted Mara, wanted her so badly he hurt inside. When he'd joined the Boston State Police he hadn't ever imagined he'd meet a woman he'd want to settle down with, leaving him wanting more than a roll between the sheets.

Mara Luce actually had him thinking about leaving the force, going into witness protection with her.

Unbelievable.

His head had warned his heart how dangerous it was to give away control to the female sex. But there was no denying the way he felt about Mara. He wanted to be with her every possible moment.

Isn't this a hell of a time to realize I want a relationship?

Shaking his head to clear away all the confusing impressions, Drew sucked in a breath. Staying focused was absolutely essential right now if he intended to get them out of this mess alive.

Mara stirred against him, drifting back toward wakefulness.

"Mmm," she murmured. "Morning."

"Hey, sleepyhead." One hand sliding to the curve of her hip, Drew bent over her, nuzzling her neck. Her perfect little ass was pressed right into his hips, giving his penis a nice warm place to snuggle. If she kept up that wriggling, he wouldn't be flaccid much longer. "You sleep okay?"

Mara yawned and stretched. "Considering I made it through the night in a nice warm place instead of a cold, dark one, I'm good. You?"

Drew grinned. "Better than I thought possible."

Mara settled onto her back, bending her legs and lifting them over his. Her bare breasts rose and fell enticingly.

The scent emanating from her sleep-warm skin aroused him in an instant. Drew felt desire stir deep in his loins. His penis took notice of her warm sex, so close and easily penetrated.

His hand drifted to her breast. Using just the tip of one finger, he drew slow circles around one erect peak.

Her eyes twinkled with sleepy pleasure. "That feels good," she murmured. She tugged the sleeping bag off her body, baring it for his pleasure.

Seeing her naked made Drew's mouth run dry. His gaze searched every inch, marveling at the sheer perfection of her physique. White-hot heat bubbled up from his core. There was no doubt about his attraction. He could never look at her enough. If only she could walk around naked twenty-four hours a day, seven days a week, he'd be a happy man.

He kept up his slow caress. "This is the first time we've ever spent the night together. I want to enjoy waking you up."

Mara wiggled her rear against his hips. Desire danced in her blue eyes. "Feels like you're already awake."

Drew released a slow groan. His cock was steadily rising to the occasion. "Oh, I am." He slid his palm down her abdomen, over the smooth plane of her belly, seeking the warmth between her thighs.

Mara opened her legs. "What are you going to do?" Naughty girl. As if she didn't know.

Drew slipped a finger through the folds of her dewy labia, rubbing gently against the small hooded organ of her sex. "I'm going to make slow, lazy love to you right here."

Mara arched her back, welcoming the firmness of his touch, the sweeping strokes of his fingers against her clit. "Sounds like the perfect way to start the day." Her body was an instrument of pleasure, responding to the sensations of touch in a way that made Drew feel like a master composer.

Determined to savor the liquid heat pooling inside his cock, he slipped two fingers inside her depth. Strong muscles gripped and held. She was hot and wet, ready to be penetrated.

Mara rolled her hips in a circular motion. "What are we going to do?"

Drew dragged his fingers out, then slowly slipped them back inside her. "I think you know what we're doing."

She shook her head. "No." A long slow hiss of air slipped through her lips. "After."

Damn hard to concentrate with a raging hardon and his fingers shoved up her twat. "The plan's rough, but the first thing I need to do is get you to a safe place."

Heat throbbed around his fingers. "That makes sense," she said in a breathy, sultry voice. "Where?"

Drew groaned, pressing deeper. "I don't know yet. But I'll find a place. One thing I do know is that my contacts are tainted. Until I know who Zinetti's mole is, I can't let the feds know anything."

She tossed out a salacious giggle. "So what are you going to do?"

Letting out a shaky laugh, Drew thumbed her clit. "I have a few ideas in mind, but right now I'm going to concentrate on making you come like crazy."

Mara's hands slipped between her legs, easing his fingers out of her depth. "I don't think so."

He grinned. "Why not?"

She guided his hand to her mouth. Her tongue slipped out, tracing his cream-wet fingers. "Because I'm too hungry to come." She licked the cleft between his fingers. "I'd much rather have a taste of you."

Shifting her body around, Mara pushed the sleeping bag aside to expose Drew's nude body. "Settle back," she ordered through a sultry smile.

Tucking the pillow under his head, Drew stretched out, grateful his Nissan XTerra provided plenty of room to accommodate his six-foot frame. He'd spent more than one night in the back of his SUV, glad for the security it offered. His penis was rock hard, the beat of his heart forcing blood into the turgid organ.

Mara settled between his legs. Her hands were warm and soft against his flesh. Fingers closing around the veined length, she brought her wet mouth down around the flared crown. The first suck from her lips took his breath away.

Body going rigid, Drew moaned like a hound in heat. Her grip on his cock was sure and firm. She knew just the right pressure to use. Oh, man! "That feels so good." He welcomed the firmness of Mara's lips, the sweeping invasion of her tongue as she explored the rim of his penis.

With an expert's move, Mara swooped lower, tongue flicking at his shaft as she deep-throated him with a technique that would make a porn star blush.

Drew groaned, threading his fingers through her hair, holding her head, silently wishing the sparkling fire pouring through his veins would last an eternity. There were too many sensations to process at once, an oncoming rush of vibrations that threatened to drive his mind into overload.

At the moment he didn't care if his brain cells all died and his mind shorted out.

Even as Mara was going into a delicious upstroke, he was lifting his hips, holding her head so she could take him all over again. Liquid heat pooled inside his gut and his balls throbbed painfully, hard and full. He didn't fight the currents of sheer rapture, willing to let himself be entirely swept away by the powerful riptide.

"You like?" she purred. A scrape of teeth followed, delivering the most delicious spike of pain he'd ever experienced.

Sparking lights flashed behind his lids. He gasped. "Christ, baby, that mouth of yours is a lethal weapon." A tide of sensation surged through his body. Being under her sensual control was the most erotic thing he'd ever experienced. If she stopped now he'd shatter.

Mara jacked him, harder. Faster. "Glad you approve," she chuckled. A hot rush of ecstasy threatened to swamp him.

Drew's internal temperature rose toward the red, perilously

close to release. Carnal impressions fluttered in and out of his brain, almost too fast to comprehend or enjoy now that he was rising to completion. Brain cells sizzling, he felt his blood boiling hotter than molten lava.

"I don't think I can hold off," he grated. By now he wanted for the ache to ease, the intense throbbing inside his groin to stop.

"Not so fast." Mara rose up, easily bracketing his hips between her slender thighs. Instead of lowering herself right away, she held her body away from his.

A groan of anticipation eddied past Drew's lips. Her sex was so enticingly near. He closed his eyes, waiting.

Leaning forward, Mara planted her palms on his shoulders. Her gaze leveled into his. One side of her mouth curved into a saucy smile. God, she had the cutest dimple. "Do you want me?" she whispered.

Drew stared back at her, marveling at how truly exquisite her features were: the exotic slant at the corners of her eyes, the pert upturn of her nose, and the lush red lips that reminded him of ripe strawberries under a warm summer sun.

The idea of her taking control was both sensual and strangely hypnotic. Keeping his emotions disengaged was no longer an option. His mind might have said "no," but his body said "yes." His heart seconded the motion.

"Yes," he murmured without hesitation.

Mara lifted a hand, her fingers scraping his whisker-covered chin, then his mouth. Her heated gaze never wavered from his. "I knew you were trouble the moment I laid eyes on you." She gave a fatalistic shrug. "You weren't supposed to mean anything to me, Drew. Just another thug in my life, another man I'd fuck a little and then walk away from."

Stomach muscles contracting with a brutal clench he felt all the way to his core, Drew knew there was only one answer he could give. "I'm not walking away, babe," he said through the lump building in his throat. "That's not the way I do things."

Mara's probing gaze softened. "You never treated me like trash, Drew," she murmured. Lowering her hips, she guided her honeyed sex down onto his waiting shaft. "Other men used me, treated me like a whore because I let them. But you—oh my!—never did . . ." Her words trailed off into a succulent moan of pure enjoyment.

Drew's moan of pleasure mingled with hers as he made his entry through the gates of heaven on earth. The glide into her slick heat was as easy as it was sweet. Her hips settled on top of his, seating his cock as far inside her as physically possible. Their two bodies were one, moving together perfectly.

Needing more, Drew cupped her breasts. Her nipples tightened at the first brush of his thumbs. He sucked in a ragged breath. "I never thought of you like that," he murmured.

Eyes fluttering shut, Mara shifted her hips. Her inner muscles contracted, rippled voraciously around his cock. The sensation was like a jolt of pure electricity surging through him. "Really?"

Drew plucked at the bead-hard tips. "The only thing I ever saw was a vital, stunning woman taking what she wanted in a man's world. You've walked with dangerous men, Mara, and you've held your own."

A single, unexpected tear slipped down Mara's pale cheek. "I can't do it anymore," she whispered, her voice suddenly cracking from emotional strain.

Taking control, Drew rolled them over, pressing Mara down. Their bodies parted for only a moment. "We're going to get through this." Supporting his weight on outstretched arms, his hips settled between her thighs. Guiding the crown of his cock to her slit, he thrust back inside her.

Catching hold of his shoulders, Mara tipped back her head. "Promise?"

Drew dipped his head for a taste of her lips. "You can count on me." Her mouth parted willingly under his, allowing him to taste her unique flavors, including a hint of her own tangy spices.

Their bodies glided into a smooth motion, the practiced waltz of two people who knew each other's needs and how to satisfy them. What had started as a base satisfaction of primal instincts had unexpectedly turned into something more, drawing them into a black hole, threatening to consume body, mind, and spirit.

Without warning, the tempo increased between them.

Suddenly there was nothing gentle about their lovemaking. It had turned fierce, wild, their needs lost in animal abandon. Every searing thrust had Drew on fire, tested his control.

Mara bucked and undulated beneath him, her cries of pleasure urging Drew to increase his speed. Rock-hard muscles flexed beneath her fingers, her nails tearing into his flesh, marking him as her exclusive property.

Drew ravaged her, pummeling her sex with everything he had. With each body-jarring stab, he felt orgasm rising. The waves inside his groin were cresting and peaking on an ocean so wild and deep that everything else was swept away.

Vaguely aware of Mara's cries of satisfaction, he closed his eyes, welcoming the starburst of climax. Hot semen jetted, its ferocious release tearing him up inside like a wild animal.

They collapsed together in a boneless heap. The only sound between them was of strained lungs seeking air. Soaked with perspiration, their heated bodies started to cool down.

Reality slammed back in, punching him squarely in the gut. His conscience wiggled like a worm on a hook. Now that his libido was satisfied, sanity was returning. The news it delivered alarmed. In the heat of the moment he'd said some things to her, things he wasn't sure he really meant.

Drew rubbed a hand over his eyes, attempting to blot out

the disquieting jumble inside his head. He'd forgotten what raw lust could do to a man's judgment. Of course a man's reason always trickled away when the blood in his head rushed to his dick. Talk about sex making the male species brain dead. Cocks weren't known for their ability to think coherently.

Staying with Mara will probably cost me my entire career.

Testifying against her murderous boss meant she'd have to go into hiding. To stay with her, he'd have to go, too. Once he walked away from the force, he wouldn't ever be able to go back into law enforcement.

A shiver cut through him. He swallowed thickly, wondering why he'd let himself get carried away in the moment. Was having Mara worth trading in his badge? She fed something ravenous, something insatiable, inside him.

But is it enough?

The question loomed inside his skull, echoing endlessly.

8

Drew wasn't taking any chances. Though the city of Boston was a large one, Clement Zinetti had a lot of influence within the community, which apparently included certain members of law enforcement. The first thing he did was ditch his cell, knowing the feds had access to all his records. Not only that, a person's location could be easily tracked via the towers picking up the signals from the calls. It was also too damn easy for anyone with a shortwave radio to pick up and record calls, a security breach he just couldn't risk.

His SUV posed a bigger security risk, but there was little he could do short of abandoning the vehicle and stealing another. A quick solution was to switch plates, jacking them from a vehicle of similar make and model. As long as no cops pulled them over and ran the plates, they should be fine. He doubted the owner of the other SUV would even notice the switch. Most people didn't even know their own license plate numbers.

Taking care of Mara's lack of clothing proved to be the easiest solution.

Since Drew couldn't exactly take her shopping, they had to

settle for the next best thing: the local Goodwill drop-off. While not exactly designer, the clothing they dug out of the donation box did the trick. A pair of faded jeans, a couple of T-shirts, and a jacket got her dressed in something more than a pair of panties and his leather coat. The clothes weren't new, but they were clean and those tight jeans covered her shapely ass just fine in Drew's opinion. The bonus was a pair of leather boots, out of style but better than barefoot.

They just didn't have a place to go. Checking into a motel was too risky. Zinetti's men had found Mara once. Finding her again wouldn't be hard. No, Drew and Mara had to get out of the city, find a safe, quiet place, and hole up until the source of the leak could be found and plugged.

Drew felt he could trust only one man: the commander who'd volunteered him for the job when the feds had come knocking for a cop with enough street cred and connections to believably go undercover. Knowing Drew's background, Captain Lewis Abbot had helped mastermind the details behind Drew's fall from grace within the force.

Right now, that plan seemed to be falling apart, shredding faster than a paper kite in a high wind.

All he could do was call Abbot and hope there was a plan C. Plan A and plan B were already shot all to hell.

Parking the SUV outside a convenience store with a gas station in front, Drew hopped out and made his way to a pay phone. Levering a quarter into the slot, he punched in a series of numbers. When the dispatcher came on the line, he asked for Abbot.

"Who's calling?" she asked, pleasant but bored.

Drew swallowed. "Hardage," he said. "Drew Hardage."

The dispatcher didn't seem to recognize his name. That was a surprise, given his infamous public routing as a cop.

She must be new, he thought sourly.

A familiar voice picked up. "Hardage?"

Thank God. "Yeah."

"What the hell are you doing calling me direct?" Abbot demanded, clearly unhappy.

Drew grimaced. "Had to. Ran into a little problem with Zinetti."

That got Abbot's interest. "How screwed are we?" he asked, knowing there would be only one reason Drew would break his silence.

Drew rubbed his eyes, mentally putting together the best way to deliver bad news. "Zinetti's got a mole on the inside with the feds. He just got the tip about Mara Luce sleeping with a federal agent." He sketched out what he knew, which wasn't very damn much.

A rush of air escaped Abbot's lips. "Shit. Does he know it's you?"

"Not yet," Drew said. He paused, then blurted. "But he will once he finds Joey Salvatore."

More cussing; very expressive expletives escaped from Abbot. "What's up with Salvatore?"

Drew had to smile a little. "He's in the trunk of his car."

Abbot's voice took on a terse strain. Committing murder on a fellow wise guy wasn't part of working undercover. Unless absolutely necessary, that is. "Dead?"

Drew shook his head. "No, he's still among the living for now." He paused, drawing a breath. He needed to explain things. Fast. "But once Zinetti finds him, my ass will most likely be grass and he'll want to mow it."

"Definitely," Abbot echoed.

Another fast breath. "Listen, Zinetti knows Mara Luce was sleeping with an agent, and that she was close to bolting. He put a hit on her." He paused, jaw tightening. "I was his man for the job, me and Joey Salvatore. We were supposed to make her disappear. You know what I mean."

"Shit. Is she okay?" Abbot asked.

Drew's grip tightened on the receiver. "Yeah. She's with me. Best thing to do is get her out of town until we can find out who the mole is. Until then we can't turn Mara over to the feds."

Abbot agreed. "If Zinetti's got someone cuing him from the inside, chances are she'd be picked off even under protection."

The space between the rock and the hard place narrowed.

"As for me, well, the minute he finds Joey, he'll know who the agent is." Drew grimaced against the images of carnage filling his head. If Zinetti's men caught up with them, they'd both be dog meat.

"That makes sense," Abbot said. "Got a plan?"

Drew had hoped Abbot had one. "We have to go underground until the leak is found and plugged. Obviously if the feds know where we are, Zinetti will be tipped off by his informant. It won't be anything for him to find us and send us on a vacation we won't want to take."

Abbot drew a breath. "Yeah, and we all know how Zinetti gets even. Cop or not, he'll ice you without thinking twice."

Drew nodded. "Just like Bruce Nordstrom. Yeah. Remember him? Hacked to pieces and not a damn shred of proof that would put a finger on Zinetti."

"I remember." Abbot sighed. "It's a given we need to stash you and her somewhere out of sight."

"Where?" Drew asked. Any place would do.

Silence. A long, long pause. "Listen, I have a cottage on the Cape," Abbot finally said.

Drew's brows rose. He was about to say something cutting when the operator broke in. More money was needed if he wished to continue his call.

Cussing under his breath, Drew dug out a pocketful of change, sliding in a couple of dollars' worth of quarters, nickels, and dimes. That satisfied the operator and the conversation continued.

Back to his question. "A cottage on the Cape? On a police captain's salary? Sounds like you might be the stoolie."

Abbot wasn't amused. "Very funny, wise guy. The place belongs to my wife's family, her parents' place. Anyway, they're in Europe and the place is empty this time of year. Head down there and park yourselves until I can do a little sniffing around." He gave a location, along with brief driving directions.

Fumbling for a pen, Drew jotted on the back of the phone book, then ripped it away. He tucked the scrap into his pocket. "Got it." A thought occurred. "How do we get in?"

"You're a cop," Abbot came back with. "Break and enter."

"People in Cape Cod do not take kindly to strangers breaking and entering."

"Just kidding," Abbot said. "I'll call my brother-in-law. He'll open the place up for you."

"What's our story?"

Lewis Abbot considered, thinking fast. "I'll tell him I'm loaning it to a friend on his honeymoon. He'll get the place ready, buy some food and stuff."

The grip around their necks seemed to be lessening. Not bad. Not bad at all. "How long you think we'll be there?"

Abbot considered. "Don't know. Telling the feds they have a leak isn't going to be easy. They don't take kindly to being told how to do their jobs."

Drew had to laugh, take a bit of relief from the pressure. "To them the Staties are just a bunch of monkeys in blue uniforms."

"Arrogant pricks," Abbot breathed, then got back to the point. "Anyway, you've been banging Mara Luce. Now's your chance to fuck her right before putting her in witness protection."

The idea of being all alone with Mara Luce in a Cape Cod cottage wasn't exactly an unpleasant idea. In fact, it almost sounded too perfect to be a solution. Just thinking about making love to her somewhere really nice and truly private made his blood heat up.

He swallowed thickly. “I don’t know about that.”

“About what?” Abbot retorted.

About letting her go alone, Drew started to say. He quickly changed his mind. “Nothing,” he mumbled. “Just don’t let my ass hang out any farther than it has to.”

“Have I ever hung your ass out?” Abbot asked rhetorically.

Drew didn’t want to get started on that one. “Yeah,” he countered darkly. “When you pushed me into volunteering for this suicide mission. I don’t know about you, but the idea of reposing in a garbage bag on the side of the highway doesn’t make me a happy camper.”

“No doubt you would be fish food,” Abbot said. “I’ll be in touch.” He hung up.

That remark didn’t make Drew feel one bit better. He grimaced. That wasn’t an image he wanted floating around in the back of his mind for the rest of the day.

Hanging up the receiver, he did feel a bit better knowing he had a place to take Mara. All they had to do was hit the road. Cape Cod was only sixty miles away from Boston. By nightfall they could be tucked in, all warm and cozy.

We’re set.

Drew headed back toward his SUV, parked by one of the gas pumps. He’d filled up before making the call, leaving Mara in the passenger seat.

No Mara.

Drew froze, his muscles going rigid. He quickly looked around. She was nowhere to be seen. “Shit, shit, shit,” he muttered. “How’d they find us?”

Just as he was about to go into full-scale meltdown, Mara walked out of the nearby convenience store. She carried a plastic bag and a couple of soft drinks.

Drew rushed over to her, taking her arm and propelling her

toward the waiting vehicle. "Where were you?" he barked, unintentionally harsh. Catching his breath, he tried to calm his overactive pulse. Blood pressure rising, he'd damn near had a stroke right on the spot.

Mara tripped, catching herself before she fell. "I'm sorry. I had to pee."

Drew opened the passenger door, hurrying her inside. "I thought they got you," he said, voice a little hoarser than he liked. His breathing was just beginning to slow down to a normal rate. "I thought they'd taken you."

Mara looked at him, taking in his confusion and concern. "I didn't mean to scare you." She lifted the bag. "I snagged a twenty out of your stash. I needed some food or I'd faint from hunger."

Relief drizzled in.

Cupping her face in one hand, Drew thumbed her cheek with a quick caress. "I should have thought of that," he said. Truth be told he hadn't even thought about stopping to feed her. He wasn't hungry. Right now his stomach was all knots and churning acid. The only thing he could think about eating was a roll of Tums. He'd have an ulcer if this didn't let up soon.

One side of Mara's mouth curved. "I think I'm flattered. That's the first time in a long time that someone's been worried about me."

"Your parents must worry," Drew said, reluctant to move his hand.

Jaw going taut, she shook her head. "My parents died when I was a kid. I've been on my own a long time. The first thing I learned in life is that no one else is looking out for you."

He looked at her in surprise. This was one of the few times Mara had actually spoken about her past, in any capacity.

"I'll take care of you," he murmured, and meant it.

Eyes moistening with emotion, Mara shook her head. "Nothing this good lasts forever." She blinked hard, refusing to let a single tear fall. "If there's anything I've learned it's that good men like you don't hang around."

Drew looked into her crystal blue eyes, feeling another pang of longing deep inside his soul. "You could be wrong," he said, wanting to chase that sad look off her pretty face.

Without quite knowing what he was doing, he leaned forward. Touching his nose to hers, he whispered against her mouth. "You'll just have to trust me, Mara."

Her lips trembled. "Can I?" she murmured back.

Drew didn't answer. Instead he kissed her. A soft, lingering kiss, one holding the promise of heat and so many other things he couldn't even begin to think about, much less say aloud. He'd already given Mara Luce the one thing he swore he would never hand over to any woman.

His heart.

Drew already knew Mara Luce wasn't a woman he'd be putting behind him anytime soon. At the beginning of this operation, walking away when it was over had been the logical option.

There was no way he could even begin to fathom going back to those long, lonely nights he'd lived as a single man. *Even if it means throwing my career away, I'll stay with her.*

He'd made the decision on the spot.

How unbelievable was that?

9

The cottage Lewis Abbot had shrewdly offered as a hideout was charming, with its log cabin-like exterior and beautifully white-shingled roof. The patio and yard were perfectly maintained, right down to the neat white picket fence surrounding the property. The place looked like something out of a fairy tale.

Lewis Abbot's brother-in-law, Norman, greeted them on arrival, cheerfully handing over the keys to the place. He didn't seem to notice they were traveling with almost no luggage. Who said newlyweds would need extra clothes?

Drew waved him off, glad to get him gone. At this point in the day he was ready to collapse. Everything that could go wrong had gone wrong. Their trip hadn't been an easy one, hampered by a flat tire and a thunderstorm suddenly rumbling in offshore. The rain had beat the SUV at such a furious pace the windshield wipers could barely keep up with the flood of water. The big vehicle had hydroplaned a couple of times, almost sending them off the highway. Both he and Mara were tired, their nerves on edge.

The inside of the cottage was just as breathtaking as the outside, with a knotty pine interior and built-ins. Along with the usual amenities, the three-bedroom house held a mix of antiques and new furniture. Just a ten-minute walk from the Sagamore Bridge, the house represented old Cape Cod at its best.

Mara looked around, clearly pleased. "This is nice," she complimented. "I wasn't expecting anything like this."

Drew tossed the keys onto the counter. "Honestly, me neither." He couldn't fail to notice Norman had left a bottle of champagne sitting on ice. Two crystal glasses waited to be filled.

"Nice touch," she murmured, wiping the rain out of her eyes. Just getting inside had given them all a nice drenching. Her hair, damp and disheveled, hung in frizzy little ringlets around her face and shoulder, creating the appearance that she was much younger than her thirty-one years. Without cosmetics, she looked dewy and fresh faced, innocent.

Drew hadn't believed Mara could get any better looking. He'd been wrong. Noticing the way her nearly transparent T-shirt clung to her full breasts brought a smile to his lips. They hadn't been able to find a bra to fit her at the Goodwill dropoff. She'd been forced to go without, giving anyone who looked a nice peek at those hard little nipples poking out beneath the fabric. Dressed in those tight jeans and even tighter tee, she was every teenage boy's wet dream.

Come to think about it, she was pretty close to his wet dream, too. "Lewis told his brother-in-law we were newlyweds, hence the loan of the place."

Running her fingers through her hair to smooth it away from her face, Mara smiled. "Would be a place for one."

A smile tugged at Drew's lips. As far as a hiding place went, they'd hit pay dirt. Might as well take advantage of it.

He opened the fridge, hoping there would be enough food to last them a few days. Abbot's brother-in-law hadn't disappointed. A platter of cut fruit and cheeses, a baguette, and a platter of deli sliced roast beef waited to be consumed. Cabinets held nonperishable foods, at least enough for a week. They wouldn't be eating gourmet, but they'd be eating.

Closing the fridge, Drew hoped they wouldn't be confined to the place for an endless stretch. As much as he liked the quiet, he was a city boy at heart. Being stuck in a place so tranquil was guaranteed to grate on his nerves.

Not to mention, there was Mara. The more time they spent together, the harder it would be to walk away when this whole operation was over. One thing was for sure. It was a chance to find out if they had anything in common besides a desire to fuck like bunnies. Without the specter of the Mob boss hanging over their heads, would they even stand a chance as a couple?

Is that even something I should be considering? The thought wasn't as vague as it should be. Working undercover meant keeping a distance, not getting involved. By climbing into Mara Luce's bed, he'd violated a rule that, while not exactly sacrosanct, did throw him into a gray area concerning undercover operations. An agent wasn't supposed to have sex with potential witnesses. It was too easy for an agent to criminally implicate himself in a case he was investigating.

Part of his cover involved leading a realistic life as a thug. Getting to Mara meant getting into her bed. One wouldn't work without the other. Now he was in too damn deep and it felt like the water was coming up over his head.

Despite his earlier resolve, he was already second-guessing his earlier decision, wondering if he was letting his dick rule his head.

Do I cut her and swim, or do we go down together?

At this point, Drew wasn't sure what his feelings were. He'd wanted to wake up beside her. Now it seemed fate was attempting to hand him that chance.

Mara walked around, looking the place over. "How long do you think we'll be here?"

Drew shrugged. "I don't know. Abbot's looking into the leak. Until they know who it is, we can't be seen."

"But they'll find out who it is?" she asked.

"I hope so."

"Then what?" she demanded.

"Witness protection."

"So I'll really have to go into hiding?" she asked.

He nodded. "It would probably be best."

"I see." She paused, thinking a minute. "So what happens to, you know, us?"

It was the question he'd been dreading. On one hand he wanted to be with Mara. Forever. On the other hand, he didn't want to be seen as tucking his tail between his legs, running off because he was afraid of the Mob retaliating after the testimony he'd be duty bound and sworn to give in a court of law.

"I don't know," Drew answered honestly. "I suppose I'll go back to work."

She cocked her head. "Then you don't think Zinetti's men will come after you, too?"

He shrugged again. "That's hard to know. What I do know is I'm not the kind of man who likes to hide."

Mara levered her gaze into his. "And what if I don't want to go into witness protection?"

Was she saying what he thought she was?

Drew stared at her. A thousand impressions tangled inside, but he choked on every one like they were shards of glass. "Nobody can force you to," he said slowly. "But you'd be safer, Mara. It's one thing for a man to take a risk with danger. It's another thing for a woman."

Nostrils flaring, her mouth settled into a grim line. "Guess it's a chance I'll have to take."

Aware of his heart raging in his chest and his blood pounding through his veins, Drew stared at her. "You can't—" he started to say.

Mara insisted on pushing. "Why not?" She stared back at him, gaze snapping sparks, her breasts rising and falling with each angry breath.

"Because it's too damn dangerous," he said between clenched teeth.

Her stubbornness kicked up a notch. She raised her hands as if to strike punishing blows. "I'm not afraid of Zinetti," she insisted. "And I won't hide either."

Drew resisted the urge to grab her shoulders, shake some sense into her.

"That's stupid," he snapped, nerves suddenly fraying to the point of breaking. "You're not thinking." How could she refuse the safety of federal protection? Couldn't she see he loved her, damn it? That he wanted her to be safe? Even if it meant he'd have to give her up to keep her alive.

She's being stupid, he raged.

She offered a compromise. "I'll go if you will. Otherwise, I'm staying in Boston and going on with my life."

His heart deflated. "Are you saying you won't testify?"

Resolve glinted bright and hot in her eyes. "I'll testify," she said flatly. "And I'll take my chances."

Drew stared at her hard, all of a sudden knowing without a doubt he loved Mara with all his heart. Instead of asking him to sacrifice his career for her, this stubborn and infuriating woman was taking things one step farther. She'd offered to forego federal protection to stay with him.

But, oh heavens, would he be able to bear it if something happened to her?

An earsplitting rumble of thunder temporarily ended the conversation.

Caught in the grip of a fresh wave of emotions, Drew sat down in a nearby chair. Exhaustion, anger, anxiety, and a dozen other emotions were threatening to combust inside his skull.

This isn't what he wanted to be talking about.

This isn't what I wanted to be doing.

Drew looked at Mara, her clothes and hair still damp from the rain. Her clothes clung, making him hyperaware of her every lush curve.

"We might as well be married," he snapped. "We're fighting instead of fucking."

Mara stared at him, wide eyed. A small smile of mutual surrender parted her lips. "We do it really well, don't we?"

"Fight?" he asked.

"Fuck." Mara arched a suggestive brow toward the icy bottle. "It's all ugly outside and so nice and cozy inside," she continued, turning on her female charm. "Why don't we take advantage of a nice cold glass of champagne"—she reached for the edge of her damp T-shirt, peeling it up over her breasts—"and a nice hot shower?" She let the tee drop to the floor at her feet.

A tremor rippled through him. Her bare breasts alone were a sheer force of nature.

Gaze locking with hers, Drew rose from his chair. Just looking at her perfect features caused a rippling sensation deep in his guts, one that sent a wonderful pulse through his loins.

Closing the distance separating them, his pulse kicked into high gear as he cupped her pert breasts. They were beautiful, a work of art that defied gravity. "Forget the drink."

Mara caught her breath, biting down on her bottom lip as he thumbed her erect nipples, the sensations clearly swamping her.

"I take it you want to fuck?" She trembled more than a little, her body's heat seemingly melding his palms to her skin.

Drew slowly kneaded her breasts, expertly teasing the little nubs. Need jolted through him. Forget food. This was what he was hungry for. "Fucking isn't what we're doing, babe. This is making love."

Slipping one strong arm around her waist, Drew bent Mara back. His head dipped and his lips closed around one perfect peak.

Releasing a low moan, Mara's hand found his shoulders, fingers digging into his skin as his mouth worked at her breasts. "Oh, yessss . . ." she sighed. "That's perfect."

Drew circled one tented peak with his tongue. His cock grew heavier as an erotic sensation began pooling in his loins, causing his organ to swell.

His hand slipped between her legs, cupping her intimately against the crotch of her tight jeans. Feeling her heat, he rubbed harder. The seam of the jeans was right against her clit, giving her a nice bit of friction.

"I've been dying to screw you since you put those tight jeans on," he said, voice a husky register he didn't recognize as his own. "God, the way they cling to your ass . . ." He pressed against her crotch, drawing more slow circles. "Makes me hard just thinking about pulling them down over your hips and sticking my cock right into that tight little hole of yours."

The idea apparently appealed to her on several levels. "Then do it," she urged. "Show me what a good fucking feels like."

Heart beating as fast and furious as the rain beating the roof, Drew shook with unrestrained need. "I intend to."

Letting her go, he pushed her back against the counter. "Place your hands on the edge and don't move." Just looking at her, ready to please, sent a thrill through him.

Mara giggled. "What?"

Drew guided her hands down. "Hands on the counter, lady."

Her gaze glittered. "Are you playing big bad cop with me?" she teased, eyeing him with a grin.

"That's exactly what I'm doing. Only this pat-down isn't the one they taught us in training."

Mara took a deep breath and maneuvered her body into the position he indicated, leaning back against the counter. "Like this?"

"Like that." Drew knelt, his face level with her smooth belly. Running his palm against the flat of her abdomen, he followed the caress with a long slow nibble beside her navel.

"Ohhhh . . ." she murmured. "Sexy."

"Not half as sexy as this." Drew unsnapped the top of her jeans, then guided the zipper down. The top of her pants came apart, giving a peek at the panties covering her bare mound.

More blood drizzled out of his head, pooling around his groin. His erection strained against the front of his pants, suddenly too damn tight for comfort. They were going to have to come off soon, or he'd be cut in half.

A smile twitched at her lips as he tugged her jeans and underwear down. When they were about halfway to her knees, he stopped.

Drawing a deep breath, Mara looked down at him. "I can't open my legs," she complained.

Drew grinned. "I know. That's exactly what I want."

"Why?" she asked.

He showed her.

Using two fingers, Drew parted her soft folds. His tongue delved into the narrow cleft of her sex.

Moaning with abandon, Mara welcome the madness of his oral lovemaking. Her body shook with every stroke of his tongue, flicking out and invading her most intimate places.

Her knuckles went white around the edges of the cabinet. "Damn you," she cried out between great gulps of air. "You know just how to drive me wild." Her hips bucked, fighting the wet strokes he levered across her clit.

Knowing how deep and hard she clenched during orgasm,

Drew didn't want to miss her climax; he wanted her to come while he was inside her.

Turning Mara around, he bent her over the counter. He fumbled with his jeans, somehow getting them open, freeing his insistent erection. Aiming his hips at hers, he thrust. Her eager sex welcomed his shaft.

Drew almost whimpered with relief and satisfaction. God, she was tight. And snug, fitting him like a custom-tailored suit. It was all he could do not to cry out with the exquisite pleasure of the resulting carnal sensation.

Drew's left hand slipped around her body, covering her breast. He tugged at the sensitive nipple even as his hips pressed against hers.

With difficulty, Mara planted her palms flat, lifting her body back against his. "Is that all you've got?" she challenged.

Heart crashing against his ribs, Drew's breath raged in and out of his lungs. "I'm doing the best I can." Pleasure built with every dedicated thrust.

Fingers digging against the marble countertop, Mara whimpered. "Do better." Her voice was taut, ragged as his.

Drew caught her by the throat, pulling her up against him. "Like this?" His thick shaft shuttled in and out, delivering long ramming strokes. Orgasm coiled at the base of his spine.

Mara's vaginal muscles rippled delightfully around his penis even as the need to climax created exquisite sensations of agony deep inside his core. Head bent backward, throat straining, she cried out. "I'm coming—" Her words leveled off into a low moan of sheer pleasure.

Caught in her grip, Drew's blood sizzled, red-hot sparks threatening to incinerate him from the inside out. The pressure in his balls increased, drawing them tighter against his body. Release arrived and his entire body shuddered. Rapture picked him up, tossing him into a sky filled with shooting stars. He'd reached for the heavens and touched the face of creation.

A moment later, he and Mara collapsed together. They lay sprawled and dazed on the kitchen floor. They hadn't even made it anywhere near the bedroom.

No matter. The day was still young.

Drawing her close, Drew released a long shuddery breath. The only other sound in the house was the rain pinging against the windows, gentler now that the worst of the storm had passed.

"Somehow we're going to work this out," he said, trying to catch his breath.

Mara curled into him and offered an exhausted smile. "How?"

"Getting rid of Zinetti is a start," he murmured.

Mara turned those big blue eyes his way. Her pupils were dilated. A hint of tears shimmered at the edge of her lids. "What if we can't?"

Drew smoothed her tangled hair away from her face.

Guilt punched through him at the sight of those ugly bruises staining her skin. She'd taken the beating to protect him, kept her mouth shut when all she had to do was give him up to save herself.

Drew's anger spiked all over again. His fury was so sharp he couldn't catch his breath. *Any man who beats on a woman deserves to have more than the shit kicked out of him,* he silently fumed. Whether he wanted to admit it or not, his whole world had somehow come to center around Mara Luce, and he couldn't bear the thought of anyone hurting her ever again.

"I'll kill him if I have to," he growled, surprised by the force behind his words.

At that second Drew had no doubt. He could definitely pull the trigger on Zinetti.

And smile as he did it.

10

Half conscious, Drew hovered between waking and sleeping, too comfortably exhausted to move a single achy muscle. He and Mara had spent the afternoon making love, enjoying each other in ways he'd never dreamed possible.

Hours later, they'd dropped into bed wrapped in each other's arms. If ever his life had come close to any sort of perfection, this felt like the moment.

Sometime during the night, Drew was vaguely aware of Mara slipping out of bed, gliding silently out of the bedroom. In his twilight-dazed state he thought he heard whispers, a woman's voice, low and muffled, in the distance.

Vaguely thinking he must be dreaming, Drew didn't give the whispers a second thought. Especially when Mara slid back between the sheets. Her body pressed against his. Warm hands roamed his naked flesh.

Mmm. What a way to fall asleep.

The sandman crept in, wrapping his senses in the silken veil of sleep. Relief washed over him as he finally let go of the day's tension.

A minute later, Drew was peacefully unconscious.

11

The lamp beside the bed snapped on. A blinding shaft of light hit Drew squarely in the face. Neon shards stabbed his eyelids, temporarily blinding him.

"This time I arrived ten minutes early." The voice cutting through the silence was all too familiar.

Suddenly aware an uninvited element had crept into the bedroom, Drew opened his eyes. Hand flying to his face to cut the illumination, he blinked hard, struggling to cast off the shackles of exhaustion binding his mind.

A familiar figure loomed over him. Despite the early morning hour, the mobster was turned out in one of his impeccable suits.

Drew bolted upright. His hand shot under the pillow where he'd stashed his 9mm Glock subcompact before going to bed.

The gun wasn't there.

Shock rattled him to the teeth. "Damn."

Zinetti's dark eyes snapped with hatred and murderous intent. "You looking for something, Hardage?"

Discovering he was totally unarmed, a chill of horror rippled down Drew's spine. Given the look on the gangster's face, he logically deduced he was probably about to be sent right back into a zone of unconsciousness.

One he'd never wake up from.

Drew laughed, disgusted with himself for being such a fool.

Zinetti's wicked gaze danced. "Looks like we got the drop on you," he observed coolly.

Panic coiling inside, Drew sucked in a quick breath before releasing a brief but obscene curse. "Son of a whore."

He looked around, focusing on the next move he could logically make. He didn't have many options.

Jimmy Mancuso stood a few feet away, gun leveled at his gut. He grinned. "Wakey-wakey, sleepyhead." Outside, the sun wasn't even cracking the horizon.

For the first time in his career, Drew's life flashed in front of his eyes, unspooling in slow motion across his mind's screen. "Fuck you."

Zinetti's features tightened. "Fucking's over for the night. I'm afraid Mara's gone bye-bye."

A glance over his shoulder informed Drew he was in bed alone. "What did you do to her?" he growled, too aware he was stark-ass naked under the sheets—and totally helpless to defend himself.

A wolfish grin widened Zinetti's mouth. "She's okay. In fact, she's perfect." He turned toward the adjoining bathroom off the master suite. "You can come out now, babe."

The door opened.

Dressed in a flimsy negligee she'd borrowed, Mara Luce glided out. Hair twirled up in a knot, a few strands strayed down around her face and neck. Her skin glowed with a fresh sheen, still damp from her recent shower. The see-through robe clung to her body, gloriously naked underneath.

Drew's brain registered what his eyes saw, leaving him speechless. Mara had his Glock clutched firmly in one pretty little hand.

Shock washing over him, his eyes widened. In his own hand the weapon didn't seem so menacing. In hers, the weapon looked a lot bigger, more dangerous and deadlier than ever.

Drew's heart slammed against his ribs. The breath he'd been struggling to take left him in a rush, leaving his lungs bereft of oxygen. Nausea rose, turning his insides to acid. Cold-blooded, choke-the bitch-to-death rage surged through him at the sight of his lover holding his gun.

"What the hell is going on?" he stammered, vaguely dredging up the hushed one-sided conversation he'd believed to be part of a dream. All Mara had to do was pick up the phone and make a call.

Without a word, or even a second glance his way, Mara silently glided around the bed, joining her murderous boyfriend.

Zinetti slipped an arm around her waist, pushing a smile into place. "My little girl gave us a call last night." He gave her a quick kiss on the temple.

Betrayal felt like a sharp knife shoved right through his rib cage. "Why?"

Mara's grip tightened on the Glock. "I wanted my life back," she murmured, her voice strangely vague. She seemed to be making it a point not to look directly at Drew, or speak directly to him.

Her detachment chilled. *She's going to blow my fucking brains out,* he thought vaguely.

Shit. He'd lost her.

Somehow Mara had slipped though his fingers. It vaguely occurred to Drew she'd probably planned on setting him up from the beginning. He wondered if she'd felt anything when he bought the farm, or if she was truly as cold hearted as she'd been when they'd first met. She'd warned him she always took care of Mara first.

Apparently she was still living by that credo. Turning him over to her boss had certainly saved her pretty little ass.

Drew wasn't afraid of dying. But he was appalled that Mara might be the one to pull the trigger on him.

God, he felt so dirty. Used. If only he'd known what she was really capable of, he'd have played things differently. As it was, he'd let her burrow under his skin, infect him like a disease. A fatal disease.

Zinetti used the tip of the cane to prod Drew, lifting up the sheet to reveal his otherwise nudity. "So that's the cock she's been playing with." A low whistle escaped his lips. "Not bad, cop." He laughed. "But not enough to keep her happy."

Drew felt his cheeks go ten shades of red. He slapped Zinetti's cane away. "Maybe you should have been a little earlier," he snapped. "Then you could have seen me pounding her sweet little cunt." He tossed a glare at Mara. "It seems to me you enjoyed it every time you came. How many times?" He pretended to think. "Four—or was it five?"

The gun in Mara's hand wavered, but didn't drop. "I'm sorry, Drew," she murmured. "I have to take care of things my own way." Her bottom lip trembled, the first sign of emotion she'd shown toward him. "I only hope someday you'll understand."

Drew snorted. Fat chance he'd understand! Like he even had a verifiable future on the face of this earth. If there was a time to bend over and kiss his ass good-bye, now was it.

He felt stupid, like the biggest dunce in the world. He'd let his guard down, believed Mara when she'd said she wanted out of the Mob life.

She'd double-crossed him. Good. Damn her, she played like a pro. Cold, ruthless, and very efficient.

So much for letting a woman niggle her way into his heart.

Drew reached for his pants, pooled on the floor beside the bed. "You mind?"

Jimmy Mancuso gestured with his weapon. "Be my guest. I can't go riding around the Cape with a naked man." He grinned like a shark-eating chum.

Drew sighed and pushed to his feet. He slipped into his pants, tugging the zipper shut and buttoning up. Having his ass covered made him feel a little bit better, salvaging his dignity. He didn't relish the idea of being found floating naked in the ocean. "I take it we're going for a little ride."

Jimmy Mancuso scowled coldly. "You got it. Far be it from me to mess this nice place up."

Drew pulled on yesterday's socks, then put on his boots. "Guess I don't get any points for not plugging Joey."

Mancuso shrugged. "You had your chance." He waved his gun. "Hurry up and get dressed. We need to get gone before the sun rises."

Looking at Mara, Drew slipped his shirt on. "Don't guess I get a kiss good-bye."

Zinetti grinned like a piranha. "Feel lucky you got to fuck such a terrific piece of tail." He spread his hands to show generosity. "But hey, you can't say I am not a charitable man. Consider it my gift to you."

Drew snorted. "Some gift."

Mancuso gestured with his gun. "I haven't got all goddamned day," he said with more than a little annoyance. "Let's get going."

Drew stepped past Zinetti, not bothering to give Mara a second glance. His throat tightened. He swallowed thickly, but could think of nothing he wanted to say to the traitorous bitch.

Good-bye and good riddance.

It hurt to breathe, hurt to think. He'd known all along falling in love with Mara Luce was bad for his health.

In more ways than one.

Mara's voice stopped him mid-step. "Drew, wait."

Drew turned, not feeling very generous toward her at all. "Yeah?" he snapped.

Mara lifted the gun she'd nabbed right out from under his head as he slept. "I'm going to make this right." She shoved the gun right into Zinetti's gut.

"What the hell?" the mobster cried, clearly stunned.

Thinking fast, Mancuso lifted his weapon, clearly intending to take Mara out. Temporarily distracted, he took his sights off Drew.

That was all the motivation Drew needed to save his own ass. Blood roaring in his ears, he didn't bother with any of the fancy moves he'd learned in the academy. He acted on instinct, curling his hand into a fist. Without stopping to think, he whirled toward Mancuso, delivering a roundhouse blow and catching the smaller man squarely in the temple.

Mancuso reeled blindly, squeezing off a reckless, unsighted shot. "Bastard!"

Drew dodged. The heat of a bullet passing by grazed his left bicep. The bullet lodged in the wall behind him.

Gathering his wits, Mancuso prepared to fire again. "This time I won't miss," he snarled.

Mara Luce's voice rang loud and clear. "Stop it, Jimmy!" she ordered. "Drop it or I'll kill him."

Mancuso started to point the gun at her. "I'll take you out, Mara," he warned.

No amateur with a gun, Mara Luce squeezed the trigger. Without flinching, she expertly plugged Jimmy Mancuso with a slug of lead right through the heart.

Mancuso toppled backward, landing on his back with a solid thump on the floor. A small corona of blood began to seep across his chest, staining his shirt a bright cherry red. He still held his gun, fingers convulsing around the grip as he struggled to pull the trigger one last time.

He never managed. Giving a small final gasp, Jimmy Mancuso died.

Zinetti made a running grab for the fallen weapon.

Palm clamped against his bleeding shoulder, Drew beat the mobster to the weapon. Ignoring the searing pain in his arm, he punted Mancuso's gun with his boot. The gun skittered across the carpet. Out of Zinetti's reach.

Cane held in a death grip, Zinetti's gaze flickered toward the dead man at his feet. Disbelief written across his pale face, he turned to Mara. "Shit. You killed him." He brandished the cane, clearly intending to strike her.

Mara pointed the gun toward her boss without flinching. "I want my life back." Eyes narrowing, a fine trembling enveloped her body. "I want a life where I'm not hiding. Where I'm not afraid any more."

Zinetti scoffed, leveling his chin to an imperious angle of defiance. "You think you have enough nerve, little girl, then go ahead." His grip tightened on his cane. "I don't think you have it in you."

Mara stared at her former lover with sheer hate in her snapping blue gaze. "Oh, I think I have the nerve," she snapped viciously. "I know just how to shoot a man down in cold blood. I'm going to shoot you, just like you shot my father."

Zinetti shrugged. "So what?"

Drew saw Mara's grip tighten on the gun, steeling her determination to carry through her threat. "They say don't get mad, get even. I'm getting even, you bastard. Or don't you remember Josh and Angelina Lucas?"

Zinetti physically grimaced. The names had obviously touched a nerve somewhere deep inside his sociopathic brain. "You can't know them."

Two intense gazes clashed.

Mara's grin was skeletal, an unsettling grimace stretched across her lips. "Oh, I do. They were my parents. You shot my father dead right in front of my mother, or don't you remember her begging for his life? She pleaded, but you just laughed and took her out, too, like a dog on the street."

Drew saw Zinetti's face go dead white. The old man started to sway. "No one was there."

Mara looked at him, clearly bewildered by his words. When she spoke again, her voice sounded curiously small, childlike. "I was in the closet . . . I-I . . ." She started to falter. "Saw everything . . ." A single tear tracked down her cheek, then another.

Drew stared at her hard, seeing her in a new light. Now he knew why Mara never mentioned her childhood, why she'd clam up and go silent when questioned about her life. She'd clearly come up the hard way, a way no little girl deserved to.

Pain cut through him, spearing his heart. It felt like all the blood was draining out of his body. Oh, God. No one, especially a child, should ever witness such carnage delivered by the hands of another human being.

Mara angrily swiped her tears away with the flat of one palm. She looked scared. Desperate. Like a very young girl and not a woman of thirty-one. "Daddy made me hide." The final confession tumbled out of her mouth, her words stumbling over one another.

Drew realized she wasn't speaking as a grown woman. She was eight years old again. Mara Luce had been damaged early in life, a damage that was most likely irreparable.

"Jesus Christ," he spat toward Zinetti. "How could you?"

Apparently beyond hearing anyone, Zinetti closed his eyes for a moment in sheer frustration. He'd gotten caught, red handed. A murder he'd committed over twenty years ago had come back, rising like a specter from an unquiet grave to point a damning, deadly finger.

"Josh Lucas stole a lot of money," he tried to explain. "It was just business."

Mara shook her head. More tears slid down her cheeks. By the expression on her face, she wouldn't be deterred come hell or high water. "I've waited to get even with you, find the perfect moment to put you in the ground. Now is that time." Steeling herself for the recoil, her finger tightened on the trigger.

Mind whirling with dark thoughts, Drew looked from one to the other, the woman he loved and a man he hated. He wouldn't blame her a bit for pulling the trigger. Were their positions reversed, he probably would have done the same thing.

Zinetti deserved to die. That was clear enough. But there was a right way to handle this, a right way to make him pay for his crimes.

Making a sudden decision, Drew stepped closer to Zinetti. They were both behind the trigger now. If she chose to fire, there was no way she'd miss.

The bedroom suddenly felt too damn small, too damn close for comfort. "Mara, no." He shook his head. "Killing him isn't the way to get your life back."

Eyes writhing with desperation turned his way. "It is," Mara insisted. "It's the only way to get him out of our lives. Then we can be together."

Acutely aware she could fire at any second, Drew slowly held out a hand. "We'll get him out of our lives," he said slowly. "But we have to do this the right way, the legal way. Justice deserves a chance to work here."

Mara's gaze darkened. "There is no justice," she snapped back viciously. She brandished the Glock, looking from the gun to the man she fully intended to kill. "This is the only thing that works in his world."

Blood running cold, Drew shook his head. He had to hold steady, convince Mara that two wrongs didn't make a right. Murdering Zinetti wouldn't make her feel any better.

Murder was murder.

Period.

The cuffs would go around her delicate little wrists the same way. She'd go to jail. Justice didn't reward vigilantes, no matter how defensible the violence.

Damn. It tied him in knots just to think of Mara Luce sitting behind bars. That wasn't where she belonged.

A need to protect her from her own madness flowed through his veins. His arms ached to close around her, holding her close and stroking away her pain.

First he had to talk her out of killing Zinetti.

"Justice depends on good people like you and me standing up to bad men like him," Drew said slowly. "Killing him only brings you down to his level, makes you like him."

"You aren't doing me any favors, cop," Zinetti barked under his breath.

Drew could smell the old man's fear, sweat mingling with a sour, pungent odor. "Shut up," he snarled back. "Otherwise I'll turn my head and say I never saw a damn thing."

Mara's gaze chilled dangerously. Swallowing hard, she summoned her courage. She was ready to commit murder and pay the penalty. "Just close your eyes." Her voice broke briefly. "You don't have to see a thing, know a thing."

There was no doubt in Drew's mind that she meant what she said.

He stared at her, so small, fragile, and utterly beautiful in her ruthless determination. The room suddenly felt overly warm as heat settled inside his gut. Somehow she'd turned things around in her mind. She was protecting him, taking care of him.

"I'll know the truth," he said softly. "I'll know it was you, Mara." He slowly shook his head. "That's not something the woman I love could ever do."

Mara's blue gaze settled on him, searching for answers. "You l-love me," she whispered, her voice a-tremble.

Drew nodded. "Yeah." He offered a tentative smile. "I do. Completely and absolutely, I do."

Crumbling from inside, Mara's tears fell unchecked. She started to sob. "I love you, too." The hand holding the gun faltered, beginning a slow slide from her grip.

Catching the gun, Drew eased it from her lax fingers. "Careful now. Just let me have it." His reassurance swirled through the narrow space separating them. She let the deadly weapon go without protest.

Gaze glazing over, Mara sagged in weary defeat. Every bit of anger she'd possessed suddenly drained away, leaving her limp and exhausted. "It had to be over." Leaning against his solid frame, she took a deep breath. "Just make him go away." Her fingers clenched into his shirt, holding on tight. "Please."

Drew's arm quickly circled her waist, drawing her close.

He hadn't been wrong about her after all. Underneath her hard exterior was a frightened little girl. One he wanted to take care of.

For the rest of his life.

He leveled the gun at his prisoner. "Don't move if you want to stay above ground."

Zinetti's shoulders sagged. Suddenly he was nothing more than an old man with a cane. No threat to anyone anymore. Standing up to him sucked away the Mob boss's power.

Mara smiled up at Drew, her love shimmering in her eyes. "I think I can handle that idea now." Her hold on him tightened. "I think I can handle it as long as you're with me."

Exactly the words Drew wanted to hear.

The mobster frowned. "You fucker," he snarled.

Swallowing down the lump building at the back of his throat, Drew smiled back. "Yeah, I am." He gave Mara a little squeeze. *And I'm loving every minute of it.*

Though he didn't relax a muscle, he felt the tension twisting his guts unknot, draining away. His chest expanded, his lungs drawing in much-needed oxygen. His arm hurt like hell, but he barely noticed the insistent throb.

Now that he had Mara back on his side, and back in his arms, he intended to keep her safe. To do so, he'd willingly pledge his heart, his soul . . . and his badge.

SATURDAY NIGHT SPECIAL

Myla Jackson

1

"Happened about seven hours ago, based on current body temp." John Mokiua, Medical Examiner, straightened from the naked body of a well-muscled man in his late twenties, found dead in the Outrigger Hotel on Waikiki Beach. He glanced at his watch. "That would put time of death around 3:25 A.M." The M.E. removed a notepad from his front shirt pocket and jotted down the information.

The crime scene investigators shot photos and carefully gathered evidence in the room. They combed through the sheets, floor, and bathroom for hairs, fibers, fingerprints, or anything else that would help them identify the murderer.

Honolulu police officer Mano Kekehuna inhaled the faint, bitter scent of almonds and blew it out. "Black Widow?"

"Same M.O." John nodded to the night table. "Candlelight, nice hotel, no signs of struggle, looks to have had sex recently, and if I test that wineglass, I'll bet you my shirt I'd find it laced with cyanide."

"That makes three in the past three days." Mano's gut clenched. He knew what the news would bring to the department, and what his next assignment entailed. He fought to keep from groaning out loud.

Brad Weis, Mano's partner, slapped him on the back and grinned. "Just got off the phone with HQ. Our stiff worked as a stripper for the Cabana Boys Club. Guess you know what this means."

Hell yeah, he knew and didn't need reminding. Mano glared at Brad. "Shut the fuck up."

Dr. Mokiua's brows twisted into a curious frown. "What does it mean?"

"Our man, Mano, here, gets to strut his stuff to find our Black Widow."

John's frown disappeared and a smile spread from ear to ear. "Mano undercover as a stripper? I'd pay good money to see that."

Mano directed his glare at the mild-mannered M.E. with enough venom to make the man take a step backward. "Don't."

"Okay, okay. Don't get your G-string in a twist." John laughed at his own joke, gathered his bag of tricks, and nodded to the waiting EMT team. "Load 'em up. I'll have the autopsy wrapped up by tomorrow."

Mano scanned the room, his gaze taking in every detail, from the tossed sheets to the bottle of champagne in the ice bucket. A night of sex, a little cyanide as a chaser, and it's done. No fuss, no muss, just death. He had to admire the woman for her deadly precision. She'd left behind nothing to go on.

"Bingo!" One of the Crime Scene Investigators straightened from his position hovering over the bed. He held something between his rubber-gloved fingers. "Our first clue since this started."

Mano and Brad waited just inside the door of the suite for the technician to bring it over and dangle it in front of them, a grin of triumph on his face. "One long, silky red hair. Must be one hot little redhead to get a guy like this into bed."

Brad nudged Mano. "Goes with what the porter said. A woman about five foot five, nice curves, dressed in a black, slim-fitting dress and dark sunglasses with . . . long red hair. We have our description; all you have to do is provide the bait."

"The porter could have been mistaken. The redhead might have been a guest of guests here at the Outrigger."

"Escorted by a muscle-bound man who meets the description of our victim?" Brad's brows rose. "Are you nervous? Do I detect reluctance? I thought you wanted to work undercover."

"I do, but not as a fucking stripper."

"I'd trade places with you in a heartbeat, but you're the one with the Mr. Universe body and professional dancing experience." Brad's gaze traveled Mano's length from head to toe. "If I didn't love women so much, I'd go for you myself. You're a gay man's wet dream."

Mano's fists clenched. "Shut the fuck up."

Brad raised his hands and backed away. "Easy. Down boy. Save the tough guy look for the women. They're gonna love it. I'll bet you beat out the rest of the strippers in tips." Brad heaved an affected sigh. "I'd give my left nut to be in your shoes. Uh. Make that G-string." Brad leapt away from Mano's flying fist. "Touchy, touchy."

Mano worked out to stay in shape and he took his job seriously. His first break to work an undercover operation and he'd become the laughingstock of the department. Who would take the Big Kahuna seriously after he'd danced practically nude at an exotic dancers' club? He wished the hell he hadn't let his mother talk him into taking traditional Hawaiian dancing lessons as a kid. The little-known fact had sealed the deal. The chief fell on it like a starving man on a T-bone steak.

"Cheer up. The women are going to love you." Brad led the way out to the squad car.

"As long as one of them is the Black Widow. We don't even know what club she'll show at next."

"So far she's spread the wealth among the clubs along the Waikiki Strip. She hasn't gone back to the same club, and she seems to be working her way south from the north end of Kalakaua Avenue. I bet she hits the Man, Oh Man! Male Strip Club next."

Mano had done the math as well and he'd bet his badge the Black Widow would show up there next. As much as he wanted to nail the bitch who preyed on male strippers, he didn't want to dance on a stage in front of a hundred crazed women, all screaming and groping. His cock shriveled at the thought. How men got off on that, he didn't understand. A quiet room, maybe candlelight, a little wine, and a beautiful woman were all he needed to get himself off.

His footsteps faltered. His internal description of the perfect setting for making love was an exact duplicate of the one he'd just left. The one with the dead man lying on the sheets, his lips blue and body stiff.

Mano's back straightened. This particular undercover job was as important as they came. His number-one goal: catch a cold-blooded killer with long red hair.

"I can't do this." Rachel sat in the backseat of the taxi, refusing to get out on Kalakaua Avenue at the Man, Oh Man! Male Strip Club. "At least come with me."

"No way. I'm an almost-married woman." Hayley smiled. "Besides, mine's waiting for me as we speak. He's got the bubbly chilling and the sheets warming."

"Too much information. Do you know how weird that sounds to hear your little sister talking dirty?"

"We're both adults."

"To me, you'll always be my kid sister." Rachel stared out at the club. "At this point, I don't even like men!"

"No, honey, you don't like *some* men. The lying, cheating bastards who lead you on and then dump you with no explanation." Hayley smiled. "Not all men are like that."

Rachel glared. "You just got lucky with your fiancé. You know I've never been lucky."

Her sister's smile widened, its sweet optimism enough to make Rachel want to upchuck. "Maybe tonight will change all that. What do you have to lose? You've got no one back in Minnesota waiting for you. Why not let loose, have a little fun?"

Sadly, Hayley was right. Since their parents' deaths five years ago in a car accident, neither one of them had any reason to stay in Minnesota. Hayley had jumped at the opportunity to work in Hawaii. Rachel had stayed because she thought she had a future with the vice principal of her school—the dirty, rotten liar. His dumping her had been the best thing to ever happen to her. Or so Hayley kept saying. Rachel was only beginning to be convinced.

Still, she wasn't ready to swim on her own in a nightclub. Rachel crossed her arms over her chest and refused to budge from the taxi, her stomach twisted in knots. "I can't do this."

"Sure you can. You're good at organizing things. Look at all those middle school students you keep in line. One stripper should be a piece of cake. Beefcake." She laughed.

Rachel didn't. "You're the one who wants the stripper at your bachelorette party. *You* go get him."

"Only as entertainment for the rest of the girls. I have my hunka hunka burnin' lover already." She hugged her sister. "It's the only thing I've asked you to do for this entire wedding. Please don't let me down."

Rachel's fingers clenched around the little black handbag she carried. The impractical accessory had barely enough room for the tiny notepad with her sister's list of requirements and cash. She hoped she had sufficient funds for a few drinks, the cab ride back, and hopefully to secure the services of one, as her younger sister put it, *hunkilicious* stripper to dance at her bachelorette party. Nothing like leaving the entertainment till the last minute with the party only three nights away. "Let me serve the punch or decorate the pavilion. Anything but this."

"Rachel Grant, are you chickening out?" Hayley crossed her arms over her chest, a stern frown forming on her beautiful pale forehead, the look incongruous with her angelic blond-haired, blue-eyed beauty. "You're my older sister; I look up to you. Please, show me you have the backbone to do this one itty-bitty thing for your favorite sister." She batted her lashes using the look that always worked when she was a little girl. Hayley always got her way when she pulled the sweet angel act. And as an adult, the affect was no different.

"Itty-bitty, my ass," Rachel muttered. "I don't know anyone here."

"Exactly. If you act a little"—she coughed—"out of character, no one will ever know back home in Minnesota."

She was right. No one would ever know straitlaced, middle-school librarian Rachel Grant had gone to a strip club in Honolulu. Elk River, Minnesota and Oahu were thousands of miles and an ocean apart. "Well, I guess I could try. . . ."

"Good!" Hayley leaned hard on Rachel's back and shoved her out of the cab. "You have the number of the cab company. If you're not back at the hotel by two A.M. I'll assume you found better accommodations. Be daring, for once. It's about time you let your hair down, for Pete's sake, and don't forget to have fun." Then she leaned over the back of the cabbie's seat. "Drive!"

"No, wait!" Rachel reached for the door, only to have it slammed before she could grab onto the metal frame. Tires squealed against pavement as the cabbie shot into the steady stream of traffic moving along Kalakaua Avenue. If she ran, Rachel might be able to catch up to the cab, but the sidewalks were just as crowded as the street and she'd have to push her way through in the ridiculous five-inch heels her sister had insisted she needed in order to look like a woman on the hunt.

On the hunt for what? Rape? Someone bumped into her, and she staggered dangerously close to the curb. A Mustang convertible, overflowing with young men, chose that moment to pass by. When the passengers spotted her, they let out a loud whoop.

One leaned out so far Rachel feared he'd fall out onto the pavement. "How much, babe?"

"Hey, Red, what say you and me, you know . . ." He pumped his hand in a rude, sexual gesture.

Rachel's face burned with humiliation and anger. Well, what did she expect? She'd let her sister dress her in what was more or less a hooker-worthy look: too much makeup and a neckline that would make her mother turn over in her grave.

Maybe going inside the bar would be better than standing outside on a busy street in the shorter-than-short black dress and killer high heels. Her feet ached and she couldn't breathe in the snug-fitting strapless bra that pushed every ounce of her breasts up and out of the low-cut neckline.

How had she let Hayley talk her into this? The baby blue eyes had done it, damn it. She'd been just as much of a sucker as everyone else in the world when confronted with Hayley's baby blues. Hayley had inherited their mother's soft angelic look, while Rachel took after her father's mother with the deep red hair and brown doe-eyes that she normally hid behind thick-lens glasses.

Rachel wasn't ugly, but she didn't have the same classic beauty of her sister Hayley, and everyone reminded her of it when they questioned whether or not they were really sisters.

Tonight she wore the contact lenses she usually reserved for matches on the tennis court. Hayley had insisted on doing her hair, letting the silky tresses drape over one shoulder in long, loose waves instead of her usual tidy bun at the nape of her neck. She'd layered on soft brown and pink eye shadow, drawing out the color of her brown eyes. When she'd seen herself in the mirror, Rachel hadn't recognized the beautiful woman and couldn't wait until she could fade back into her middle-school librarian role in Minnesota. The sooner the better. All she had to do was make it through the wedding and then she was on the airplane back to the Midwest.

First, though, she had to secure the services of one hunkilicious stripper for the bachelorette party.

Rachel squared her shoulders, which had the effect of pushing her boobs out even farther, and marched into the Man, Oh Man! Male Strip Club prepared for battle. She refused to come out without a stripper.

The music boomed loud enough to make Mano's ears ring within the first fifteen minutes. He'd be deaf after just one night of this undercover operation. When he got back to headquarters, he'd demand earplugs and hazardous-duty pay for his part in this undercover sting.

Like that would make a difference. Between Brad and the other cops, he'd been ribbed so much he wanted to punch someone in the face. Didn't they understand the importance of this mission? It wasn't about the women throwing themselves at him. It was about the right woman throwing herself at him and trying to kill him. Mano would be ready.

At the Man, Oh Man! Male Strip Club, he quickly undressed down to his skivvies, then stared at the costume the owner, Mrs. Jones, had left for him to wear: a tuxedo with Velcro strips down the legs to allow him to strip them off with a flick of the wrist. "I'm not fuckin' believing this." He yanked the trousers off the hanger and slipped one leg up his calf.

"Did you read the rules? No tighty whiteys allowed." Mrs. Jones—or Jonesy, as the other guys called her—pointed at his white briefs. She held up a package containing a brand new black G-string. "This is the rest of your costume."

Mano stared at the package, his head shaking. "You're kidding, right?"

Her faded green eyes regarded him without humor. "Do I look like someone who kids?"

He studied the deeply lined face of a hardened woman who'd smoked a million packs of cigarettes too many. "No, ma'am."

"Then put the damn G-string on. The less you wear, the more they drink and the more tips you make."

"I don't give a d—" He almost told the woman he didn't give a damn, until he remembered he was supposed to be a down-and-out personal trainer in need of quick cash—his cover for this operation. He grabbed the G-string. "Yes, ma'am."

"And cut it with the ma'am stuff, you're making me feel old. They call me Jonesy. You can call me that or Gladys."

"Yes, ma—Jonesy." He waited for her to leave, but when she didn't make a move to do so, he dropped his briefs, ripped open the package, and shook out the miniscule scrap of black silk fabric.

Jonesy whistled, her gaze fixed firmly on his cock. "Yessiree, we're going to make a fortune in sales tonight."

He glared at her. "Do you mind?"

She grinned, long yellow teeth matching her yellow-leather skin. "Not at all." She leaned on the wall, prepared to stay the duration. "Don't worry, you don't have anything I haven't seen before. Although, I have to admit, your packaging is commendable."

"Thanks, I think." Mano turned his back to her and stepped into the thin straps of the G-string and slid them up his thighs. When the string pressed between his buttocks, his ass puckered. "Geezus! How do the guys stand these things?" He plucked the string from his crack and let go, the elastic popping him.

Jonesy chuckled. "You may not like it, but I guarantee the women out there are animals. They'll be all over you."

Mano swallowed the groan rising in his throat. He needed to play the part like he meant it. He turned to face the boss, his cock and the dark black thatch of pubic hair barely concealed in the triangle of black silk. With the cockiness of a professional dancer—he hoped—he pushed out his chest and flashed his pearly whites. "How's that?"

"Baby, I'm seeing dollar signs and creamed panties all over the place." She grabbed her own crotch. "Might even contribute a dollar or two myself. You have all the right equipment." Her eyes narrowed. "Now I just hope you can dance. What's your act?"

"Act?"

"You need a stage name."

Mano scratched his brain for a name, coming up with what the guys at work called him. "How about the Big Kahuna?"

Jonesy's eyes narrowed even more as her gaze passed over him from head to toe. Then her face brightened. "It works. All that dark Hawaiian skin and muscles, you'll be a hit with the tourists for sure. Okay, then. Climb into your tuxedo and get ready."

The music ground to a halt, women screamed and catcalled until one of the dancers, a blond-haired surfer, ducked behind the stage, plucking bills from his baby blue G-string. "Hey, new guy. Look out, they're rabid tonight. One woman actually grabbed my 'nads."

Mano cringed. "What did you do?"

"Let her!" He waived a bill in Mano's face. "She gave me a twenty for the privilege."

Great. A chant rose from the audience, growing louder and louder until the emcee walked out on the stage. "And now, for a taste of what Hawaii has to offer, put your hands together for the Big Kahuna!"

Sweet Jesus, that was his cue. How was he supposed to step out on that stage and dance in front of all those women? Never one to shirk his duty or shy away from bullets, Mano now found himself shaking in his proverbial boots.

Get a grip, buddy, it's the job. You're here to find a killer.

The first bars of the music rang out and women clapped in time, yelling for him to appear.

Mano took a deep breath, adjusted his scratchy tuxedo, and flexed his butt cheeks, wincing at the G-string riding up his ass. *Well, here goes nothing.*

He closed his eyes, listened for a moment to the music, and then stepped out onto the stage, applying what he'd learned as a boy dancing to traditional Hawaiian music, swaying to the sexy, steamy beat of the bump and grind now playing. *Give them what they came for.* The last three strippers had been the best in each of their clubs. He had to compete against the others to win the Black Widow's attention.

The stage lights glared into his eyes, making it difficult to see the women on the other side. He moved to the end of a short runway that jutted out into the crowd of ladies, rocking his hips and pumping his crotch at them. The ladies hooted and crowded around the stage, waving bills at him.

"Over here. Give me some of that, you big Kahuna!" An older woman with gray hair and a fistful of dollars called out louder than the others.

Frankly, she scared the hell out of Mano. He swerved to miss her, but she reached out and grabbed his ankle. "Shake it, baby, shake it!"

He forced a smile and did as she asked, shaking his ass, rocking his crotch in the woman's face.

The woman yanked on his pant leg. "Take it off. Take it all off!"

For a woman old enough to be his grandmother, she had surprising strength and managed to yank all the Velcro loose on the side of one leg. His thigh bulged out of the leg and another roar rose from the crowd.

How was he supposed to search for the killer when these women were out of control? He twisted his ankle loose, and stepped out of the old woman's reach, hurrying back to center stage and out of range of grabbing hands.

From there he danced, gyrated, and studied the crowd while slowly peeling the tuxedo jacket from his broad shoulders.

A woman in a red dress with long, straight bleach-blond hair studied him like a side of beef, calmly watching him from her table just beyond the crowd. Despite her cool demeanor, she had that barracuda look to her, with narrowed eyes as if calculating a dangerous move. As he panned the rest of the crowd, he caught a glimpse of deep red hair and a black dress. Just a glimpse as the crowd swayed as one in time to the music, arms in the air with fists clutching bills ready to stuff in some poor guy's shorts.

His pulse quickened. Was that his target? Was it her? The woman who'd killed three men in the course of as many days? *Shit. Where'd she go?*

He danced to the edge of the stage, his hips gyrating, his fingers unbuttoning the tux shirt, with little regard to the women shoving bills into the top of the G-string peeking out of his trousers.

There she was again!

The crowd parted just enough so that he caught a clear image of a woman in her late twenties sitting at a table sipping from a straw. She had long dark red hair and a skimpy black dress that clung to all her curves in just the right places.

Mano's cock twitched.

The Black Widow was a fuckin' knockout. No wonder the victims went along with her. Red hair, pale skin, and a body any man would want to fuck, she was a damn siren leading them to their doom.

His cock swelled as he imagined her long, tapered legs wrapped around each one of her victims. He'd bet she'd demand to be on top, riding them like prize bulls in a rodeo.

Adrenalin and something else pulsed through his veins. Still dancing, he yanked the shirt off his shoulders and, aiming for the woman in black, tossed it over the reaching hands of the ladies crowded around the stage. The shirt landed on the table in front of the redhead. *That ought to get her attention.*

2

Rachel leaped to her feet, her ginger ale soaking through the thin fabric of the black dress her sister had loaned her, the slice of lime plopping to the floor. "Damn, Hayley's going to kill me." She brushed at the liquid with her cocktail napkin and stared down at the spot. In the dim lighting, the damage appeared minimal.

"Damn." She'd hoped a ruined dress would be her ticket out of her current situation. Three strippers into this "taste test" and she still hadn't found the right one for the job. Until The Big Kahuna strutted his stuff onto the stage.

She lifted the shirt he'd thrown, a shirt big enough to swallow her twice. The man had linebacker shoulders and a narrow waist. And his butt didn't disappoint. A firm, tight ass swelled out in the back, perfect for pinching or slapping.

And some of the women near the runway were testing its tautness.

As her gaze lifted to the dark-skinned Hawaiian, Rachel held the shirt to her nose, expecting stinky sweat but catching a whiff of exotic Hawaiian musk. The scent plus the decidedly beautiful and downright sexy moves he performed on stage made her consider choosing this particular stripper.

She stepped closer to the stage, still holding his shirt, wanting to inspect the merchandise a little closer before buying.

"If you don't want that, I'll take it." A woman dressed in red stood at the edge of the crowd of women shoving and jostling each other to get closer to the Hawaiian hottie.

Rachel clutched the shirt closer. "No. I think I'll keep it."

The woman shrugged. "Suit yourself." But she hovered close to Rachel as though waiting for her to set the shirt on a table or something so she could steal it while Rachel wasn't looking.

With deliberate and overemphasized moves, Rachel tied the shirt around her waist. Then she double knotted it, just for good measure. *Take that, you blonde bitch.*

The Big Kahuna leaped from the stage into the audience.

Women screamed their lust and excitement, crowding in on him. He towered over them, smiling and dancing with each one as he worked his way around the room.

His movements were sensual, his naked chest perfectly tanned a deep coffee brown, the muscles glistening in the stage lights. His short dark hair spiked up, accentuating the strong lines of his cheekbones and jaw.

Rachel's heart raced and beads of perspiration formed at her temples and upper lip. She pushed her hair back off her face. It had to be the temperature in the room. Other ladies were perspiring, except the cool blonde in the red dress. She stood at Rachel's side, her face devoid of expression, her gaze following every move Mr. Kahuna made.

If the lady in red isn't sweating, why am I? Rachel grabbed the tiny notepad from her too-small-to-be-practical purse and tried to bring order to chaotic thoughts where The Big Kahuna was concerned. Did he meet all of Hayley's requirements?

Exotic. Rachel glanced at his black eyes, dark hair, and rich, smooth, dark skin a woman could run her fingers over, again and again. The man reeked of Exotic. She placed a check next to Exotic.

Built. She glanced up. *Oh, yeah, he's built like a contestant in the Ironman competition, every muscle on his body distinct and bulging in all the right places.* Rachel's tongue swept across her suddenly dry lips as her gaze swept him from head to toe, stopping somewhere around midpoint.

At that exact moment, the crazy old woman with the handful of bills grabbed the tuxedo pants and ripped them off.

For a brief second, the Big Kahuna's eyes widened and his hands jerked to cover his crotch. Just as quickly as he did, his gaze captured hers, his eyelids drooped over his inky-black eyes and his hands lifted into the form of a Hawaiian Hula dancer. Which left his crotch for all to see in the tiniest scrap of fabric imaginable. His cock pressed against it, his balls practically bulging out the sides.

Rachel's breath caught in her throat and a slow steady ache swelled low in her belly. "Oh, sister, he's the one."

"Got that right." The blonde next to her pushed her out of the way and stalked toward the crowd of women shoving each other to get their chance at touching the Big Kahuna. By the time he broke through the throng and worked his way around to where Rachel stood, he sported a G-string bulging at the elastic bands with every bill from ones to fifties. Okay, so he was bulging for other reasons besides the bills stuffed in that itty-bitty, I-can-see-almost-everything scrap of whatever.

Holy crap! He appeared to be headed directly for her!

Rachel backed up a step, her hand going to her throat, which had dried to ten-days-in-the-desert parched. She swallowed, or at least tried to, but a lump of shear terror lodged and stayed in her throat.

Not that she was afraid of the Big Kahuna. No, she was afraid of saying or doing something stupid the closer he came.

Like licking his pectoral muscles or sliding her leg up his massive thigh just to feel her pussy rub against it.

Holy crap! She'd just creamed her panties! That had never happened to her in her entire life. Not in a public place, for Pete's sake. Her cheeks heated. Would anyone notice? Would he notice?

She tried to shake reason back into her staid librarian head. Of course he wouldn't notice. How would he see inside her panties? Not that he'd want to. Surely he'd grown bored with women throwing themselves at him. What would he care about the flaming redhead from Minnesota?

Rachel tore her gaze away from him, hoping beyond hope he'd bypass her and move on to some more appreciative and less flustered woman than she.

But if she ignored him, how would she contract him to perform at the party? Her hand tightened around the notepad she'd been clutching in her grip. Perfect!

She'd write a note and stuff it in his G-string. They could meet outside the club and discuss terms there. Away from the frenzy of music and foaming-at-the-mouth women.

Speaking of which. Rachel swallowed, surprised at the amount of saliva (okay, call it what it was: drool) that had accumulated since Mr. Kahuna had begun his dance of seduction.

She grabbed a pen from her purse and scribbled the note, her hands shaking as the music intensified to the point that her blood beat to the rhythm of the island song.

"Hey, beautiful, feeling lucky?"

A stampede of galloping horses ripped through Rachel's veins, her breath catching in her lungs.

The man of her immediate wet fantasy stood beside her, his hand slipping around her waist, his hips swaying, bumping against hers in time to the music.

She turned, her nose inches from the most beautiful brown chest she'd ever laid eyes on. Right there. Within licking distance.

A moan slid up her throat and out. She swept her tongue across her lips, the urge to lean forward and taste the smooth, taut skin almost irresistible. Her body swayed toward him. If not for her nerveless fingers dropping the pen to the floor, Rachel wasn't sure what would have happened.

Heat flared in her cheeks and she dropped to her haunches to find the pen. Not that she really cared if she lost it. She'd picked up the pen at the hotel with the Hyatt logo written all over it. She really didn't want to find the pen. She just wanted to crawl beneath the tables to the exit, avoiding the man hovering next to her, whose calves were just as sexy as his chest.

Dizziness swept over her before she realized she'd been holding her breath a bit too long.

Then the Big Kahuna squatted on the floor beside her. His knees wide, his crotch there for the staring.

And Rachel stared.

Which was her first mistake. Now all she could focus on was the shift of the G-string and the rapidly expanding triangle of black silk. And the pen lay on the floor directly beneath his—Rachel gulped—scrotum.

Abandon the pen, her mind pleaded. But her hand had a will of its own and reached below him, her knuckles skimming his balls.

Was that her imagination, or had he gotten even bigger?

Her nasty, nonlibrarian thoughts revved into overdrive. What would that stiff ridge beneath the silk feel like in her hands? Would it be as hard as the muscles in his chest and thighs? Was the man hard all over? Again, her tongue flicked out to moisten dry lips.

Then she realized what she'd done. Rachel Grant, middle school librarian, had touched a strange man's balls. In public, no less. She glanced up to see a swarm of women panting over the Big Kahuna, shoving more bills beneath the black silk string.

The old lady, carrying considerably fewer bills than when she'd started, glared at her. "You know it's against the rules to touch the entertainment, bitch, so back off."

In her haste to rise to her feet, Rachel lost her balance and would have toppled over if Kahuna hadn't reached out and grabbed her elbow. Of course, the elbow of the hand with the note in it.

A low chuckle could be heard over the music. "Writing me a love letter?" He took the note from her and pulled the front of his G-string out far enough to expose the tremendous cock straining to get out of the silk confinement.

Rachel gulped. Even if he read the note, she couldn't go through with this. The man had her so tied in knots she couldn't pry words from her throat. How was she supposed to talk terms?

The woman in the red dress leaned close to his ear and whispered something.

A flare of rage charged Rachel's blood. What was that hussy telling him? A sickening thought struck Rachel. What if she wasn't telling him anything so much as offering him sex?

Rachel straightened. Hadn't her sister told her to have fun? Hadn't she told her that no one in Elk River, Minnesota, would ever hear a word of her exploits on Oahu? Hadn't Hayley said it was about time she let her hair down and had some outrageous fun?

Hell, yeah! And that red-dressed bitch was horning in on her fun.

Rachel straightened her dress, inching the hemline upward, showing more of one of her best features. Her thighs. She walked five miles a day to allow her to eat pretty much anything she liked. She had the perfectly taut, beautifully shaped thighs to prove it. *Red dress lady, watch and learn.*

With courage she never knew she possessed, Rachel fluffed her over-the-shoulder hairdo, dropped her chin, and assumed the vamp mode. Now she just had to get through the steadily increasing barricade of fans to the man she had every intention of making a pass at. Even if she didn't intend to sleep with him.

She told herself it was all for the cause—her sister's bachelorette party. But Rachel couldn't delude herself. She wanted the Big Kahuna. Here and now.

Mano peeled hand after hand off his ass as he waded through the throng of horny women in an attempt to find the Black Widow. Where the hell had she gone?

The barracuda in the red dress determinedly elbowed her way through the crowd until she clung to his arm like a boa constrictor to a tree branch. God save him from pushy broads. Rather than slinging women right and left, he gently pried loose the fingers gripping him like the tentacles of a hundred octopuses.

"Come with me and I'll show you things you've never seen before." The red-dressed woman stuffed a one-hundred-dollar bill into Mano's open palm and curled his fingers around it. She leaned close to his ear and said in a throaty voice, "There's more where that came from."

"Uh, thanks, lady. But keep your money." He held out the bill.

The lady in red hid her hands behind her back. "Oh, no. I want you, and I'm willing to pay big bucks."

"Thanks, but I'm not interested." Because she refused to take the bill back, Mano did the only thing he could: he plucked the front of her dress open and stuffed the bill into her cleavage. "I appreciate the offer, but I like to pick my own entertainment."

And that entertainment was the red-haired woman working her way back through the crowd toward him. Was this assignment going to be that easy? Was the Black Widow that snowed by his performance as a stripper that she would walk right into his trap?

Whoever she was, she put on a great act. That air of innocence and clumsy shyness would endear even the most hardened of strippers. He had to admit he wasn't immune. When he'd stood next to her, he'd wanted to pull her into his arms, to feel the touch of her tongue on his body, to teach her the art of making love, to bring her to orgasm. But most of all to drive his cock deep inside her delicious warmth. If he didn't already know how evil she was, he'd swear she really was an innocent, a fish out of water in a male strip joint.

The music ground to a halt before the Black Widow could reach him. The women in the crowd voiced their disappointment in a collective "ah." But just as soon as the music ended the next act took center stage. Most of the women shifted in that direction, eager to see what else Man, oh Man! had to offer.

Which left him to the stragglers: the glaring woman in red and the sexy, innocent-acting Black Widow. Now he could memorize every detail of the woman who'd already killed three men and for all he knew would attempt to kill again tonight. Hopefully she'd go for him.

And he'd be ready.

His cock twitched, reminding him he wore next to nothing, and suddenly it wasn't enough.

The redhead in the black dress stood in front of him, twin patches of red brightening her cheekbones. "Could I speak with you, Mr. Kahuna?"

The woman in the red dress frowned and tried to shove the redhead away. She stared down her nose at the redhead. "Make yourself scarce, loser."

Mano almost laughed at the changing expressions on the Black Widow's face. From wide-eyed shock to frowning anger to a determined pressing of her lips, she stood there for a full minute before responding. "I believe he told you he wasn't interested."

So she'd been listening as well. Interesting. She'd definitely taken to bait. Now he needed to reel her in. After he ditched the blonde.

The red-dressed woman's eyes narrowed. "He'd be plenty interested if you wouldn't keep butting in. Wouldn't you, darling?" She draped her breasts against his arm and slid her trim calf up his bare leg.

"No, sweetheart," Mano said. "I believe Red here had it right the first time. I'm not interested." He peeled her hands off his arm and set her to the side. "Please don't embarrass yourself with another attempt to claim me. It isn't happening."

The blonde's jaw tightened, her lips clamping into a straight line. "Have it your way." She turned, muttering beneath her breath something that sounded like ". . . sorry." Well, good, at least she understood manners and when a person should apologize for stalking another.

The Black Widow's brows puckered. "Are you sure you have time for me?"

"All night if that's what you want. Let me change into something street-worthy and we can leave." Even though pretty much anything went on Waikiki Beach, Mano had his standards and a G-string on Kalakaua Avenue wasn't it.

"Okay." She stood with her little black purse clutched in her fingers, twisting the catch on it.

He'd have to get inside that purse to find her stash of cyanide. Or maybe she kept it in a ring or locket. His gaze went to the gold chain around her neck. A locket dangled low in the valley between her breasts.

Oh, yes, getting into that would be a breeze. Her lashes fluttered over deep, brown eyes.

Mano's heartbeat quickened and his groin tightened. He sucked in a deep breath and let it out slowly. This job might be a little harder than he thought.

This woman had him as hard as a hammer, just by standing in front of him. Imagine how hard he'd be when she climbed up on him and rode him like a stallion. "If you'll wait out here, I'll only be a minute."

"Sure. Only, if it's all right with you, I'll wait out front of the club."

"Deal."

He grabbed a towel off the shoulder of one of the busboys and held it in front of himself as he hurried through the tables, his backside pinched more than once on his way backstage. No doubt he'd have bruises. He felt bad about taking the ladies' money when he really wasn't a stripper. For all he knew the old woman who'd stuffed so many bills into his string was probably using her Social Security check to feed her dirty little habit. If he gave it back to her, she'd probably cop a feel of another dancer in her pathetic ploy to stuff bills into his crotch.

Mano had to strike while the iron was hot, get in and gather his clothes and belongings. He'd have to get the owner to let him get his gym bag out of her safe. His nine millimeter Sig Sauer pistol was wrapped in a pair of shorts beneath a pair of smelly sweat socks. He might need the gun tonight if the Black Widow made a move more dangerous than poisoning his drink.

He could completely relate with the men who'd lost their lives to the woman.

Damn, she was a good actress. He couldn't wait to see what other moves she'd make before the big showdown. It almost seemed a shame to arrest her for murder.

3

Rachel wiped her hands on her dress for the tenth time since she'd stepped out of the club. Despite the cool breeze off the Pacific Ocean, she'd worked up a sweat thinking about the Big Kahuna and what he could do for her.

No. That wasn't right. It was what he could do for Hayley. No, that wasn't it either. It was what he could do for all the women scheduled to attend Hayley's bachelorette party. No, no, no.

For the eleventh time Rachel wiped her hands down the sides of her dress. What was taking him so long? She'd hand him the money, make him sign something stating he'd be there on Friday night, and they'd shake on it. How hard could that be? Nothing more than a business transaction. She'd dealt with businesses as the main purchaser of books for the middle-school library. She knew how to bargain and set dates and expectations. What was so different in this situation?

Six feet of dark-skinned bulked-out male with enough charisma to light her hair on fire. She fanned her face with her purse. Maybe a little practice would be in order.

Where to start, where to start? Pricing? Music? Time? Place? The options swirled in her mind, the lights of the street blurring as she once again forgot to breathe.

Rachel sucked in a deep breath. *Pricing.*

"How much do you charge?" she asked out loud.

At that moment three older men were walking past her, eyeing her like potential customers at the deli counter.

The one closest to her grinned. "For you, babe, I'd do it for free."

She glared at them. "I wasn't talking to you."

The next one in the trio shoved the first guy to the side. "Step aside, the lady was clearly speaking to me."

She couldn't help the grin tweaking the corners of her lips. The guys meant no harm. "Wrong again."

When the third man muscled through the first two, all three got into a scuffle.

Rachel crossed her arms over her chest and raised her brow. "So mature. But just to set the record straight, I wasn't talking to any of you."

"She was talking to me." The deep voice rumbled behind her, the tone unmistakably dismissing the three gentlemen before they could voice a protest.

Her humor of a moment before skipped town, replaced by sheer terror. Not to mention the raging awareness skimming across her skin and throughout her body. Awareness of the man standing so close to her, his breath fluttering the flyaway strands of hair brushing her cheek.

Deep breath, Rach. Her breath caught halfway into her lungs and stuck; she coughed to clear her airways. *Again.* This time she managed to get oxygen to her dying brain cells. Forcing a smile to her lips, she turned to face the man she'd come to acquire . . . er . . . hire.

Nothing in her Minnesota upbringing around farm-fed boys prepared her for the sun-kissed perfection of the man filling her vision. The smile slipped as her jaw slacked to the drooling-groupie position.

He wore a lightweight brown jacket with a loose-fitting white shirt beneath that he hadn't bothered to button. Every inch of his exquisite torso was exposed, from his broad, contoured chest to washboard abs and lower to the waistband of black denim jeans. The hard metal button was strategically unbuttoned as well.

Rachel's fingers itched to reach out and unzip to expose the bulge beneath, wondering if he still wore the black silk G-string or if he'd abandoned it to go commando. Her hand was halfway there before she realized what the hell she was doing and jerked it back.

Business. Strictly business. Even when her mouth watered and other places grew damp just by close proximity to the man.

"How much—" Rachel squeaked. Horrified at her nervous beginning to an otherwise simple transaction, she clamped her lips and eyelids closed for a second, gathered her wits, and started over.

A large, warm hand brushed along her bare arm. "It's okay. I don't bite. Take a deep breath and start over."

Her eyes flew open at his touch and everywhere his fingers had been tingled with electric currents, spreading the wealth over rapid-fire nerve endings. "I'm sorry. I'm new at this." *That's right, tell him the obvious. He could have guessed by your blubbering beginning you were small town.* "What I meant to say is how much do you charge?"

Mr. Kahuna looked away, his gaze panning the steady flow of people and traffic on the sidewalks and streets. "Wouldn't you rather go somewhere more private to discuss . . . er . . . business?"

As if on cue, a drunken girl still wearing her bikini and wraparound skirt from the day at the beach slammed into Rachel, knocking her into the sexy Hawaiian's chest.

His arm clamped around her waist, holding her upright while she struggled to catch her breath and get her five-inch heels back under her.

"Oops! Sorry!" The blonde giggled, shot a glance at them, and did a double-take when she looked up into the dark eyes of the Big Kahuna. "Wow, are you for real?" She reached out and poked a finger at his chest.

The urge to scratch the girl's eyes out attacked Rachel so fast, she'd reached out and grabbed the girl's wrists before she could think about her actions. "Don't touch." As quickly as she reacted, she let go, her cheeks flaming at her harsh response.

The girl swayed and giggled again. "Sorry again. Didn't know he was claimed. Lucky you! If you change your mind about him, let me know." She waved her fingers. "Tootles!" Her friends grabbed her elbows and hustled her away, promising her a cold shower when they got back to their room.

"As I was saying." Kahuna hooked her elbow and walked her to the corner. "I think what we have to talk about would be best handled in a quiet place."

"Do you have one in mind?" Before he answered, the light changed and the little man on the crosswalk display glowed white.

The big Hawaiian hurried her across Kalakaua Ave, reaching the other side as the red hand started blinking. Once on the other side, he slipped an arm around her waist and smiled down at her. "I have just the place where we won't be interrupted."

"Good. I'd really like to get this over with." *Before I do something stupid like jump your bones and make a bigger fool of myself than I already have!*

Aware that her heart rate bordered on ballistic and her breathing had yet to return to normal, the sooner she got his agreement to perform for the party, the better. Then she could get back to her room, shut the door, and explode into a million sexually dissatisfied pieces.

Not until she stood in the lobby of the Regal Hawaiian waiting for an elevator did she come to her senses. "Uh . . . where are we going?"

"To my room." He smiled. "Don't worry. It's just business. I won't do anything you don't want me to do."

Her eyes almost rolled back in her head at the infinite possibilities his one statement implied. She could think of a lot of things he could do to her and none of them were business related. How, oh, how was she supposed to keep this on a transaction level when all she wanted to do was explore every inch of his body, first with her fingers, then with her tongue?

The elevator dinged their arrival on the fourth floor. As the doors slid open, Mano had to remind himself he was there to catch a killer. Whatever it took, he had to convince the Black Widow that he was a stripper looking for a little extra cash.

That the killer played the part of a country bumpkin too well had him second-guessing himself. Was she really the Black Widow? Lots of women had red hair and wore sexy black dresses.

But not all redheads in black dresses wanted to discuss business with a stripper the night after three previous nights of killings.

It had to be her.

He shoved the key into the lock and glanced down at her.

Her hands twisted the strap of the ridiculously small purse and her teeth bit into her bottom lip until it was red and a little swollen.

Mano's cock twitched.

Her lips were pretty delicious to look at: soft, full, tempting. As typical with true redheads, her skin was pale, almost translucent, with a light dusting of freckles barely visible, but there for those who got close enough to find them.

She glanced up at him, giving him a nervous smile. "Are you sure we can't conduct our business downstairs?"

"Positive. Let me order a bottle of wine from room service to make the deal more agreeable." He pushed the door open, his gaze going immediately to the camera mounted behind the fake fire alarm disc. Nothing like performing for the crowd of schmucks at the station. He'd have to shift the cameras away from the bed. Some parts of the job weren't meant for departmental consumption.

It's the job, just like any other stakeout where he played the part of someone other than himself. Whether he pretended to be a drug dealer or a stripper-gigolo, he could pull it off, because he was the job.

Had he already thought that? Geez, he was repeating himself in his head. How psychotic was that? With a beautiful woman hanging on his arm, possibly about to strip naked and make love to him like there was no tomorrow (for him, at least), he had to keep reminding himself that this wasn't playtime. This was a real life-or-death situation. He had to be ahead of her every step of the way to ensure he didn't ingest the cyanide she preferred as her weapon of choice.

She stopped in the doorframe, pulling free of his arm, panic written in the roundness of her rich, brown eyes. "Maybe I could just call you with the details. No need to do this now."

He took her arm and urged her over the threshold, closing the door behind her. Now she couldn't just back out. She'd have to make a conscious effort to leave. The trap was set; all he had to do was lure her through the maze of deception to the bait. Him.

The tough part being where he had to let her seduce him and pretend to enjoy it while she poured the poison into his wine.

Mano stood in front of the door, basically blocking her exit. The woman edged into the room, clutching her purse, looking for all intents and purposes like a lamb being led to the slaughter.

Damn, she was good at the poor innocent act. Mano shoved a hand through his spiked hair, shrugging off the sense of being the lion awaiting his share of lamb steak. If the scenario played out like he thought it would, he would be the victim, not the other way around.

No time like the present to get the ball rolling. He had to tamp down the sudden surge of anticipation filling his cock. He couldn't make love to the woman, he just had to bring her close enough that she wanted to do the dirty deed—the deed being poisoning him.

Mano dropped his jacket to the floor, careful not to let the gun in the pocket thunk against the carpet.

The woman turned as he stalked toward her. Her eyes rounded and a soft gasp escaped her full, pouty lips. "M-M-Mr. Kahuna, shouldn't we discuss business?"

"Why talk when I can show you what I have to offer?"

"L-l-like a menu sample of your . . . skills?" Her eyes grew rounder still and her throat worked convulsively. "That won't be necessary. I know what I want."

He stopped in front of her, reached out and stroked her hair, the fine strands feathering through his fingers. His jeans grew impossibly tight and he had to remind himself she was the prime suspect in three murders.

When he reached the ends of her hair, his fingers brushed the tip of her breast, the nipple puckering beneath the thin black fabric of her dress.

"Do you like what you see?"

"Oh, yes," she moaned, her next breath lifting her chest outward to fit into his palm. "But I'm not the only one you have to please."

Interesting. Was this her confession of motivation for the

killings? "Tell me." He stroked her hair again, his hand circling behind her neck, tipping her head upward.

Her breathing became erratic and she held her purse in front of her like a shield. "There will be more women eager to see what you have." Her gaze met his, the light brown of her irises darkening as her tongue flicked out to wet her lips.

Mano fought the urge to take those lips, to capture her tongue, taste and twist it with his own. One of his large hands spanned the width of her lower back, pressing against it, holding her in place as his body leaned into hers. When his cock bumped into her belly, a groan rose up in his throat. He swallowed it and managed to say, "And you'd rather not share?"

Her eyelids drooped half-mast and her gaze shifted from his eyes to his lips. "No," she whispered, warm breath skimming across his mouth.

His lips descended, taking her. At first gentle, the kiss turned passionate, his mouth slanting over hers.

Then she stood on her toes, her hands reaching up to bury in his hair and bring him closer, the purse pressing against his back. She tasted sweet, of ginger ale and cherries. Kissable, too easily kissable. This is why the other men were lured to their deaths. She was irresistible.

Mano shifted, his crotch constricted by denim. This act was going to be more difficult than he'd originally anticipated. He hadn't considered the woman might be a complete knockout, someone he'd want to take to bed and fuck all night long.

Right now, his strongest urge wasn't to serve justice, but to serve up a helping of the petite redhead, naked and spread open for him.

In the back of his mind, Mano thought of the hidden cameras and the cops in the viewing room, witnessing his every move. A smile curled his lips. He wondered how many of them had a hardon. He shouldn't feel so uptight. At least he had good reason for his. Being alone in a hotel room with a beautiful woman tended to have that effect on a man's cock. The other cops only lived vicariously through the video screen.

In the meantime, Mano had a job to do. He had one fine-looking killer he had to coax into the mood to make her move.

He ended the kiss by dragging his lips along the smooth line of her jaw and taking her ear between his teeth. Unfortunately, this part was too easy and yet too hard. He could go on kissing her.

"Oh, you're good. Do you do this part for all the ladies?" the redhead asked.

"Only for the ones I like." He nibbled at the lobe, rolling it with his tongue.

"That's nice." As her eyes reopened, a look of shock replaced the soft, just-been-kissed dazed look. "Oh." She backed away, slipping free of his embrace. "Oh. I'm sorry. I didn't mean . . ."

"What? Did I say or do something you didn't like?"

"No, no. It's not that. It's just that I haven't paid you." She lifted her purse again, bringing the ineffectual shield up between them. "I shouldn't have done that." The back of her hand pressed to her lips, her eyes peering over the top. "I'm sorry, this isn't how it was supposed to work out."

"No? Why not? We're both consenting adults, aren't we? I have something you want; you have something I want; we should be able to come to some agreement."

"Exactly. But you don't have to show me everything you have. I can take your word on most, and after your demonstration in the club, I'm sure you'll suit my needs perfectly. Here." She shoved a wad of bills at him. "Take this. I'll need you to be—"

Mano curled his hand around hers, forcing her to keep the money. "I don't collect until I deliver. Keep your money for now."

"But—" She stared down at his hand covering hers.

"No buts." He kissed the tip of her nose and tipped her chin up with one hand. "Now, where were we?"

"I don't know . . ." Her voice breathed against his lips.

With slow and careful precision, he leaned into her again and pressed his lips to hers, then lifted his mouth to within a hair's breadth of hers.

"There, we were there," she said, her gaze locked on his mouth.

"Are you sure?" He dragged his lips down her chin to the pulsing vein in her neck. "Are you sure we weren't here?"

"Yes," she said, the word blown out on a puff of pent-up air.

His hand slid down her arms to her waist, pulling her up against his, her soft curves fitting perfectly against the hard planes of his body. He cupped the nape of her neck and tipped her head back, giving him full access to her throat and the shadowy valley between her lush breasts where her locket lay.

"What have you got in here?"

Her hand reached up to take the locket from his. "Just a locket."

Alert and ready to rip the necklace from her neck, Mano tried another tactic. "May I?" He held out his hand. If she refused, he might have to insist. Maybe this was where she kept the poison.

Her face reddened, but she handed the locket over.

Inside wasn't what he'd expected. Instead of a stash of poison, he found a photo of a couple. "Someone special to you?"

She smiled, her eyes glazing with moisture. "My parents."

Mano shook his head. Definitely not what he expected.

"They died five years ago." She shrugged. "Not sexy, huh?"

The soft look of love in her eyes was about the sexiest look Mano had ever seen on any woman's face. He could have kicked himself for letting his thoughts go that direction.

Only a sick man would enjoy making love to a killer. If that were the case, he was a very sick man, judging by the swell of his cock and the way his blood ricocheted inside his veins. She'd woven her spell on him and he couldn't seem to break free. Somewhere in the lust-filled corner of his brain he wondered if this was how she drugged her victims. Blinded by lust, they never saw it coming. If he wasn't careful, he'd be next.

4

Where did the Big Kahuna leave off and Rachel begin? She didn't know. They seemed joined in more than a physical sense, or so her body told her.

His lips traveled to the swell of her right breast. He took the pointed nipple between his teeth, nipping at it gently through the thin folds of the black dress.

She couldn't think. She couldn't breathe.

All she could do was feel. The warmth of his breath, the moist heat of his mouth on her breast. She wanted to push her top lower to allow him to take her, lick her, tongue that turgid peak. Somewhere between leaving the taxi earlier that evening and now, the little black dress had transformed from not enough fabric covering her body to too much in the way of the Big Kahuna and her. Surely his real name wasn't Kahuna. That was some surfer movie made-up name. "I don't even know your real name." She thought she should care, but she didn't as long as he continued doing what he was doing to her.

He let go of her breast, leaving a wet spot on the black fabric. "My name is Mano. And you?" He didn't wait for her answer, slipping the thin spaghetti straps down over her shoulders. "What's your name?"

"Rachel." She sucked in a sharp breath, the touch of his fingers against the side of her breasts almost painful it felt so good.

His hand stilled. "Do you want me to stop?"

"I shouldn't be doing this," she said and pressed his hand to her skin.

His lips descended to her bare shoulder, slipping down over the mound of her breast, his fingers scraping the bodice to the side, exposing her. He paused before taking her into his mouth. "Just say the word and I'll quit."

Every nerve burned beneath her skin, every ounce of flesh begged to be touched, eager for more. "No, please. Don't stop." She grasped his head, pulling him to her.

He sucked her nipple into his mouth, rolling the hardened nub between his teeth, flicking it with his tongue, again and again.

Without conscious thought, Rachel's leg slid up the back of Mano's, her pussy pressing against the rough denim of his thigh, her panties wet with her cream.

Deep in the shadowy recesses of her librarian's mind she wondered what the hell she was doing. Hadn't her dear departed mother taught her better than to have a one-night stand with a man she only knew by his first name?

Her sister's words echoed in her head louder than any lecture her mother had ever given. "Let your hair down, be reckless for once."

A surge of desire shoved aside all her mother's warnings, pushing away the echo of middle-school children shouting in the hallways of the school and the humming of the gossip of the close-knit community back in Minnesota where everyone knew everyone's business. Here in Honolulu, no one knew her. Here, no one cared if she got laid by a gorgeous Hawaiian. But she cared. For once in her life she'd reach out and grab what she wanted with both hands.

Her fingers trailed up his chest and entwined behind his head. "I'm on fire."

His chuckle rumbled against her chest. "Me, too, babe; me, too." When he raised his head to her lips, his hands maneuvered to cup her breasts. "Why don't I order that wine?" he said, his mouth hovering over hers. Then he proceeded to kiss her in the most soul-shaking connection Rachel had ever experienced.

His lips left hers, his face flushed, his eyes glazed. "I promised you wine." Mano pulled Rachel's straps up her arms, securing the bodice of the dress over her before he stepped to the desk in the suite. He lifted the phone and dialed room service, ordering up a bottle of their best merlot. Before he hung up, he glanced across at her. "You do like merlot, don't you?"

Rachel nodded. She didn't know her merlot from her chablis, but she didn't want to show her ignorance in yet another area. Not tonight. Besides, she didn't need the wine. Her heart beat so fast, her thoughts and vision blurred as though on a natural high. But the longer she stood out of the circle of Mano's arms, the colder her feet got.

And for once, she didn't want that. She wanted to be risqué, live in the moment like her younger sister. But how did she accomplish that with a man so much more practiced than herself?

She turned to the window, her shyness rearing its ugly head and threatening to steal away an experience of a lifetime. Her hands rubbed up and down her bare arms to chase away the chill of the air conditioning.

"Windows work best when opened." Mano reached around her and pulled the drawstring that slid the heavy curtains aside. The room had a spectacular view of the ocean and, to the left, lights from the other structures lining Waikiki Beach twinkled in the darkness.

Rachel's breath caught. "It's so beautiful."

Large, calloused hands covered hers on her arms and pulled her back into his chest. "Yes, you're beautiful."

Her first instinct was to disagree. All her life, she'd been compared to her younger sister: the pale redhead and the young girl with the spun gold hair of an angel and features so delicate everyone wanted to take care of her. Including Rachel. She loved Hayley and wasn't a bit jealous of her. But sometimes, she wanted to be regarded as beautiful. Like tonight.

His lips skimmed the curve of her neck and continued downward, pressing against her shoulder. "You have skin the texture of silk and the color of cream." He stared at her reflection in the window, his gaze capturing hers, mesmerizing in its dark intensity. "Your eyes sparkle like the stars twinkling in the night." The back of his hand skimmed the line of her jaw, running down her neck to her shoulder.

Rachel's eyelids drooped, the stars in the sky grew brighter, and she leaned into him, the ridge of his jeans pressing into her buttocks. She wanted him to take her there. In front of the open windows, with the exotic view, the scent of the sea, and the palm trees swaying in the breeze. "I've never felt so alive."

A knock on the door jolted her back to earth.

Mano stiffened, then brushed a kiss to her temple. "That must be the wine."

Once again standing alone, Rachel wavered. What did she know about seducing a man? She needed advice, someone to walk her through it, give her tips, pointers. Something!

Mano held the door open while one of the hotel staff pushed a small cart into the room. The woman wore a brightly patterned Hawaiian muu-muu, with a starched white apron tied around her middle and a name tag that read LEI. Her short gray hair hung in a bob around her ears, brushing her cheeks, the bangs half covering her eyes.

She wheeled the cart into the bedroom and parked it at the

foot of the bed. With a flourish, she lit a fat cream-colored candle and set it on the nightstand. Then she lifted a napkin and wrapped it around the neck of the bottle nestled in the bucket of ice and twisted it to chill the liquid inside. Keeping her eyes averted from Rachel and Mano, she hurried out, closing the door behind her.

Mano said, "Would you like to pour?"

"I'll let you do the honors." Rachel stared at the bottle of wine. If she wanted this night to be memorable for the good times, she'd have to get some help. She didn't want her one fling on the wild side to be something to be laughed about later. "If you'll excuse me, I need to use the bathroom."

"Take your time." He lifted the bottle out of the bucket, pulled the loosened cork out of the opening, and tipped some of the dark red liquid into each glass. The candle's scent curled around her senses. The warm nutty fragrance stirred her passion. God, she wanted him!

Rachel scrambled for the bathroom. As soon as she closed the door, she turned on the water in the sink, dug out her cell phone, and speed-dialed her sister.

"Rachel? What's wrong? Are you all right?" Hayley's questions grew sharper as Rachel fought to push words past her constricted throat.

"I'm in a hotel with one of the strippers."

"Are you okay? He didn't hurt you, did he? Want me to come get you?"

"No! He's been very nice." She clutched the phone in her hand, her grip so tight she was afraid she'd snap it right in two. "What do I do? I've never seduced a man before?" She tried to keep the panic out of her voice, but some of it must have escaped.

"You'll do fine, Rach. Just be yourself. Everything else will come naturally. If he's a stripper, he'll know the ropes, just go with the flow." She giggled. "I can't believe you're going to make it with a stripper. I wish it were me. No, just kidding. I've got all the man I need in Bryan. But a stripper? Now, that takes guts."

A brief flare of pride surged through Rachel before she remembered the man was still out there. If she took too long in the bathroom, he might lose interest or leave. A different panic filled her after that thought. She wanted this one night of passion more than she'd wanted anything in her life. So what was she waiting for?

To know what to do next.

"I can't go out there without a plan; tell me what I can do to get the ball rolling, please!"

"Okay, take a deep breath and listen carefully. . . ."

Mano fished his cell phone from the back pocket of his jeans and hit the speed dial for the station.

"This is Officer Kekehuna, let me speak to Officer Weis."

As soon as the line clicked it filled with the raucous shouts and laughter of a group of guys filling the war room, no doubt gathered around the video display of the show Mano had been putting on with the suspect.

"Mano, how's it going?" Brad's voice held a hint of humor.

"You know as much as I do, what with the front-row seating to the freak show."

"Now, now, don't get your G-string in a wad." Was that a snort? From Weis? Mano clenched his fist, wanting to hit something so badly it hurt.

Laughter echoed in the background.

"I've got news on that hair sample we found in the room with the last vic," Brad said. "The red hair was real but had glue on the end like that used in wigs. Your killer was wearing a wig. She probably isn't a redhead at all."

Mano stared at the closed door to the bathroom, fighting disappointment that he'd picked the wrong girl and relief for the same reason. Rachel's mannerisms and innocence didn't seem like those of a killer. She probably didn't even like to step on ants.

One of the boys back at the station yelled into Mano's ear. "Leave the cameras on, we want to watch! The redhead is hot!"

Biting hard on his tongue, Mano didn't tell the guy exactly what he thought of that idea. He'd already exposed Rachel enough to their lecherous hearts. He didn't need to give them reason to think there might be something more going on between them than a cop trying to seduce a criminal into committing a crime.

"Fuck off, Joe." Brad told the guy off, then in a calm voice continued. "The room's paid for, you might as well enjoy the rest of the night. I'm pulling the backup and sending them home."

"What a fucked-up mess." Mano shoved a hand through his hair. "I hope the Black Widow isn't out there killing another stripper as we speak."

"You and me both. But we had to give it a shot. Too bad it didn't work out."

Mano flipped his phone shut at the same time Rachel emerged from the bathroom, draped in a towel—and nothing else.

When her hands moved to release the terry cloth knot at her breasts, Mano leaped forward and snatched her hands before they could open the towel. "Wait!"

Her eyes widened, her cheeks flushing bright red. "You don't . . . I didn't mean . . ." She turned to run back into the bathroom, her eyes suspiciously bright.

He'd hurt her feelings by his clumsy move. "No, don't go. I'm flattered you came out here like that. I just don't think it fair that I still have on so many clothes." He ripped his shirt off his back and sent it flying straight for the smoke detector where the hidden camera ran on, capturing everything in digital.

The shirt hit the wall and slid down, catching on the round plastic smoke detector.

With a sigh, Mano reached out and pulled Rachel into his arms. "There, now we're on more equal terms."

She blinked up at him, her cheeks still a fiery red. "I don't know if I can go through with this. I don't usually throw myself at men."

He could believe that and he found her shyness as charming as her determination to conquer it and throw her inhibitions to the wind. "Come here." He gathered her into his arms, his hands sliding down past her waist to cup her ass and pull her against his straining cock. "You see what you do to me?"

The shine in her eyes glazed and her tongue slipped out to swipe a path of moisture across her coral-colored lips. Lips Mano could kiss without worrying about being poisoned.

A weight lifted off his chest as he realized he could make love to this woman with a clear conscience. He wasn't trying to trap her into admitting she'd killed someone. With slow determination, he relieved her fingers of their grip on the towel. Then he let go, the fluffy white terrycloth slipping over her skin to pool at her bare feet.

Although he hadn't snared his killer, the night couldn't have turned out better. Rachel seemed to be a gentle soul on the edge of passion and Mano looked forward to pushing her over the edge. His cock twitched behind the thick denim, his gaze panning her length, from the deep red hair to the pale peachy-pink of her toenail polish. This woman was a true redhead down to the thatch of curly red hair between her legs. No one could fake that very convincingly. "You're beautiful."

Her gaze rested on his chest. "I think you are." Tentatively at first, her hands rose to his chest, then with surer movements she traced the contours of his muscles, her palms scraping over his nipples, making them harden to dark brown points. He sucked in a deep breath, pushing his chest into her palms. With more certainty, her hand skimmed downward to the skin stretched tautly over his abdomen. Down even farther to the metal rivet on his jeans that he'd buttoned during the walk from the club to the hotel. For a moment she paused, the tips of her fingernails scraping his belly.

She glanced up, her gaze meeting his. "Do you want me to do this?"

Mano sucked in a deep breath, closed his eyes, and tried to think thoughts geared toward shrinking his swollen dick. He let out the breath in a harsh whoosh. "Yes. I want you to do that. I've wanted you to do that since I saw you at the club. In fact I'll help you." He reached for the rivet, but her hand stopped him.

A slow smile curled her lips. "No, let me. I've never undressed a man before."

"Never?"

"I know that must sound lame to someone like you." Her brows furrowed. "Do you want to change your mind?"

"Good God, no." She still thought he was a stripper. He really should tell her. Confess the part he'd been playing. Move forward with a clear conscience.

Her fingers flicked the metal button open and unzipped his jeans, allowing his cock to spring forward, hot and heavy with need.

When Rachel circled his penis with both hands, Mano's thoughts of lies and confessions scattered to the four winds.

"Wow." She stared down at him, her eyes wide, her breath coming in short rasps. "Wow."

He slipped her hair behind her ears and chuckled. "Keep that up and you're going to embarrass me."

"I thought you'd stuffed your G-string." No man could be that big. Her fingers slid upward to the tip and back down to where his balls disappeared into his jeans. She slipped her hands around his backside to cup his ass. Then she pushed his jeans down, shoving them past his thighs, dropping to her knees to peel them off his legs one at a time. When he stepped free, she didn't rise; instead, she cupped his balls and rolled them between her fingers.

She laid her cheek against his cock, dragging her soft skin along the length until the tip hit the corner of her mouth. Her tongue flicked out and tasted the mushroomed head.

A stimulating jolt of electricity jerked through him. He clenched his hands at his sides to keep from forcing her to take him into her mouth and suck him hard and fast.

He guessed she'd never gone down on a man and he didn't want her first experience with him to be bad. He feathered his fingers through her hair urging her closer, but leaving it all in her power to accept or deny his direction, even though the effort nearly made him explode.

Rachel touched her tongue to his penis again, this time licking a long swirl around the rim of the head, flicking at the sensitive points.

Mano's fingers tightened in her hair.

"Like that?" She smiled up at him as her hands hooked behind his calves and slipped upward to his thighs. When she reached his ass, she pressed her palms against his cheeks and took his cock into her mouth until it bumped against the back of her throat.

The warm wetness of her mouth on him almost pitched him over the edge. What kind of lover would he be if he didn't get her there first? "No." Mano's hands dropped to her shoulders and he pushed her away. "I'm about to explode."

"Am I doing it wrong? My sister said a man couldn't resist a woman who'd suck his cock."

Mano choked. "She did? Your sister?" He clutched her arms

and brought her to her feet, pressing a kiss to the tip of her nose. "What else did your sister tell you?"

"That I didn't have to have an orgasm to have fun, but if it's all right by you, I'd like one." Again her cheeks brightened to an adorable shade of peachy-pink.

"One orgasm coming right up."

5

Before Rachel could guess his next move, Mano scooped his arm behind her knees and lifted her high.

She admired the way her naked body fit against his, how her pale skin stood out in stark contrast to his burnt coffee coloring. He strode to the bed and laid her down on the mattress.

With her body on fire, she couldn't wait for more of Mano. Her knees fell to the sides, exposing herself to him.

The hungry gleam in his eyes echoed the ache in her core.

Mano traced her pale skin from the top of her hip down to her ankles then back up, brushing his knuckles along the inside of her thigh, making her skin burn, her nerves ignite, and her heart pound.

His fingers tangled in the mound of hair covering her mons, threading through the coppery curls, digging deeper to part her folds.

Yes, there, touch me, she pleaded silently, willing him closer still.

There he found the little strip of flesh packed tightly with nerve endings. One flick of his finger and her heels dug into the mattress, raising her ass off the comforter.

"Oh, yes!" she cried out, mindless of any shame or self-consciousness.

When Mano paused before his next trick, Rachel sank back down, drawing in a shaky breath, wondering if she would come apart before this was over and not caring at all if she did. Just as long as he kept doing what he did so well.

He stroked her clit again and she cried out, rising up to meet his touch. She couldn't breathe, the pleasure was so intense.

"Please. Don't tease me," she begged. Her hand glided over her belly to that place he'd discovered. Her fingers touched the spot, swirling around the nubbin. "Please."

"Uh-uh." He pushed her fingers aside. "That's my job." Then he pulled her to the edge of the bed where her knees dropped over the sides. Pushing her legs wider apart, he knelt on the floor, draping her legs over his shoulders, touching her pussy with the tip of his tongue.

Rachel moaned, her fingers digging into his scalp, alternating between pushing him away and dragging him closer. Never in her life had anything been this wonderful. Never had she come so close to ecstasy.

He tongued her clit, flicking, licking, and sucking until she thought it couldn't possibly get better.

Then he swirled a finger around her cunt, bathing it in juices, lubricating it for . . .

His fingers slid inside her at the same time he sucked her clit into his mouth and nipped the tip between his teeth.

Pleasure so intense it hurt burst through her groin, releasing a flood of cum onto his finger. His finger slid free only to be joined by two more, sliding deep inside her where his knuckles scraped deliciously against her inner channel.

She wanted more. His fingers weren't enough. An overwhelming need to be filled by him overcame her. Rachel's fingers pulled his hair.

"Ouch!" He grinned up at her. "Like to play rough, do you?"

The gleam in his eyes made her shiver with anticipation. "Yes, oh, yes. I like to play rough." Was that her voice saying those words? Had she lost her mind? She really didn't even know this man. But it didn't matter. In that moment, she knew what she wanted. She wanted him to play rough with her. Right now. "Bring it on, Big Kahuna."

He stood, straight and naked, his chest bulging with hard, dark, muscles, his cock jutting out like a conqueror's sword.

And she wanted it. Wanted him.

Then he bent over her, claiming her mouth, the taste of her cum on his lips adding flames to the burning core of her desire. His hands clamped over her breasts, squeezing hard enough to hurt a little, but not enough to make her want him to stop.

He dragged his fingers over her ribs, into the curve of her waist and back out to the swell of her hips. In the blink of an eye, he flipped her onto her stomach.

A puff of air whooshed out of her lungs as she landed against the mattress. He shoved three pillows under her belly, hiking her ass into the air.

"What are you doing?"

"You wanted rough, didn't you?" He slapped her ass with his large palm.

He'd spanked her! At once alarmed, Rachel couldn't deny the added excitement. No one had ever spanked her, unless you'd count her parents when she'd been a little girl. And this felt nothing like that. Her daddy would be horrified at the way her body flushed with increased need. She wanted him to do it again.

She pushed up on her hands and stared back over her shoulder. "What are you going to do, you big bully? Spank me again?" *Yes, please, yes!* She gave him what she hoped was a sultry look.

He grabbed both cheeks of her ass and massaged them, digging in with his finger tips. When he let go, she almost cried out. A big hand came down sharply against her other cheek, the loud pop more noise than pain.

"Is that the best you can do?" she taunted, loving playing the role of a sexpot, something she'd never thought she had in her. She twisted around to watch the expressions on his face and to admire the jut of his cock. "You think you're so tough. Well, you're not."

He growled, a smile twitching at the corners of his lips. "I'll show you tough." He slapped her again and dove in to touch his tongue to her pussy, lapping at the cum dripping out.

Her belly clenched and her eyes closed at the exquisite feel of him. "Show me more, Big Kahuna. I'm not convinced," she managed to get out between gasps.

Mano slapped her other cheek, following the sting by cupping her pussy with his palm, dragging it back until his finger hovered over the opening. Swirling the juices over her nether lips, he pumped one finger, then two fingers, make that three, and finally four big fingers into her cunt.

"Not good enough, Mano. I want more," she whispered, so close to orgasm she might explode at his next touch.

"Did you say something?" He lay over her body, his cock nudging against her entrance. "I couldn't hear you?" he breathed into her neck, then nipped at the back of her neck.

"Please," she whimpered, pressing back until her pussy surrounded his cock.

"You want some of this?" he said, dipping his dick into her juices.

"Yeeesssss." She closed her eyes, tears threatening. She'd never wanted something as badly as she wanted him inside her now.

Mano straightened, his hands clenched around her hips, and he rammed into her, filling her, stretching her with his hard, thick shaft.

"Thank you," Rachel gasped, her body tensing, catapulting her into orgasm.

Mano almost laughed out loud when Rachel thanked him for finally consummating their lovemaking. But his focus centered on his own release. Her channel squeezed around his cock, tight, wet, and hot.

Her creamy white ass bounced against his groin as he pumped in and out of her, too far gone to question his sanity making love to a woman he didn't know, in a hotel room paid for by the department.

No, he was running on instinct. The primal instinct of the male of the human species. The internal drive to mate with a woman. That she had fiery red hair and skin the texture of silk went a long way toward fanning the flames of his lust. Her rich, light brown eyes sparkled with desire when she looked at him, making his cock thicken, his body crave what she had to offer.

His desire rocketed out of control, shooting him over the top. At the last minute, he yanked out of her channel, his seed spilling onto her ass instead of inside her. How he'd wanted to stay where he'd been, his cock buried deep in her pussy, pulsing his cum into her.

When he came back to earth, he collapsed beside her, dragging the pillows from beneath her.

She snuggled against him, her head nestled in the crook of his arm, a slim, pale arm draped over his chest.

Yeah, he liked this.

Exhaustion pulled at him, but he wanted to stay awake and get to know more about this woman. The only fact he knew about her was her first name. Rachel. It suited her. Sweet, yet passionate.

She sighed, her breath teasing his nipple. "Do you always perform so . . . energetically?"

He chuckled, tightening his arm around her, bringing her closer to him. "No, not actually."

"But you must have loads of experience."

Guilt twisted a knot in his belly. He'd yet to tell her why he'd seduced her in the first place. Although she couldn't possibly be the Black Widow, how much did she really need to know? "Not as much as you'd think." Once revived, the guilt didn't back down. Still, he wanted to get to know her better. "Tell me more about you."

"Why?" She didn't ask with suspicion in her tone, just curiosity. "I thought guys like you liked to keep things somewhat anonymous."

Oh, yeah, she thought he was some kind of gigolo, sex for hire and all that. "Sometimes, but not this time. I want to know you better."

She chewed on her lip. "You know we haven't even discussed payment." Pushing up on her elbow, she stared down into his face, her forehead creased in a frown. "I'm not even sure I can afford you."

"Did I ask you for anything?"

"No, but—"

He touched a finger to her lips. "None required."

Her forehead cleared and she sank back into the crook of his arm. "Thank goodness. I don't think I'd have near enough money to pay you enough for . . . for . . . well, what you did." Her hand slid across his chest, stopping at the far nipple where she tweaked it gently. "How many women have you been with? Or is that too personal?"

"Again, not as many as you'd think." The lies didn't get any easier. In fact, they stuck to his tongue, making it harder for him to reply to her.

"Does that mean you only pick the ones you like?" Her

voice faded off into a whisper, her breath warming the tiny spot where she breathed against his chest.

"Definitely." Ah, at least this answer wasn't a lie. He liked what was in his arms. He liked her and he wanted to know more about her. "Do you live in Hawaii?"

"No." She pinched his nipple between her thumb and forefinger. "I'm from Minnesota."

Damn. Disappointment edged out some of his pleasure. "Let me guess. You're here on vacation and wanted to have a little fun before you head back home." Back home to a mainlander boyfriend. That was the trouble with dating strangers in Hawaii: the relationships were short lived. He sighed. He always managed to fall for the unattainable.

"Something like that. Only not on vacation. I'm here for my sister's wedding."

At the very least he could enjoy the few short hours he had left with her. "Minnesota, huh? That would explain the accent."

Her forehead scrunched. "That bad?"

"No, that good." He kissed away the frown, his lips pressing against her temple, her cheek, and finally to the dewy softness of her lips. Yeah, it was a shame she wouldn't be around long.

His chest tightened and his kiss deepened, his tongue sliding into her mouth to stroke hers.

Already his cock twitched, hardening. But he didn't want to appear too eager, too needy. No use investing in an emotional connection with Rachel.

"Want some wine?" he asked, ready to make the night last a whole lot longer, imagining the many more things they could do in this bed, and at the same time, trying to distance himself from her. Not that guys were emotional when it came to sex. Well, not usually.

"Yes, that would be nice." Her hand skimmed over his back and down to his ass.

Oh, yeah, guys thought with their dicks, not their hearts. He just had to remind himself a couple more times before he got it.

He climbed out of the bed and stretched, working the muscles he'd just abused in his wild ride with a beautiful redhead.

Rachel sat up, scooted to the end of the bed, and slid off, standing in front of him.

"You didn't have to get up."

She smiled. "I got lonely."

He closed the distance, stepping over the towel she'd dropped earlier. "Can't have that."

"I've never been this . . ." She waved a hand. "I don't know."

"Cold, exposed, naked?" He rubbed the pad of his thumb over her peaked nipple.

"Ummm." She moved closer. "No, I think the word I'm looking for is 'naughty.' " Her leg wrapped around the back of his calf. "And I think I'm liking it way too much."

"I didn't think a person could like being naughty too much." He kissed the tip of her nose, then brushed her lips with his. His cock hardened, pressing against her hip.

"Really?" She looked up into his eyes. "Wanting to be spanked is normal?" Her hand cupped his ass and she slapped him.

Mano's fingers tightened around her breasts. "Very normal. So normal, we'll never make it to that wine if you keep that up."

"Oh." Rachel backed away. Maybe she was taking it too fast. If she wasn't careful, he'd be thinking she was some kind of slut or something. A little flustered and feeling a bit foolish standing there naked in front of him, she fought to keep from covering herself.

Desperate for something to do with her hands other than run them over Mano's gorgeous coffee-colored skin, she grasped at anything. "Let me get the wine." She ducked around him and hurried toward the little cart with the two glasses of wine already poured and waiting for them. In her hurry, she didn't notice the towel on the floor until her feet caught in the terrycloth.

Mano reached out too late. "Watch out for the—"

No! Even as she struggled to stay upright, Rachel fell, the slow motion of her fall forcing her to take in the minute details. Yeah, she was going to hit the little wine cart with the two shiny glasses full of red liquid sparkling in the light as if laughing at her. The wine bottle lying in the bucket of ice and the full glasses were in equal amounts of danger, based on the direction of her uncontrolled fall.

She hit the tray full on, all of her weight sending the little cart toppling over onto the creamy white carpet. Red wine sloshed out, soaking into the fibers. The glasses emptied; the bottle landed a few feet away, rolling across the carpet, leaving a bright red trail like blood from a ragged cut.

Rachel landed on the cart, the metal edges slamming into her chest and arms. Her knees hit the carpet and skidded, guaranteeing rug burn. When the movement stopped, she lay still assessing the pain erupting from all points and wondering if there was any way to salvage her dignity. At least the candle's flame snuffed out before it could catch the carpet on fire. The nutty scent rose in a swirl of smoke.

6

When he saw Rachel pitch forward, Mano reached out. She fell so fast, he couldn't catch her. The cart, Rachel, and the wine flew in all directions.

When he got to her, she lay on top of the cart, moaning.

"Oh, baby, let me help you." Mano knelt on the floor beside her, wondering whether he should move her or call an ambulance.

Rachel tried to laugh, and winced, her hand going to where her rib lay against a sharp edge of the cart. "When I fall for a guy, I like to make a big impression."

"If that was your goal, you've succeeded magnificently." He smiled when he'd rather gather her in his arms and crush the air out of her. She'd scared the shit out of him and he was still shaking. "Think anything's injured?"

"Not much, mostly my pride."

Mano shook his head and scooped his arms beneath her, lifting her off the cart.

"Okay, this is much better than lying on the cart." She rested her cheek against his chest. "Only I think that's my blood on the carpet." She pointed to the bright burgundy stain in front of the cart, the wine stain being completely different.

Warm, wet liquid oozed down over Mano's arm and his chest tightened. "Let's get you into the bathroom."

"I'm okay. It's just a little cut." She ran a hand over his chest. "I'll live, but I don't think you're getting that wine you ordered."

"Screw the wine." He kicked open the bathroom door and sat her on the counter beside the sink.

"I can stand," she protested, wiggling her cute little naked butt close to the edge in an attempt to climb down.

"Stay." He reached for the snowy white washcloth hanging on a towel rack beside the sink and ran it under the water, squeezing out the excess.

"I can take care of myself, you know. We need to do something about the stains on the carpet or your bill is going to include replacement."

"Screw the bill. This may sting." He dabbed at the cut on her side, cleaning the edges of the wound carefully.

"See? Just a scratch. All that bleeding for nothing." She eyed the shower. "If it's all the same to you, though, I'd like to get the blood and wine off me. It's all getting kind of sticky."

"You sure you're not hurt anywhere else?"

She smiled. "No, but thanks for caring." She scooted to the edge of the counter again.

Every time she scooted across the cool granite, Mano wanted to be the counter, and his cock, which had deflated with the fall, revived substantially.

"Stay." He pointed a finger in her face. "I'm not done yet." He ripped back the curtain and turned on the shower, adjusting the temperature, careful not to look at Rachel as she sat there naked and more desirable than ever.

When he turned to face her, her legs were spread wide and her fingers were toying with her clit, a rosy blush on her cheeks. "This counter is making me crazy." She dragged her finger across her pussy and up into the folds where her clit nestled, her eyes squeezing shut. "Who would have thought cold, hard granite could be so sexy?"

Mano groaned and stepped up to the counter, his cock sliding into the wet offering of her pussy. "I don't know, but it's making me crazy, too." He buried his face in her neck, lavishing kisses across her collarbone and up her throat. When he reached her mouth, he paused. "You scared me for a moment there."

"I scared myself." She reached out for his hips and pulled him more fully inside her. "I thought you'd run screaming from someone so clumsy."

"Never." His lips descended, claiming hers, drinking in the warmth of her mouth and the tangy flavor of lime. He was careful not to touch the cut on her side. In slow, steady movements, he glided in and out of her. The slow speed, coupled with the rising heat, made him so hard he thought he'd explode any second.

"I'm not going to break, you know." Her hands climbed up his back and circled his neck.

"I don't want to hurt you."

"You're hurting me by holding back."

Mano grasped her hips and pumped into her, the rapid fire action bordering on manic. He had to have her, had to be buried inside her, all the way. When he exploded over the top, he almost forgot to pull back. Almost. At the last second, he slid free and pumped his cock with his hand, cum spurting out on her thigh.

Rachel pushed his hands aside and picked up where he left off, coaxing the last little bit of seed from him, her fingers slick and shiny. She leaned forward and licked the last drop from the tip of his penis.

Mano dragged in a deep breath and let it out. He couldn't

remember the last time he'd felt this good, so satiated. He grabbed Rachel off the counter and carried her into the shower, counting his blessings.

He let her slide down his body until her feet touched the floor. "You are amazing."

She smiled up at him. "So are you."

He reached for the bar of soap, lathered it in his hands, and then handed it to her. Standing beneath the spray, he spread the foam over her body, exploring every inch and crevice until she moaned for more.

Her hands slid over his chest and down to the patch of hair surrounding his cock. "How many times can you orgasm in a night?" she asked as his cock lengthened and hardened beneath her caress.

He laughed. "Why? Are you trying to break a record?"

She shrugged. "No, just wondered." Her hands circled and stroked his length. Then she cupped his balls, massaging them between her fingers.

When he could take it no more, he lifted her up, wrapping her legs around his waist. "Let's find out."

He fucked her in the shower with her back pinned to the cool tile walls, enjoying the way water dripped off the tips of her breasts into his mouth. He loved everything about her and didn't want to stop. Even after he came, he held her against him, kissing her and sliding his tongue across her smooth skin. Not until the hot water cooled did he make a move to leave the shower.

When he did, he used the towel to pat her dry, starting with her long red hair, squeezing the moisture from the locks. All her makeup had dissolved, leaving her face fresh and clean, her natural beauty even more breathtaking than before. He worked the towel over her shoulders, down her arms, and back up to cup each breast reverently, stopping long enough to kiss the tips and nibble until she cried out. As he worked his way down her torso to the thatch of red curly hair between her thighs, he took extra care to touch and stroke her.

Before long her breath came in ragged gasps and she threw her head back, moaning. "God, you're amazing."

"Glad to please you."

Her head came up and she advanced on him with a dry towel. "My turn."

Thirty minutes later, they lay in the bed, the stain on the rug forgotten, their legs tangled in the sheets.

Mano couldn't shake the feeling of impending loss. His chest tightened with each thought of Rachel walking out the door. After just one night, he didn't want to let her go. He wanted to get to know her, take her out on a real date. Walk on the beaches and show her the Hawaii he'd grown up in and loved. But she'd only be there a few days, and she had a wedding to prepare for and attend. When would she have time to see him?

"Rachel?" He stroked his hand over her breast, teasing the nipple to a peak.

"Ummm."

What would he ask her? *Want to stay in Hawaii and fuck with me forever?* Those were words a woman couldn't resist. Not. What could he offer her? She probably had family back on the mainland. Hawaii was a world of its own out in the middle of the ocean, far from everything she knew and people she loved.

He didn't even know her.

Well, he did know that she liked to make love on granite. And he knew she'd learned that with him. He also knew she liked the feel of soap sliding between her legs in the shower.

"Are you staying with me all night?" As soon as he asked, he regretted it.

She turned toward the clock on the nightstand. "Why? What time is it?"

"Two in the morning."

"Two?" She sat up straight. "Two? Good grief. My sister will be beside herself. My aunt and uncle are flying in today. I need to be awake enough to pick them up at the airport." Rachel leaped from the bed and began pulling on her clothes. She came across the bottle of wine still tipped over in the carpet and grimaced. "I bet that leaves a stain." She carried the bottle to the bathroom and emptied the remainder into the sink, returning with a washcloth.

Mano stood, slipping into his jeans. Their time together had come to an end and his chest hurt. "Leave it."

"I have to try and get it out."

"I said leave it." He reached down and captured her hand, pulling her to her feet. "It doesn't matter."

"No?"

He pulled her against his body, irritated by the clothing between them. "Will I see you again?" He had to know the answer to this question. It burned in his gut. Mano wasn't a one-night-stand kind of guy.

"I don't know. The wedding is in a few days."

He kissed her earlobe, drawing it between his teeth and biting down gently. "There has to be a day in there you can meet me."

"I think I can manage," she laughed and pulled his mouth to hers, kissing him hard. "I have to go now."

"Where are you staying?"

"The Hyatt." She kissed him again. "Call me."

"I will."

"Now, I really should go." Her lips left his and she hurried for the door, turning as she stood in the threshold. "Thanks for a wonderful night."

Mano stared at the door's wood paneling even after she left, wishing the night wasn't over. As he wandered around the room, collecting his clothes and removing the shirt from the camera on the wall, a thought struck him. How was he supposed to contact her when he didn't know her last name!

Mano ran to the door and flung it open.

Rachel was long gone, the hallway standing silent and empty. He ran down to the elevator, but the numbers indicated she'd already reached the lobby.

Damn! Mano retraced his footsteps to the hotel room, already thinking a day ahead.

If he had to, he'd stake out the lobby of the Hyatt Hotel until he found her. Shoot, he was a cop. He ought to be able to find a redheaded guest. Someone would know something. His thoughts brightened as he reached the open doorway and stepped through.

Not until he'd half-closed the door behind him did he realize he wasn't alone.

A woman in a red dress emerged from the shadows, her blond hair strangely askew, a Saturday Night Special pistol held cocked and ready, its three-inch barrel aimed at his chest.

Mano's first instinct was to shove the door in her face.

The woman stepped out of range of the heavy hotel door before he could make his move. "Don't do anything stupid. I know how to use this thing."

With his hand still on the doorknob, he left it open just enough so the lock wouldn't engage. Then he released the knob and raised his hands in the air, his mind racing, searching for an opportunity to regain control of the situation and the small but equally deadly weapon. His own gun rested in the pocket of his jacket on the floor on the other side of the bedroom.

Her eyes narrowed and she moved in a wide arc around him, her gaze taking him in from the top of his head to the bulge at his fly. "Already tired of the redhead? You strippers are all insatiable sex addicts, aren't you?"

Her question didn't bear answering. Mano maintained his silence, looking for his opportunity.

"You're much better looking than the average stripper. Why is that?" Her gaze scraped him from top to bottom again.

He shrugged, realizing the truth would be easier to remember than a lie. "I haven't been stripping long."

"Really?" She snorted. "You could have fooled me. The way those women were touching and petting you, you looked like a professional."

"Maybe a natural, but not a professional."

"You're just like the others." Her hand shook, her finger tightening on the trigger. "Only they were smart enough to drink the wine."

Keep her talking. Mano moved away from the door, hoping to get close enough to knock the gun from her hands. He'd seen the woman earlier at the club. She'd flirted with him, tried to get him to leave with her, but he'd been so intent on the lady he thought was the Black Widow, he hadn't given the blonde in the red dress much more than a passing thought. A shame he hadn't given her more attention. If he wasn't mistaken the woman in front of him had to be none other than the Black Widow.

7

Floating on air, Rachel left the hotel, intent on walking the ten blocks to her own hotel. She needed the time to come down from the cloud she'd been floating on since she'd met Mano.

A rush of joy and excitement filled her chest and she pressed her hands to her flushed cheeks. Had she really slept with a perfect stranger? She dropped her hands and laughed out loud. Yes! He'd been the perfect stranger, too.

Passersby stared at her and smiled, probably thinking she was high or something. And wasn't she? High on life. High on sex. High on living! All because of one very sexy Hawaiian stripper. A stripper who'd wanted to see her again. Her! A boring middle-school librarian from Minnesota.

Three blocks away from his hotel, her feet slowed and reality set in. He didn't know her last name. He hadn't asked for her room or telephone number. Had she imagined his continued interest? Or was he playing her like he did all the women he slept with? And just how many women was that? Questions jumbled in her mind, bringing her high on life down with a thud to the solid concrete of the sidewalk on Kalakaua Avenue.

If he didn't know her last name, how was he supposed to contact her? She stopped and turned. Should she hurry back and give him her hotel number, her last name, her home phone in Minnesota, her date of birth, and favorite color?

Her shoulders hunched, Rachel resumed her walk back to her hotel, her feet dragging. No, he'd think she was some kind of pathetic groupie, chasing him when he really never had any intention of following through with a second date. Not that the first one had been a date.

It had started out as a business deal. Rachel ground to a stop.

The couple following too closely behind her bumped into her. "Hey, will you make up your mind, already?" The girl gave her a dirty look and hurried around her.

Damn! She'd forgotten the whole reason for her visit to the strip club to begin with. She was supposed to secure the services of a stripper for her sister's bachelorette party. She'd never hear the end of it if she didn't come through on the one and only task her sister had given her for the entire wedding.

Question was, should she go back and ask Mano if he would perform for the girls? It would give her another opportunity to gauge his sincerity about seeing her again. She had a perfectly valid reason for giving him her hotel room number and her last name without appearing like a pathetic groupie.

Hadn't her sister said to seize the moment? An opportunity had presented itself; shouldn't she grab it?

Rachel spun on her high-heeled sandals and hurried back to the hotel where Mano was staying, her mood brighter, hopeful. Maybe she could recapture some of her earlier euphoria.

All that would depend on Mano's reaction to seeing her again.

Retracing her steps, the three blocks seemed longer than before. She hoped he hadn't already gone to sleep. He might not be happy about being woken up.

Once again, doubt settled in, slowing her pace. What if he didn't want to see her again? What if he wasn't thrilled about performing for the girls? Would this have been the last time she'd see the oh-so-incredible Hawaiian?

The hotel entrance loomed ahead, the brightly lit lobby welcoming her, mocking her insecurities in a warm and friendly glow.

She'd never know what he thought if she didn't get her chicken butt up there and find out.

Rachel squared her shoulders and marched through the lobby, on a mission to learn the truth, no matter what it was.

"May I help you, miss?" An older Hawaiian gentleman dressed in a brightly colored Hawaiian shirt stepped away from the concierge's desk.

"I need to get to the fourth floor."

He smiled, but stood between her and the elevator, unmoving. "What room are you staying in?"

What was with this guy? Had he appointed himself the Hotel Inquisition? "I'm not actually staying here." Okay, that didn't sound good, and by the frown on the man's face, he considered it a problem, too. Rachel took a deep breath and tried again. "A friend of mine is in room 421. I just need to speak to him for a moment."

The concierge took her elbow and guided her to his desk where a computer monitor shown through the glass surface. "Could I have his name, please?" He slid a keyboard out from under the desk, his fingers poised over the keys.

Rachel's stomach dropped to her knees. She didn't know Mano's full name any better than he knew hers. What a complete idiot she'd been. She smiled up at the concierge. "Mano," she said with as much confidence as her sinking spirits could muster.

"Last name, please."

She shrugged, her face scrunching. "Would you believe it, my mind's a complete blank? Must have been the wine at the club."

The concierge's brows drew together. "I'm sorry, miss. No room key, no access."

"Could you at least ring room 421? I'm sure he'd come down to see me." She crossed her fingers behind her back, hoping her little story wasn't a complete lie. All this time she'd been worried about Mano's reception; she hadn't considered it would be a problem getting back into the hotel to see him.

"I'm sorry, miss. We don't disturb our guests after midnight unless it's an emergency." His brows rose on his dark forehead.

Rachel opened her mouth, paused, and closed it. Defeated.

Getting a commitment for a stripper to perform at her sister's bachelorette party probably didn't constitute an emergency on the concierge's part.

"If you'd care to leave a message, I'll be sure to deliver it to room 421 in the morning."

"No, thank you." Rachel headed for the door, her steps slow, her body sagging under the weight of her failure. How could she go back to her sister empty-handed? What excuse did she have? *I had hot, nasty sex with the stripper and forgot to schedule the party or get his number.* Yeah, her sister would never believe it for a moment.

Rachel looked back over her shoulder at the hotel Nazi standing between her and the elevator, his arms crossed over his chest.

A couple stepped through the lobby doors, their raucous laughter jarring in the quiet of the tastefully decorated entrance.

As they stumbled past her, Rachel snuck another glance at the concierge. He'd returned to his station, no longer standing in front of the elevator. Not that Rachel had a chance of sneaking by him without capturing his attention. Then she noticed a staircase almost hidden by a large, potted royal poinciana tree. The bright red flowers of the beautiful tree camouflaged the entrance to the stairwell. Although not far from the elevator, the stairs were easily out of sight of the concierge's desk.

When the couple leaned over the concierge's desk asking for the addresses of clubs open all night, Rachel jumped at the chance to duck past the vigilant elevator guard and make a run for the stairs.

"Hey!"

Rachel didn't stop, but kept running, taking the stairs two at a time to the first landing. By the time she reached the third floor, she was definitely back to one step at a time, dragging her way up to the fourth floor, reminding herself to get back on her stair-stepper when she returned to Minnesota.

Her breath rasped in and out of her lungs from her mad dash up the stairs. The stairwell opened onto the fourth floor in a little vestibule around the corner from the main hallway leading to Mano's room. The concierge had seen her make a run for the stairs. Would he be waiting around the corner to head her off before she got to room 421?

She sure as hell hoped not. After walking and now climbing in the cute little killer sandals her sister had loaned her for the occasion, Rachel wasn't sure she had it in her to race for Mano's door.

All this to give the man her phone number. Sheesh! She should have left a message at the desk as the concierge had suggested.

Rachel peeked out into the hallway. So far the coast was clear. No security guard, no elevator Nazi. No one.

Her heart rate had almost returned to normal at the relief of not being caught until she took one step out into the hallway. Room 421 was only five doors down and behind it was Mano.

Her breathing went into hyperventilation mode at the prospect of facing the stranger she'd made love to, not once but three times in less than two hours! So much for a slowed heartbeat. He probably thought she was a slut or nymphomaniac.

Her hands covered her burning cheeks and she stopped midway down the hall.

The ding of the elevator arriving on the fourth floor made her jump. Stifling a scream, her feet skipped ahead until she was running toward room 421, more afraid of the hotel staff stopping her or throwing her in jail than being rebuffed by the handsome Hawaiian she'd come to see.

The whoosh of the elevator doors coincided with her arrival at the door she'd exited not fifteen minutes ago. Her hand closed around the handle as she glanced back over her shoulder. A man dressed in a black security guard uniform emerged.

The hotel concierge stepped out at the same time and pointed down the hallway to where she stood with her hand in the proverbial cookie jar (or in this case, on the doorknob). "There she is!"

Rachel pushed hard against the door. Expecting to have to bang on it to get Mano's attention, she didn't expect it to fly open at her touch. All her weight pitched forward, sending her flying across the floor, face first. In the second it took for her to crash land, the vision of a woman in a red dress with a gun pointing at Mano flashed by. Now the woman's hand, the one holding the gun, swung toward Rachel! Not that Rachel could do anything but finish her fall.

A loud bang echoed off the walls of the room.

Rachel hit the ground on all fours, the carpet burning a skid mark on her knees. Pain made her roll to her side, clutching her skinned knees.

Mano's foot swung out and clipped the woman's hand,

sending the gun flying from her fingertips to smash into the wall.

Just because Mano had disarmed her didn't stop the woman in red from reacting. She flung herself at Mano, kicking and scratching, screaming at the top of her voice. Mano held her at arm's length, but the woman had gone completely wild.

Rachel picked herself up off the ground and ran across to where Mano stood, grunting at the impact of the woman's pointed-toe shoes connecting with his shins.

Rachel had seen a female student go after another at school just like this. From behind, she grabbed the crazed woman around her waist, locking her arms to her sides.

"Thanks," Mano reached into his back pocket and pulled out a plastic zip tie.

The woman bucked and kicked out at Mano. Rachel held on, surprised at the woman's strength. She definitely wasn't a fifth grader.

Mano laid his hands on the woman's arm and nodded at Rachel. "I've got it now."

Rachel didn't want to let go, sure the woman would attack again. "Are you sure?"

"I'm sure."

Rachel let go and jumped out of range.

Mano spun the woman in the red dress around, locking her arms together behind her, wrapping the zip tie tight enough around her wrists that she couldn't escape.

"What are you doing? You have no right to tie me up." The woman screeched, kicking out again, aiming for Mano's shins.

He held her with her back to him, careful to stay out of range. Then he turned to Rachel. "Could you dial 9-1-1?"

She nodded and headed for the phone on the desk.

Mano spoke to the woman in a calm, steady voice. "You're under arrest for murder. You have the right to remain silent . . ."

Rachel's stomach performed a full gainer and she stopped with her hand outstretched toward the phone. She spun to face Mano, her mouth gaping open. Before she could say anything another voice interrupted.

"Mr. Kekehuna, is everything all right in there?" the security guard called out from around the corner of the doorway, out of sight and bullet range.

Mano stared from Rachel to the door and sighed. "Yes, although we could use some backup."

The security guard and the hotel concierge appeared in the doorway.

The concierge glared at Rachel, then his gaze took in Mano and the woman in red. "What the hell happened?"

Mano ignored the question, taking charge of the scene as if he knew exactly what to do and had done it before. "Call the Honolulu Police Department and have them send a unit."

As if in a fog of pea-soup proportions, Rachel advanced toward Mano. "You're not a stripper?"

Mano smiled and shook his head. "I'll tell you about it in just a minute." He picked up where he'd left off, reciting the Miranda warning to the woman who'd tried to put a hole through Rachel a moment before.

"But I thought . . ." What *had* she thought? That Mano was a loose and easy stripper ready to pleasure any woman for a price?

The blood drained out of her face. He could arrest her for solicitation or something, couldn't he? Or could he? He hadn't taken her money, she hadn't given him any. Still . . . "Why me?"

He'd finished the recitation.

The woman in red, whom Rachel assumed was the Black Widow, spit at Mano. "Bastard! I knew there was something wrong with you." She tried to turn, glaring over her shoulder at Rachel until a wicked smile curled her lips. "You thought *she* was the Black Widow, didn't you?" Her laugh reminded Rachel of the Wicked Witch of the West on the *Wizard of Oz*. The entire scene was like one out of a dream or a very bad movie.

"You thought I was the Black Widow?" Rachel had read about the murderer in the complimentary copy of the *Honolulu Star-Bulletin* left outside her hotel room door the previous morning. She'd taken her third victim in as many days.

Mano's lips pressed together and he nodded. "At first."

Rachel's heart squeezed in her chest and her eyes burned. "And at what point did you realize I wasn't the Black Widow?"

He paused, his gaze boring into hers. "Can we discuss this later?"

What was there to discuss? Mano lured her to the hotel to arrest her as a murderer. He'd probably seduced her to see if the Black Widow would make love to him then kill him like she had all her other victims. The entire night had been one big joke with her as the butt of it all. "No need to discuss anything. I have to go. My family will be worried."

Even before she'd said the last word, Mano was shaking his head. "You're a witness, Rachel. The detectives will want to take your statement."

The next moment, the room filled with police in uniform, everyone talking at once. Another officer took her name and information. When she promised to show up at the station the next day to give her statement, they let her go.

Surrounded by other officers, Mano didn't see her leave. And that was just the way Rachel wanted it. She needed to sneak out and avoid the embarrassment of telling him why she'd come back to his room.

She'd wanted to hire a cop to perform as a stripper at a bachelorette party. Ha! The entire police force would have gotten a good laugh out of that.

Rachel stepped into the elevator, swallowing the sob rising in her throat. The only reason Mano invited her up to his room was because he'd thought she was the Black Widow. Not because he'd been instantly attracted to her or thought she was the woman of his dreams. A laugh bubbled up in her chest, choking off her air. He'd thought she was a murderer. She'd been played for a fool. She should have known better than to take that step on the wild side.

8

Mano paced in the war room at the police station, his cell phone pressed to his ear. The line rang four times and cut to the answering machine at the hotel. Rachel should have gotten back to her hotel six hours ago, but she wasn't answering.

"Still no answer?" Brad Weis entered carrying a box of donuts. "Want breakfast?"

The thought of donuts in his knotted stomach made Mano want to puke. "No, thanks."

"I learned something interesting."

"What's that?"

"Why Rachel Grant was at the strip club by herself last night." Brad bit into a donut as if he had not a care in the world beyond digesting the sugary confection.

Mano's fists bunched, ready to wipe the smug expression from his partner's face. "Why was she there?"

Taking his time chewing and swallowing, Brad finally replied, "She was there to interview strippers for her sister's bachelorette party." He grinned. "Apparently, she chose you." He clapped Mano on the back. "Congratulations, buddy. If you ever want to quit the cop business, you have another career to consider."

Mano stood still, holding back his rising temper. "Back off, Brad."

Brad raised his hands. "Calm down, Kekehuna. It's not as if the whole department knows. Yet."

"And they better not find out," Mano warned.

Dave Pendleton grinned in the doorway, holding up a DVD disc. "Got the video from the hotel last night. Noticed you threw a shirt over the lens for a while there. Too bad it didn't block out the sound, you baaaadddd boy. If I ask you nicely, will you spank me, too?"

Mano groaned and grabbed for the disc. "Give me that."

Pendleton danced away. "Oh, oh, wait. I liked this one better. 'One orgasm coming right up!' " The cop laughed out loud. "Do girls really fall for all that?"

"Give." Mano held out his hand, refusing to grab for the damning disc.

Dave held it out of Mano's reach. "Sorry. It's evidence. It's a good thing you took the shirt down before the real Black Widow stepped in."

Great. Everyone and his brother would know by the sounds what he and Rachel had done in the room that night. Just what he needed to make his life at the office unbearable. He scrubbed his hand down over his tired face and redirected the conversation to safer ground. "What's the story on our suspect?"

Dave nodded toward the outer offices. "The Chief's taking her statement now. Looks like our suspect, Ellen Brown, aka The Black Widow, is spilling her guts."

Mano's brows rose. "She confessed?"

"Yeah." Dave tapped the DVD against his palm. "Seems she was dumped by her first vic after a one-night stand. Must have triggered something, because she went off the deep end and started taking out strippers. A real winner."

"What about the other chick from last night? You gonna see her again?" Dave held the DVD up and smiled. "She's pretty easy on the eyes. And those legs. Ummmm. Wouldn't mind having those wrapped around me real snuglike."

"Shut up, Pendleton," Mano warned.

Brad leaned toward Dave. "He's been trying to get her on the phone."

"No luck, huh?"

"Hello? I'm still in the room." Mano inhaled and let out his breath and glared at Dave. "Don't you have something better to do?"

Dave shrugged. "Not really, but I guess I should get this video over to property."

After Dave left, Mano resumed his pacing and tried Rachel's number for the tenth time. When she didn't answer yet again, he almost threw the phone against the wall. "This is crazy. I don't know why I even bother. She's obviously not interested."

"I know a way you can get in to see her." Brad's mouth twisted into a wicked grin.

Mano glared at him. "This better not be another one of your stupid ideas."

"Not stupid at all. It just involves your second career."

Mano's gut tightened. "I'm not liking it already."

Brad shrugged. "All I'm saying is that she didn't get her man. Why not let it be you?"

As he considered the implied suggestion, Mano allowed a smile to finally lift his lips. "If we do this, we do it my way."

Brad's eyes widened and he gulped. "We?"

"I'm really sorry I let you down, Hayley." Rachel hugged her sister from behind and handed her the gift she'd picked up at the International Market, a box topped by a fresh plumeria flower to pin in her hair and a flower lei for the bachelorette party. Inside the box were sexy G-string panties that reminded her of Mano and the black silk G-string he'd worn at the Man, Oh Man! Male Strip Club.

Hell, everything reminded her of Mano. Every time she took a deep breath, her breasts rubbed against the inside of her bra and tingled at the memory of Mano's beard-roughened chin scraping over her nipples, his tongue teasing her into a frenzy of need.

But the man had lied to her. Had set her up, taken advantage of her, and then expected her to listen as he explained? Not on her life.

"Why don't you call him?" Hayley secured the bright yellow and red plumeria flower behind her ear and stared at her sister in the mirror. "I know he's tried to call you at least twenty times in the past two days."

"Hayley, he lied to me!" Rachel swung away from her sister's gaze. "He was pretending all the time to like me just to get me to confess to murder or to attempt to murder him. I don't know! I just feel so used."

"You should at least give him the chance to apologize. I'm sure he feels bad about it all." Hayley rose from her seat in front of the dressing table and took Rachel's hands. "He can't be all that bad if you're still thinking about him."

"I'm not thinking about him." Rachel squeezed her sister's hands, determined to put her troubles aside for her sister's last night as a single woman. "This is your night. Let's go out there and enjoy it."

Hayley grinned. "Oh, I plan to. And I was able to find just the right entertainment." Her gaze shifted away from Rachel's.

She'd done that before when she'd planned something really sneaky when they were girls. "What are you up to, Little Sis?"

Headed for the door, Hayley waved her hand. "Oh, nothing you can't handle." She paused in the doorway and turned to face Rachel. "Are you ready to shed that sour face and have a little fun?" Her eyes twinkled in challenge.

Rachel's stomach knotted. The thought of joining the roomful of rowdy women in a night of debauchery didn't even appeal to Rachel. Not when her thoughts kept straying to one tall, sexy Hawaiian with arms the size of tree trunks and . . . Oh, hell, there she went again. Maybe a little diversion was what she needed. Tomorrow she could change her flight home so that she could leave immediately instead of sticking it out another week in depressing, sunny Hawaii.

Rachel nodded at her sister and pasted a smile on her face. "Is this better?"

Hayley's brows twisted. "If you like looking like you just bit into a sour mango. Come on. It won't kill you to smile."

"Okay, Okay." She laughed, letting her sister's enthusiasm revive her somewhat. "I guess I'm as ready as I'll ever be. Let's go party."

As soon as they entered the darkened banquet room, decorated Hawaiian style with flowers in the drinks and candles lighting every table, Rachel planned to sneak off to a shadowy corner and hide.

She only made it to the first table when the music started, then she stopped and groaned. Of all the music to play, it had to be the very song Mano had danced to out on the stage at the Man, Oh Man! Male Strip Club the other night. The night he'd made passionate love to her. The night he'd lied to her.

Unable to take another step, Rachel collapsed into the nearest chair and laid her face on her arms.

A whoop rose from the roomful of women, the cheering doing anything but cheering Rachel's mood.

The music switched to a traditional Hawaiian hula dance, the music soothing and more fitting with the location and occasion.

The rattling of an uli uli gourd broke through Rachel's depression, almost tempting her to lift her head and look for the source.

"Rachel, come on!" Hayley called out. "At least look at the entertainment! Sheesh!"

She couldn't, knowing it wouldn't be Mano with his larger-than-life dark muscles, jet-black hair, and eyes the color of a moonless night. It would probably be a less-than-adequate replacement.

The table beneath her arms shook as if a great weight had jumped onto it.

Rachel jerked upright.

Standing before her like solid tree trunks were two well-defined calves, rock hard and muscular. The feet attached to them moved to the beat of the sensuous music, the legs swaying to the beauty of the hula dance, the uli uli rattle brushing her senses with its gentle shushing sound.

As her gaze traveled upward to thick, brawny thighs, a swarm of butterflies invaded her belly, turning it inside out with their disturbing flutters.

When she got to his midsection, she collapsed back against the chair, her gaze climbing ever upward.

The Hawaiian wore the traditional garb of the hula dancer, with the plumeria lei around his neck, the haku lei wreath of leaves on his head. On his wrists and ankles he wore the leafy kupe'e. Tied around his hips hung the traditional kapa, the fabric pounded out of tree bark fashioned into a loincloth covering the important parts.

This was no stripper standing before Rachel. The man before her was a Hawaiian trained in the art of Hula, his muscles proof of his manhood, his grace and beauty in tune with his culture.

"Mano . . ." she breathed.

He smiled down at her, lifting the lei from around his neck. He dropped to his knees on the tabletop, his broad shoulders thrown back. With great care, he settled the fresh lei around

Rachel's neck and bent to seal the gift with a kiss, pressed to her lips. Leaning close, he whispered, "Come. Dance with me."

Mano rose to his feet and held out a hand.

Hayley jumped up onto another table with another man dressed similarly to Mano, except the other man didn't look as natural in the attire, his features more European than Hawaiian. He smiled and laughed good-naturedly and gave a poor imitation of Mano's flowing hula dance.

The ladies around the men cheered and catcalled, urging Rachel to get on the table and dance with the man before one of them took her place.

Rachel shook her head, staring up into Mano's eyes. "I can't hula."

"I'll show you."

The low insistence of his voice wrapped her in a layer of warmth and confidence she didn't recognize in herself. Before she realized what she was doing, she'd climbed onto the table and stood in front of Mano. "Why am I doing this?" She turned to climb back down, her face burning.

He caught her from behind and circled her waist with one brawny arm. "Because we fit together and because you want this."

She stiffened, her body at odds with the flow of the music. "No. I don't want this. You lied to me." She tried to face him, but he kept her spooned against his body, his cock pressing through the loincloth to the fabric of her floral skirt.

"I didn't want to lie." He took one of her hands, stretching it to the side palm up, flowing with the music. "When you went into the bathroom that night, I knew then you weren't the murderer."

She let him take her other hand and brush it out to the other side, palm up. His hips pressed against her backside, making her hips sway to the same rhythm. Her heart dared to hope. "Before we made love?"

"Yes. Before we made love, I knew you weren't the killer."

Her eyes closed and she let her body melt against his, the backs of her thighs hot from the pressure of his knees against them. "Why did you come tonight?"

"Someone wouldn't answer her phone or talk to me. I had to do something." He pressed his lips to the side of her neck. "I had to see you."

Hayley's friends hooted and cried out, "Dance, Rachel, dance!"

Their raucous calls brought Rachel back to her senses. She was dancing on a tabletop with an almost naked man and he'd come to see her!

The last thought outweighed any embarrassment. The past few days of anger and disappointment melted away.

"Why didn't you tell me?"

"That I wasn't a stripper?" He shrugged, his chest bumping against her back with the movement. "I don't know. Maybe I was afraid you'd leave when you found out I was a cop."

"Damn right." She caught his hand in hers and slid it up her bare midsection to the bikini top she'd worn for the party. "I'm glad you didn't tell me," she whispered.

"Me, too." He twirled her around to face him. "Can we get out of here?"

Rachel cast a glance at the other man dirty dancing with Hayley on the other tabletop. "Will my sister be all right with your friend?"

Mano laughed. "Yeah. He's all right. He's my partner."

Rachel raised an eyebrow. "And that's supposed to reassure me?"

Mano leaped from the table and pulled Rachel into his arms. "Not at all. But your sister's a big girl. Now, what's it to be? Are we staying for the party?"

Rachel wrapped her arms around Mano's neck. "I know of a quiet little room on the tenth floor, only I don't think these women are going to let you out of here, and I really don't want to share."

"I've got a little distraction arranged." He flicked his wrist and the doors opened at the end of the room.

Five men danced in, all wearing parts of cop uniforms. One wore trousers and no shirt. Another wore the shirt and no trousers, cuffs dangling from his wrists. Others wore G-strings with metal official-looking cop badges hanging off the string.

The women went wild.

"More of your cop friends?" Rachel asked, comfortable in Mano's arms and content to remain there.

"Not quite. These are some of my new buddies from the club." He nuzzled her neck, the leafy fringe around his forehead tickling her ear. "You're here for another week, right?"

"How did you know?"

"I'm a cop. I have ways of getting information."

She shook her head, a smile creeping up on her lips. "You asked my sister, right?" A quick glance at her sister confirmed.

Hayley waved to Rachel and mouthed the word, "Leave."

Mano nodded at Hayley and returned his attention to the woman in his arms. "I owe you a date."

"Yes." Rachel wrapped her arms around Mano's neck. "You do. But do you think the date could wait? I'm only here for a week, after all." She twirled her finger around his ear and reached up to kiss him, sucking his bottom lip between her teeth and biting down gently.

"A week, huh? We'll have to see if we can change your mind. Maybe you'll want to extend your stay indefinitely." He strode through the crowd of females toward the door. "Tenth floor?"

"You got it." She let him carry her, enjoying every moment of being completely swept off her feet. "And how do you plan to change my mind?"

"I'm a cop." He waggled his dark brows. "I have ways."

He stepped into the elevator and the doors closed, trapping them inside for the trip up ten stories.

As the elevator rose, so, too, did Mano's hand rise up Rachel's skirt. He got right to showing her some of his "ways."

CUFFED HEAT

Delta Dupree

1

The way his eyes critically studied her, Raegen Crosby figured her two-bit ho style had worked. On the other hand, having the barrel of his .44 Magnum aimed at her heart raised even the cheap wig's hair at the back of her neck. Sometimes rookies had itchy fingers.

Bad enough she felt naked without her badge and weapon, but the new sky-blue tube top, with silver thread laced throughout, inched farther down with every breath she inhaled. She should've purchased a halter top or something with sturdy straps.

"Hands behind your head. Feet spread apart," Thaine McDuff said. "Both of you." He handled the show pretty well.

The commander had selected McDuff because he "looked" the part of a buyer. Not bad either. Immaculate, the tailored three-piece suit in dark rust fit him to perfection, when what Raegen had expected was a raggedy ensemble boasting pinstripes on seersucker, gangster brim, and white shoes. Instead, silk tie, off-white shirt, gold cufflinks, polished shoes . . . Wow.

Behind McDuff, six cops had lined up a quartet of suspects against the wall, frisking and cuffing the band of teenaged gunrunners, confiscating evidence. Three other unlucky devils were old enough to face major hell in prison if any one of the weapons came back positive in the deaths of two cops last month. Summer heat usually brought out the worst in people. Oppressive temperatures in Phoenix had skyrocketed to 110 and it was only the second week of June.

Perspiration already dampened Raegen's forehead. She raised her hands as high as her shoulders.

"I said lock your fingers."

Hell's bells. She glared at PeeWee the Snitch, who'd set up the meeting and the buy. She followed orders and put some inches between her stilettos, which hiked her metallic-blue miniskirt high enough to parade all she owned.

As cops escorted the teens out of the building, the tube top rolled below her boobs. Shit. In front of PeeWee, the same chump she'd put behind bars for dealing heroin a few years ago. In her opinion, he'd gotten his get-out-of-jail ticket early on false pretenses. She'd questioned the liar's integrity more than once. Didn't matter. Detective Bob Slater continued using him as street eyes.

PeeWee grinned.

Following suit, Slater's rumbling laughter filtered through the dilapidated building. No big deal there. The detective had fondled every inch of her body. Then she found out he was married. With four kids. The white boy knew his stuff, though. At least his tongue and mouth knew something good. He would rather feast than fuck. Problem was he'd been nagging her crazy about hooking up again.

Slater had sense enough to block PeeWee's view. McDuff had sense enough to block all the other eyeballers' scrutiny. Tonight was the last damn time she'd wear this particular ho getup.

When she tried to pull her top into place, McDuff, the cop that others called Duffy, said, "Don't tempt me, sister."

Strike one against him, dammit. She so wished she had been born with laser beams for eyes. By now, he would've had two perfect circles burned into his smooth forehead.

What the hell could she possibly hide? Well, she'd nestled her single-shot derringer in the green bustier, but this top was stretch knit, gripping. Her nipples were obviously *en point* for all to see.

Keeping his gun focused on her, Duffy circled silently behind her. She heard the clink of cuffs.

Raegen licked her lips. When in the hell did he plan on letting her cover her boobs? Tomorrow? "You know, sir—"

"Shut up."

The timbre of his sexy bass wrapped around her in a delicious caress. Despite the building's warmth, Raegen shivered. Still. Strike two. He'd taken this a little too damn far with his shitty orders. She took commands from only one person. Commander Vanderbilt.

Gently, Duffy swung her right hand behind her back. *Hmm,* Raegen thought. *Gently.* Somebody needed to re-educate him on handling suspects. He was lucky they were on the same side. She could've easily caught him off balance: flipped him, taken his gun, dotted both eyes, cut off air to his windpipe, and wrenched his balls.

"Too tight?" he asked.

She rolled her eyes. *That's it. Blatant red flag.* He'd jacked up her three-strikes-you're-out rule. Thaine McDuff was on his way back to school, back to the Academy. Tomorrow. Immediately, if she had any say-so.

The first time she saw the baby-faced rookie's fine—very fine—trampoline buns was from across the station's parking lot. He was bent over the trunk of his car. He wasn't tall tall, but at a distance, it appeared everything fit in the right places.

Definitely hot eye-candy, a fine specimen: broad chest, tight butt filling out his trousers, muscled from shoulders to calves. But at this rate, the same roped muscle substance had likely filled the space between his ears.

"Will you at least pull up my top?" she whispered. "Damn."

"Bend over."

"What?"

"If you want all that meat put in place," Duffy said, "you need to bend over so I can stretch and stuff."

What, and toot her nekkid tail right toward him? Normally she wore boy shorts to hide the panty line. The raid called for raciness. She'd worn a lacy white thong, had dressed the ho part in case the gang's honcho menace—who had skipped tonight's party—jumped suspicious, thinking she was wired. It'd happened before, had nearly put Raegen on the slowest gurney headed for the morgue.

If she refused Duffy's instruction with him so close to her back, his body heat hotly penetrating hers, she'd miss feeling if *he* owned enough "meat" worth her time.

Raegen bent over. *Whoa, yeah,* she thought two seconds later. And still expanding. *Thank you, Ms. Shoe Designer.* She peered between her legs. This cutie-pie surpassed well endowed. Prized stallions would be proud to have him on their team. Ooh, she loved riding.

He reached around her body, his hard stuff pressing insistently against her behind. When his big hands moved all over her breasts, stretching fabric and gently stuffing *meat*, Raegen sucked in a breath. Did he just strum her beaded nipple?

Uh-huh. He wants some of this. Tough. I don't do rookies. "Are you finished?"

"Hardly."

"I think you are." She rocked backward, bumped that hot number worth bumping. *Hel-lo.*

"Do that again and you'll regret it."

"Get your big paws off my tits," Raegen hissed, "or *you'll* regret it." He cupped her boobs as if he owned them, but he finally let loose. Slowly.

PeeWee burst out laughing.

Indignant, she reared up tall as her five feet seven allowed. The stilts put her at eye level with the snitch. She tossed the long, wavy mane out of her eyes. "Shut the fuck up, you little prick, or I'll snatch that ponytail off your peanut head. We'll see if your scalp is as white as the rest of your skinny ass."

"What else do you do with that mouth?" Duffy asked nastily. "I sure wouldn't eat with it."

"What's it to you?" She looked over her shoulder. "You can't afford me anyway."

He pulled out a wad of cash, peeled off several bills, and tossed them on the cement floor. "Too much?"

Three dollars? "Why, you—"

"Shut up before I shut you up."

Grinding the enamel off her teeth while straining against the cuffs, she *so* wanted to tag his arrogant mug. "You and whose army?"

Damned if the devil didn't spin her around, toss her over his shoulder, and march toward the rear entrance. He had some gray matter upstairs. He didn't carry her nekkid tail through the throng of cops, suspects, teenyboppers, and lookie loos.

Squirming, high-heeled feet kicking wildly, she said, "I will kill you where you stand, mother—"

He smacked her bare ass with a stinging slap. Raegen yelped.

"Game. Set," the smart-mouthed prick hollered. "And match."

"Woman, don't make me put you over my knee. Say one return piece of filth," Duffy said menacingly, "and I will gladly, *happily*, give you something to cry about."

What? The last time somebody set fire to her butt, Raegen had sassed her momma. Two decades ago.

She had been young, dense like most nine-year-olds living in the ghetto. Peer pressure was hell on kids.

Momma took smack from no one, especially from her Miss-Know-It-All youngest daughter. Widowed and cleaning middle-class family homes, she worked hard to keep her girls on the straight path to success. Her efforts paid off. All three daughters were college educated. Two joyfully married sisters had given momma six grandbabies to love and spoil.

There were only five nieces and nephews now.

"In your dreams, buster. Put me down, dammit."

Did he listen? Nope. He shoved the security door open and let it slam shut with a loud bang, casting them into darkness.

Carried like a sack of potatoes, Raegen lifted her head.

Next door, the single spotlight burned brightly toward the connecting street. She scanned the alley, caught sight of two drunks or, likely, junkies sprawled near the giant garbage bin at two o'clock in the morning.

"Where're you taking me?" she snapped. "I got suspects, interviews, book—"

"Shut up," Duffy said. "You don't have squat, unless you're planning to blow your cover."

She knew that.

His unmarked vehicle and a patrol car blocked both ends of the alley.

Duffy slid her body slowly down his into his arms, her feet dangling well above the ground. Even in darkness, she knew his penetrating brown eyes, eerily seductive, stared—or glared—into hers.

As his arms tightened around her, Raegen said, "You can put me down anytime." Hard as granite, his cock pressed against her belly. Her own damn body betrayed her. Something hot and fragile quivered deep within her core. She shifted, subtly, an enticing but teasing movement. Did he notice?

Yup.

Duffy deposited her on the car's hood. He moved his big self between her legs. Greedily, he caught her lips in a searing kiss, hot as a scorching desert afternoon, his dominating tongue darting into her mouth, retreating, darting again in a ritual imitating maddening sex and glorious sin.

Raegen matched his technique in a tongue duel escalating the frenzy. She wrapped her legs around his hips. As expected, he rocked against her sensitivity, raising brand-new tides of devastating sensations when she was completely at his mercy, unable to free her wrists of the damn handcuffs, wanting to free her hands to hold his hard cock and guide him into her heat. Tease him relentlessly, give him a tidbit of ecstasy and send him home. No way would she do a rookie.

She left teaching to others. Her men were always seasoned adults. At least, when she had time for a decent rendezvous.

"Take the cuffs off," Raegen said. Decency be damned. She wanted a little taste of Duffy.

"Not today, no."

She sputtered. "What?"

Rejection? What fresh hell was this?

2

"Hey! Freeze!"

A split second later, Thaine snatched Raegen off the car and all kinds of stuff broke loose.

Boom!

The bullet whizzed passed his head as he dragged Raegen down behind the door.

Boom! Boom!

These chumps had cannons.

"Stay put," Thaine ordered and drew his weapon.

Handcuffed and unarmed, what could she do besides run? And Raegen was not a stupid woman; she scooted behind the front wheel.

Blood pumping through his veins, Thaine took a chance, raised up beside the driver's side mirror. Two figures ran toward the main street when one slowed for the corner. With a clear shot, Thaine squeezed one off. He hit the tall runner, heard the guy's painful howl. They weren't down and out. Thaine ducked as another shot went off.

The cavalry showed up, bursting through the security door,

ducking, guns ready to unload on the perpetrators. Finally. Of course, the entire shootout had only taken about seven seconds. Three cops went in hotfoot pursuit of the shooters. Patrol cars were burning rubber, sirens screaming, joining the chase for sure.

Thaine could only imagine the rampant chatter on police radio channels. They'd hunt down the shooters with a vengeance.

Lifting Raegen to her feet, he asked, "You okay?"

"Yeah, I'll live. Get these damn cuffs off." She turned her back to him. "Did you nail somebody?"

"One. Shoulder."

"Good," she said as they moved under the spotlight. "Have the cops stake out the emergency rooms. I want them caught. Got a feeling I know who one of the fucking shooters is. The bastard."

This woman cursed more than three drunken sailors slipping on an icy ship deck on turbulent seas. "Who? I'll chase him down, cuff him, and haul his butt to the station myself."

"I bet you will," Raegen replied sarcastically. "It's *your* damn brother."

"And just where did you hear that mess?" No doubt, one guy was about the same height as Simon, but that didn't mean diddly without night-vision goggles.

She looked away.

"Don't tell me," he snapped. In the distance, the wail of sirens echoed through the neighborhood. "I don't even want to hear—PeeWee? Are you serious? You were the very person telling everybody not to listen to a word coming out of his lying mouth. Now you're relying on him? What's with you?"

Raegen stepped into his personal space. "He's not the only one hearing the word on the street, dammit. We got more than one weasel in this city."

"Who else is talking the same trash?"

"We got one of them," Smitty interrupted, barely panting. Tall and buff, he took his cap off, swiped his arm across his forehead. High temperatures took their toll on everyone.

Reagan tore her glaring gaze away from Thaine. "Where is he?"

"Headed to the hospital. Doesn't look good, either. He caught a bullet in the back. I don't know how he made it as far as he did."

Son of a . . . Shoulder, arm, even leg wound, Thaine would've been able to handle it easily, better. How could he have shot the kid in the back? Darkness? "How old?" he asked.

"Young, but hard to say."

Scrubbing his face with both hands, Thaine turned away.

"ID?" Raegen asked.

"None so far. We're combing the area for the second shooter. Purcell said she saw him toss something down the storm drain."

Thaine had asked Kimberly Purcell for a date a few months back. They went out once, became friends, nothing more. He trusted her. If she saw something tossed, the guy got rid of evidence.

"I want somebody down there to get that *something*," Raegen said.

Thaine swung around. Maybe his priorities were misplaced. "Which hospital?"

"You can't go, hotcakes," Raegen said, caressing his arm. "I know it's hard, but don't get too close to this."

"Which hospital, Smitty?"

The cop didn't dare hold back. They were longtime friends from middle school through high school and never lost contact.

Thaine went to the car. Behind him, Raegen issued orders to those processing the scene. As he started the engine, she hopped into the passenger seat.

"Get out."

"It's my case, Duffy. I could order you off of it right now and bar you from the hospital's premises."

Growling under his breath, glaring, he flipped the overhead light on.

"One more of those subtle roars, buster, and your badge will be fucking history."

Even dressed like a prostitute, showing more breast meat than the law should allow, Raegen looked too good. He never should've touched the softness of her skin. He never should've kissed the stubborn, foul-mouthed woman's sweet lips.

Agitated by his loss of willpower, he shoved the gears into drive.

From the first moment he'd seen Raegen Crosby, Thaine suspected her dynamic magnetism would reel him into her clutches without the least bit of effort. Pheromones were powerful little devils, and he'd caught a nose full of hers from afar. Other cops in the department said she'd steered clear of youngsters and rookies. Technically, he was neither. His age didn't show, but he didn't consider thirty-six an old man. As for a rookie, he had some good years on Denver's roster.

He'd hoped to keep his pants zipped, his tongue in his mouth, and to avoid Detective Crosby. If he had any sense. Too many buddies had gotten their nose ring ripped away, leaving them raw, bloodied, and in pain. Thaine had no proclivity to be a casualty—especially on account of a woman like Crosby. Word had it she chewed up men, spit them out and moved on to the next tasty morsel without looking back.

He parked near the hospital's entrance.

They caught up with a blonde nurse. She led them to the emergency room after a thorough disapproving perusal of Raegen's attire. The detective's fat grin had the woman warily eyeballing Thaine. He must look like her pimp.

"He's holding his own," the nurse said, shaking her head.

"They're prepping him for surgery. Severe internal bleeding is the doctor's main concern."

Thaine groaned.

"The next twenty-four are crucial," she continued quietly. "We still don't know the boy's name. No one has called to ask about him."

"We're working on it," Raegen said.

"Darn shame. Who would shoot a child in the back?"

"Get your goddamn facts straight before you start laying blame, spreading gossip and lies! Don't let me find out you interviewed with the press, chickie. You don't know—"

"Raegen." Thaine saw something in her eyes signifying mayhem. Her fists were clenched. Simple hair-pulling and eye-scratching catfights weren't her norm, from what he'd heard. "Take the car back to the station. I'll stick around here."

"Not." She kept her narrowed, hazel glare pinned on the nurse who appeared too frightened to move one thin muscle, even when she topped the detective's height by two or three inches. "You stay. I stay. Gotta keep my eye on the goings-on in this here hospital." She never cut anybody any slack. "Don't you have something to do, Nurse Ratchet?"

For God's sake. "Thanks for your help," Thaine added as the woman backed away. She fled down the hall. This was sure to be the longest night of his life. "I need coffee."

"Sit tight, hotcakes. I'll get it."

A variety of moaners and groaners sat in a room scented with blood, trauma, medicines, and the usual stench of disenfectants. Raegen sashayed away, hips swaying seductively while every pair of bulging male eyes watched. Some women were just as bug eyed.

Coppery skin coloring. Full hips and thighs. Booty galore. Meaty women gave a man something to hold onto. Thaine shook his head. The last thing on his mind should be Raegen Crosby's body.

He found two empty chairs and plopped down on one. Lacing his fingers together, he balanced his forehead against his thumbs. What if this kid didn't make it? Even if he did, there was sure to be an investigation. He'd be given desk duty or paid suspension, pending the outcome.

"Don't question yourself, hotcakes. You did what you did by the books." Raegen handed over the cup of automated liquid mud and sat beside him.

She chugged most of her Pepsi while Thaine replayed the incident over and over in his mind. Normally he used dialogue to talk down a situation. "I'm thinking I should've—"

"Should've what, shot him in the ass? Let the little thugs—if they're as young as you think—take us both out? I don't know about you, but I like living. Love it, in fact, and I don't plan on dying for cheap thrills. Anybody who takes a shot at me is old enough to suffer the consequences. Tit for tat."

"We're talking kids."

"Maybe so, but somebody taught them the killing trade, boosting them to adults." She shifted toward Thaine. "Let me tell you something, honey. I love kids. I got five nieces and nephews whom I adore. But, there's one baby I will always keep closest to my heart. Two years ago, somebody gunned down Richelle for no damn reason at all. She was ten. Ten! Some young punk put a bullet in her chest during a drive-by. For all I know, the boy in surgery? He's the shooter." She looked away.

Thaine wasn't sure if he'd seen tears or rancid hatred glittering in her eyes. He ran his hand down the smooth skin of her arm. If he wrapped her in his embrace, he'd probably never want to let her go. "I'm sorry."

"Don't be. You didn't murder her. You didn't take her away from my sister or Richelle's grandmother. They were after—" She swallowed, looked away again.

People weren't talking about the tragedy by the time he'd

joined the department. Listening to Raegen's version, somehow she blamed herself for the child's death.

She perked up the next second. "Ran into Ratchet's sister at the 'refreshment stand.' The kid's in surgery. They need blood."

Thaine got to his feet. "Where to?"

"Are you A-negative?"

He dropped back into the chair.

"Hold this," Raegen said, handing him the Pepsi can. "Be right back."

"Do you know someone they can match?"

She winked. "Sit tight, sweetcakes."

Fifteen minutes later, Raegen returned. "They got some, but I don't know if it's enough. Nurse said surgery's moving right along, but it'll take a while."

"Thanks for finding a donor," Thaine said. "I know how you feel about the situation."

She sat again, crossed a pair of stunning legs worthy of the stares. One fellow was on the verge of slobbering. The fool wiggled his eyebrows at Raegen.

Planting both feet on the floor, she leaned forward. "Hey, have you lost your mind? I wish I had my damn badge to flash in that sucker's face."

"Could you just chill out for once?"

Her frown had enough power to quarter a fellow's soul. "You got a problem with my attitude?"

"As a matter of fact—"

"Ms. Crosby," a heavyset black woman said. She was dressed in street clothes, one beefy arm wrapped around a clipboard. "You were supposed—"

"Buzz off."

"We require—"

"Read my lips, chickie. Buzz off."

"You might pass out," the woman snapped.

Raegen had met her match with this one. Folding his arms

over his chest, Thaine sat back to watch the fireworks snap, crackle, and explode, wondering if any other males had the balls to stop a mix-up. No doubt Raegen was game for any kind of competition.

"Then, we'd have to—"

"Jesus Christ." She shot to her feet so fast the wig's hair straightened and curled again. "What the hell does a person have to do to get respect in this place? Get off my back, lady, before I leap on yours!"

Thaine realized she'd donated blood to a suspect—to a *thug* who'd tried to kill them. Raegen Crosby's big talk was all jive. What else was this lady about?

Spunk, sass, and short on class.

With those less-than-stellar qualities, what was it about this particular woman that enticed him into pursuit when his chances of winning were slim to none? Was the chase worth the loss, the kind of pain most men handled poorly?

He caught Raegen before she hit the floor.

3

She drove the car across town to Thaine's place after they'd received bad news. The kid had succumbed while under the surgeon's knife.

Thaine wasn't handling it very well. Raegen figured he needed someone to vent his frustrations on. Even if she knew how to contact his brother, she sure as hell wasn't going to call a damn junkie. Correction. Ex-junkie, according to Thaine.

"Got any Pepsi in there?"

"Didn't you just have one? Drink milk."

Ooh. Snippy. She took the keys from his hand since he couldn't manage to connect with either keyhole.

Inside, he switched the freestanding lamplight on beside the brown leather sofa. Raegen closed the door, locked up, and slipped off her Carmen Miranda stilettos. The miniature, plastic oranges and cherries covering her toes were cute.

She scanned the living room as she followed Thaine, tossing her small purse on the sofa.

"Do you live here or did you get squatter's rights to some builder's show home?" Evidently, he hadn't heard the question.

Or maybe he spent his free time with a girlfriend who had his nose. Or maybe he was already balled and chained, dammit, with a wife. She'd vowed not to go that waste-my-time route again. "Do you—"

"Live here." He grabbed a gallon of milk from the fridge, filled two glasses and handed one to Raegen.

"Really, I prefer Pepsi. Milk is for children needing strong bones."

"Drink it anyway."

Now, what kind of one-sided hell was this? She sipped a small amount and, as usual, turned up her nose. Water from the faucet tasted better. She never touched Arizona's hydrant liquids.

"All of it."

"Now, just a minute, hotcakes. Nobody orders me around. I don't like milk, never have and never will. I get my calcium elsewhere." Just because he'd plucked her from the floor, carried her to some stinky room, and watched over her didn't give him ruling rights to her life. She set the glass on the counter and stepped toward him, prepared to tell him about himself.

"Suit yourself," Thaine said, "but don't call me any stupid names again, detective. I don't like it anymore than you like milk." He left her standing in the middle of the kitchen.

Hmm. This was not going the way she'd planned. Puckering her lips, Raegen went to the doorway. She peeked around the corner, saw Thaine plant his fine behind on the far end of the sofa. He balanced his chin on his fist, staring at the floor.

"Hey, babycakes, maybe—"

"I warned you before, detective. Don't use those pet names with me."

"Well, Mr. McDuff," she said snottily, noticing a set of playing cards on the end table. "How about a game of crazy eights to warm the air in this room since it's gotten so damn chilly?"

He ignored her.

"Checkers?" Ooh, this man was a hard one to handle. "Spin the bottle?"

He grunted this time.

"How about a few hands of strip poker?" Wearing only three articles of clothing, the game might last thirty seconds.

"Take off your clothes."

Huh?

"Forget the games. I want you and, obviously, you want me."

Well, yeah, but . . .

"I've seen the look in your eyes. Strip, Raegen." He leaned back, scooted down on the sofa. "Stand right in front of me. I've had a crappy night and I want to see you naked. I want to see if you look like you do in my dreams."

She sucked in a hot breath. His dreams?

"I want to know if you taste as good as you look."

Tentative for once, she moved farther into the room, around the sofa, past the suede armchair. His eyes were closed. Elbow propped on the sofa's arm, he balanced his chin on his fist. He wore no rings on his left hand, but that didn't mean squat.

He'd draped his jacket on the sofa, had unbuttoned his crisply ironed shirt enough to show his smooth chest. A nice chest. Really nice. Raegen swallowed, her heart fluttering, eyes roaming, just thinking about running her hands over his flesh, having that hard body all over hers, inside hers.

"Well?" he whispered.

His eyes flickered open, held her captive. Undressed her. Suddenly she already felt naked. Vulnerable.

"Don't try to tell me you're too embarrassed to take off your clothes. I know better. I've had my hands all over your breasts, felt them swell in my hands. I've felt your heat against mine."

She was panting now, her breasts swelling again from his intense gaze.

"Nipples erect. Pulse skitterish. You can't stand still. What other changes are threatening your balance?"

Her breasts were tight, aching. Why was he waiting, playing this game?

Stripping for show made her uncomfortable. Her waist was too narrow for her wide hips. Momma had said her thighs belonged to the best pass receiver because Raegen ran track through college. Her sisters claimed her butt resembled a platform.

Why was the shape of her body bothering her now?

"Come here, Raegen."

She shook her head. Not yet. "Turn the light out."

"It stays on. I want to see you in full light. I want you to strip for me. Can you do that?"

Maybe. Maybe not. When he shifted on the sofa, she noticed the growing thickness pressed against his trousers. She licked her lips, tasted the lip gloss's cherry flavor, wondered how good he tasted.

"If you want this," he said, stroking his hand down the length of his erection. "Strip." He waited two beats. "Or I'll call you a cab."

"Bastard," she muttered.

He picked up the remote phone.

Before he punched all seven numbers, Raegen yanked the tube top over her head. Yeah, she was horny after a three-month stretch of abstinence, wanting what he had to offer. She tossed the knit fabric at his lap, unhooked the skirt and wriggled free of its tight fit. The cheap fabric slid to the floor. "If you want this," she said saucily, teasing her hot spot beneath her lacy thong with two fingers, "you'll have to come and get it."

The son of a bitch sat there staring, his eyes lingering on her breasts.

"You're trembling."

"Cold," she replied too quickly. Wet. She withdrew her fingers and tucked her hand behind her back before she went too far arousing herself.

"Liar," he said with a smile. "Take off the wig. Show me your hair. I like the sassy style. Matches your temperament."

She'd told the beautician to whack it all off. She had no time or patience to fool with a curling iron every morning. Raegen tossed the fake, ash-blond hair onto his lap. Ruffling the inch-long, soft curls with all ten fingers blended the autumn frosting with her coal-black tresses.

"Perfect." His gaze—the blaze of it—heated her inside out. "Come here."

Another command. She hated taking orders, but this man had made her wet and needy with his penetrating gaze. "Put the phone down and come and get me. Show me what you can do, hotcakes. See if you can tilt my world." An impossibility. If anything he'd come knocking at her door, begging like the others whom she'd given a taste, then sent on their way. Hook, line, and sinker.

"In time."

Huh?

"Slowly. Methodically. I'm not into rushing."

Sure. "I'm not into slow. I like my sex at maximum velocity. Hard."

She held his steady gaze. Usher's sexiness, Denzel Washington's polished look, and Morgan Freeman's classic eloquence and voice, she'd take any one to her bed if she could. But here they all were, wrapped in one smoking package.

He was ready, willing and horny like her.

"Not from me."

Damn you. He thinks he can run this show. "We'll see." As stout as his cock had hardened, by the time . . . The remote phone's dial tone roared in her ears.

"I'm not hard up," Thaine said.

"Fuck you."

His glittering eyes gave her pause and Raegen stepped back, poised for confrontation. He dropped the phone and came off the sofa before she had time to finish a blink, was on her in a flash, took her breath away with another greedy kiss. The taste of mint was so clean and refreshing.

Wrapping her arms around his waist, she pressed closer, enjoying the feel of his solid contours. He unwrapped her arms and pinned them behind her back without the least bit of resistance from her.

She was so caught up in the kiss, she barely heard a whirring noise.

Pow!

Raegen screamed. The leather strap meant serious business.

"Didn't I warn you about using profanity?"

Strike two surely shredded her ass to ribbons or left a mountainous welt. She screamed again, squirming. She wouldn't be able to sit for a week.

"Bastard! So help me God, I will fucking kill you. Your ass is going to jail. Assault. Do you understand?"

Thaine spun her around before she got her knee in motion enough to cause severe damage. She readied herself for the next stinging tag. Where this time? When would she learn to keep her mouth shut?

Raegen squeezed her eyes shut. She would not shed tears for him or anyone to see.

"Assault? Who's going to see this? Who?" Thaine demanded. He rubbed the soreness she felt on her behind. "Who's going to believe you when you talk so much trash?"

She'd kill him once she got loose, but that hand moved up to her waist, to her breast. The caress was as gentle as the first time he'd put his hands on her.

"How do you plan to enjoy this if I'm dead?" he whispered

in her ear. He nipped and bit, then teased the crevices with his tongue.

Pain long forgotten, Raegen shivered. She still planned to kill him.

That hand edged farther down to her belly, down to touch the one spot capable of sending her on an express ride into orbit. "Or this." His talented fingers glided toward the gateway to her heat, retreated, teasing her sensitivity. "I can't do this if I'm dead. Let me in."

Hesitation wasn't one of her strong points. "More," she ordered and moved her hips to meet the next thrust. "Hard." She was liquid now, puddling, on the threshold of catching her falling star with this solid cock teasing the cleft of her ass.

"No."

Raegen groaned. The trek toward Jupiter came to a grinding halt, damn him, when she had intended to get her nut and leave him hanging, hard and dry.

He swung her into his arms, held her tightly, her breasts mashed against his muscled chest. Thaine marched into his bedroom. He set her in his bed. While she still shimmered, he took his time unbuttoning his shirt.

"Hurry," Raegen said. His muscles rippled, flexed, a six-pack that was easily eights. Thaine McDuff looked too good, felt even better.

He hung his shirt in the closet. Jesus. She should've ripped it off his body. At least he'd taken off his shoes and socks by the time he dimmed the bedside lamp.

"Can't you speed things up a bit?" She was as horny as a bitch in heat.

Ignoring her, he disappeared through the doorway—to the bathroom, she assumed. The door closed. For crying out loud. A woman had time to grow a new cherry. She pulled the bedding back and slipped under the sheets.

How many men made their beds? How many men slept on satin sheets?

Nosy, she tiptoed to the closet. He must have a woman living here, a classy chickie who was out of town when the booty call got the best of him.

Menswear filled the closet. Expensive suits. Silk shirts. Polished shoes. Who was this guy who looked liked a baby and dressed like a powerhouse?

"I live here," Thaine said. "Alone."

Busted. She spun around. Jesus God. Her breath caught in her throat. He was all that and more as he swaggered toward her. Buffed brown skin, taut muscles, hung like a proud stallion. He completed every fantasy dream she'd had of him.

And she was his mare for a little while. An hour.

He stopped short, staring, his eyes like melting dark chocolate. Raegen swallowed when he reached up and threaded his fingers into her hair. Drawn by his gentle touch, she moved into his embrace, absorbing him, wanting his heat inside her. When his lips delicately smoothed across hers, something burst in her belly, something fragile and wicked crept through her soul.

She knew her feet had left the floor, knew he'd set her in bed, his strong body imprisoning. Wrists pinned to the pillows, she had no energy or strength to break his hold or move when he settled between her legs. His thick cock pulsed insistently at the gateway of her enjoyment.

He had the most delectable mouth, tongue toying with hers, a wet trail coursing down the column of her neck. So skillfully. So arousing. She wrapped her legs around his hips, drawing him closer, needing what he intended to give.

He resisted.

Forcing her eyes open, she stared into smiling jewels. His face was so young and arresting, she shuddered. One mind-blowing sex fest and she would walk away. Thaine McDuff wielded too much power over her sensibilities. "I want you now. Hard. Fast. Rough." Then they would be done.

"We have the rest of the night, and I intend to make good use of every minute," he said, dropping several kisses on her lips, his hot breath mingling with her panting. "Every second. Slowly."

His body slithered down hers to her breasts, tasting, teasing, teeth grazing her nipples. Stimulating, rousing her to the next heady level. Raegen groaned, long and deeply, her legs shifting restlessly.

One night, her feeble mind demanded. Only one. And she would take the lead soon. In a minute. Drive him to the brink of delirium.

But Thaine took her on a devastating romp, working her body to a frazzle, scattering her wits.

"Duffy! Thaine?" He had yet to penetrate, had tormented every inch of her from head to toe for what seemed like forever.

Release came hard and fast.

He moved up her body. "Hold on to me."

Her mind reeling, she held on tightly as she went over the edge, shuddering, her world tilting off its axis.

Weak and panting, Raegen said, "Damn you. Damn you. What do you want from me?"

He kissed her. "I want it all." And he started all over again.

"No," she replied hostilely, shoving at his chest with little effect. She would not give up more.

Finally, he rolled on the protection they both needed.

Exhausted after three round trips across the galaxy, she said, "I won't. I can't. I have nothing left." But, as he penetrated excruciatingly slowly, her legs fell bonelessly open and her eyes closed.

Raegen lost sight of reality and slipped into uncharted territory.

4

"Phone," Thaine said. His breaths were short and broken. "Yours." They'd made passionate love, showered, and had started from the top again.

Her breathing was way more erratic than his. "Don't stop."

The musical notes faded from his mind as he continued plowing inside her. Raegen was wringing the life from him when he had intended to make slow passionate love to her, had intended to turn her inside out.

"Come with me," he breathed. "Come with me, baby."

Seconds later, they reached for the same racing comet. Caught it. He lifted her hips from the bed, sank deeper through a quaking that rattled his very being.

"Oh, God," Raegen cried out and arched on a scream.

She ran her hands up and down his back, dug her fingers into the fleshy meat of his buttocks, forcing him deeper into her divine clutches. She kissed his cheeks, ran her tongue over his lips, and kissed him hard, stealing his breath, then stole a piece of his heart as he rocked against her, prolonging the feral orgasm.

Caressing each other, they returned to sanity on a leisurely ride.

Still intimately joined, Thaine moved to his side, taking her with him. He lifted her hand, measured her small, slender fingers with his own. He kissed each knuckle and tip, licked the center of her palm. She was beautiful in every sense of the word, but . . . "You chew your nails to the quick."

"Habit," Raegen said and pulled her hand free.

Nerves. "How can a woman have pretty feet and bad fingernails?"

Shrugging, she said, "Can't grip and rapid fire a weapon on the fly when flaunting talons. I barely have time to get my eyebrows waxed."

She was noted as the second-best shooter in Phoenix, better than most men on the SWAT team.

Raegen examined his fingers and nails. "Hmpf. Prettier than a woman's. What exactly do you do off duty?"

Music chimed again.

"Have to get it this time, sweetcakes," she said. "Nobody calls this late without good reason."

She rolled Thaine to his back, sat upright, nearly slipped off his cock, and glided down his hardening length for one more tease, circling, tightening. "Ooh," she purred. "I hate to let this go."

His fingers flexed on her hips, not willing to let her go. He hissed out a breath when she finally let him loose.

"Don't go anywhere. I'll be right back for another round."

She was going to kill him, but he'd die happy.

Raegen climbed off the bed and raced to the living room for her cell phone. Ten seconds later she returned. "Slater. No playtime in the showers, babycakes. Somebody tried to torch my damn apartment."

* * *

Damage was minimal. Luckily, neighbors smelled smoke, but no one saw the intruder. Or folks opted to keep their mouths shut.

Firefighters had hosed the place down. Thaine and Raegen sloshed through water-saturated carpeting, foul-smelling gasoline permeating the air. Only the small living room was touched by fire; remnants of smoke climbed bare walls painted dull white, an already tattered couch, one scorched end table and attached lamp and a battered footstool placed in front of a metal folding chair. Apparently, furnishings took last place on Raegen's list of essentials. Nothing looked worth fretting over.

She certainly didn't seem to care about her property, kicking at a pile of clothes or bedding or whatever filled the corner into a small mountain.

"You can't stay here. Grab a suitcase," Thaine said. His house was big enough for the two of them, two master suites when they only needed one.

"Tell your brother I'll move in with him until he pays to get his mess cleaned up. I don't have renter's insurance."

His hackles stood on end. "What makes you think Simon had anything to do with this?"

She swung around. "Because he shot at me?" she asked, sarcastic. "Sounds reasonable."

"Get off that."

She tsked. "Tell you what, sweetcakes. Why don't you ask him? Think he'll tell you the truth?"

Possibly. "Simon has skirted the truth in the past, but he also has an innate fear of fire after—" His voice faltered.

Twenty-odd years ago there was an incident at their grandfather's Colorado farm. Shouldering blame, Thaine had protected his brother ever since. And Simon had never let him forget the tragic episode.

"Skirted? Hah! He's a lying sack of shit."

Thaine fingered his belt.

Eyes big as saucers narrowed thinly. "You wouldn't dare."

"Try me." He couldn't care less if firefighters, cops, or neighbors watched him tear into her fine tail. With that mouth, she deserved a solid *whupping*. "Just once."

"We found this on your bed," Slater said as he came around the corner. He held a sheet of paper by its corner.

"What's it say?" Raegen asked, and Slater held the paper at eye level for both to read.

Next time you won't be so lucky. Unsigned. Typed.

She looked squarely into Thaine's eyes. "Does your brother have a typewriter or computer and printer?"

She never quit. "I'll check."

"Today. And I want to know his whereabouts in the last twenty-four. Bring him in for questioning."

"*If* I find him," Thaine replied, his voice low and threatening. He'd forced Simon into giving him a cell number. "And I'm off duty. I'll get him in when I can."

"Slater, let's," Raegen emphasized, "get that note to Wyatt and see if he can match prints."

What a way to bring on the dawn of a new day after passionate hours with this cynical woman. Thaine waved his hand, turned his back, and walked away.

"Let's stop by the hospital, too. IA will want that bullet they pulled from the kid," Raegen said a little too loudly.

Thaine snarled. According to other cops, she had great influence on the commander.

"Hey, sweetcakes!"

He kept walking in long strides, straight to the car. As Thaine drove away, he looked in his rearview mirror. Raegen stood on the curb, staring after him.

Catching up with his brother was a feat in itself. Simon usually let voicemail answer his calls. Today was no different. Thaine left two urgent, coded messages while en route to the station. He turned in the car and dropped off his weapon, knowing Internal Affairs would require a ballistics test.

At eight-fifteen, Vanderbilt called. Desk duty until further notice, probably three days. No biggy. Thaine had nothing to hide. He'd shot a man, killed. The abysmal drama would stay with him for the rest of his life. Still, no one had come forth to identify the dead. The kid's body had been sent to the morgue and stored. No print match, either.

"You're a good cop, Duffy. Report in as usual," Vanderbilt said. "Formality is all it is, nothing more."

Sure, he knew that. Knowing didn't make him feel any better that another family would mourn for a lifetime when he had no way to offer his condolences.

Tired, antsy, and running on borrowed energy, wanting to evict Raegen from his thoughts when his mind should be on Simon, he stripped the bed and put fresh sheets on while bacon sizzled in the kitchen. Breakfast was as boring as pacing around the house. He dumped it down the garbage disposal and tried Simon's number again.

Why hadn't he returned his call?

Working swing shift, Thaine reported to duty early. The nap helped his demeanor. He barely made it through the double doors at the station when his cell vibrated.

"Where the devil have you been, Simon? Where're you now?"

"Good to talk to you, too, big brother. I love sandy beaches, love the smell of the open sea. Sunny skies, bikinis, topless ladies."

"Since when?"

"Why? What's up?"

He just might go up the river again and not for tax evasion and not for the stabbing he'd committed. Slicing off the guy's ear precluded self-defense. "You, if I don't get some answers."

"My flight doesn't arrive until seven. Now, what's up?"

Simon would never admit to his location. He traveled incognito, camouflaged, had been nicknamed Chameleon. Thaine wasn't sure how many passports his brother owned. "Call me the minute you get in. We need to talk."

"Unaccompanied, or is the cavalry backing you up?"

He'd never lied to Simon. "Alone."

"Let's meet at our usual in thirty minutes." Simon told more lies than Carter had liver pills.

Checking his watch, Thaine spun on his heels and started for his car.

"Hey, baby face. Got a minute?"

Of all times . . . Raegen looked fresh, inviting, too good in tight, black pants and fitted white blouse cupping her breasts into mounds beneath her black jacket. "Nope."

Perusing him slowly, she licked those luscious lips able to unseat a man's willpower. The solid entity hanging between his legs twitched.

"Any place special? Can I come?" she asked. "Once or twice? Three times?"

Shameless was her middle name, but his heart still pounded like a tom-tom. "Busy." He marched past Raegen, kept a distance between them, focusing on the sidewalk.

Their usual meeting place was at Starbucks. Thaine went inside, ordered a tall latte and found a corner table away from the traffic lane. Across the room, an elderly man—gray beard, bushy eyebrows, wearing a French cap—grabbed his cane hooked over the chair. He hobbled to the counter. Simon was good, but Thaine recognized his eyes no matter how classy, sedate, or raunchy he dressed. He pushed the opposite chair away from the table with the toe of his shoe when Simon approached carrying an expresso that revved him daily.

"How's it going, Old Man Winter? Been to the beach lately?"

Simon had his act down pat. He lowered himself slowly to the chair using the cane's support. "These old bones could use the humidity, sonny. Need to find me one of them cute young things to take with me. Aches and pains need soft hands."

"Plenty of young things in the big house."

Leaning forward, Simon whispered, "You know better than to threaten me."

"Where were you last night?"

"Minding my own business."

Thaine slapped the tabletop, which turned a few heads. "I need to know exactly where you were between midnight and dawn."

"Like I said, minding my own damn business."

"Not good enough."

"I don't do alibis."

Thaine narrowed his eyes. It was Smitty who'd called, informing him when Simon's name surfaced in another investigation. Family meant everything; it was the reason Thaine left Denver for Phoenix. There were no other family members able to keep an eye on Simon and his circle of friends, or keep him out of trouble. "Somebody took a shot at a cop. Somebody set fire to a cop's residence."

Simon puckered his lips. "Let me tell you the buzz you want to hear. The cop? Yeah, she made the list. It's all over the metro area, Thaine, probably all over the state. Crosby's been jacking with the wrong folks. You might find her one day, drawn, quartered, body parts scattered across the desert."

Simon knew people. He listened well. He also loved knives. But drawn and quartered? Over Thaine's dead body. Because if Simon was lying . . .

"Freeze! Hands in the air." Cops came out of nowhere. "Simon McDuff, you're under arrest for suspicion of arson and attempted murder. You have the right . . ."

Simon leaned back, resigned. "Thank you so very fucking much for burning my ass again, bro."

Livid, knowing it had to be Raegen's doing, Thaine said, "I had nothing to do with this, Simon. You know me better."

"Uh-huh. Yeah, sure." Two cops yanked him to his feet, then cuffed and led him to the door while nervous bystanders watched.

Unconcerned with Simon's dilemma, Thaine raced to the car. His brother would be back on the streets within the hour after calling his attorney. For now, he had a thing or two to say to Detective Crosby.

The commander's secretary said the meeting had been in session for the last half hour. She had no idea when it would end. Tempted to bust in and drag Raegen out, Thaine reined in his temper and reported to duty.

Checking in misfits, answering calls, soothing concerned citizens, clerking . . . all grated on his nerves. What he loved was street work. Raegen had mega-nerves having him followed. Losing Simon's trust was the worst she could do when her life was on the line. His brother held long-term grudges.

On the other hand, Raegen sashayed around the city with a bull's-eye stamped on her forehead. Thaine was angry, but never irritated enough to let a person fall into a snake pit of vipers if he had the ability to halt the tumble before it began.

He swung around toward the metal cabinet and crouched beside the bottom drawer. He hated filing.

"Sure glad I wasn't Slater," he heard someone say.

"Yeah, me, too. Crosby blistered him good. Vanderbilt let her rip him a brand-new one."

"He deserved it."

Thaine peeked over the desk, caught sight of three officers near the counter. He blocked out all other voices, listening.

"I reminded him what Crosby said before we went in. Slater told me to shut the hell up and bust McDuff. That was the plan.

Did you see the shock on Duffy's face? He didn't know it was going down. Dirty shit, in my ledger."

"Think he would've gone along with it?"

"Would you? I mean, we're talking family."

"I'd have to think on it. What about you?"

Thaine stood as the next reply bled into the loud commotion near the front doors.

5

"I'm gonna have to put the hurt on somebody if you all don't get back!" The blonde was young, twenties, with electric-blue eyes. Sweat dripped down her pale, puffy face. The pupils of her eyes had spread wide. Her breaths were short and choppy. High temperatures hadn't matted her hair to her scalp. Shaking, she couldn't stand still. Chunky junkie.

Raegen threaded her way through the dwindling crowd while officers smuggled captives and innocent citizens out of harm's way. This was the worst kind of situation. How the hell did a lunatic get inside the building with a gun, holding a child hostage?

"Calm down," an officer said. He had big balls to move closer. "Put the kid down."

"Shut up," the woman screamed. "Get your ass back, mother-fucker, or I'll shoot *you*."

Deflating, the cop backed away, melting into the masses. Like other bystanders, he watched in manic horror.

The little girl's shoulders shook. Tears spilled from huge blue eyes in rivers down her cheeks. Clutching a black teddy bear, the child could only be four or five years old. With light-brown dreadlocks and complexion, she was definitely biracial.

Blondie might be loaded, but she hadn't lost all of her mental faculties. She kept her back to the wall. The lousy, no-good *skank* also kept the barrel of the revolver against the baby's temple.

"I want the fucker who shot my man in the back."

The roomed positively hummed with audible gasps and speculative murmurs.

Raegen caught Thaine's accept-the-consequences gaze. He would. She winked and shook her head. No way in hell would she allow an unarmed, or any other, officer step into this woman's line of fire, risking his life for a thrill-seeking nut. Junkies were trigger-happy folks. Dangerously unpredictable.

Ignoring his narrowed eyes, Raegen reached inside her blouse. She slid the derringer from her cleavage and palmed the single-shot weapon. She preferred not to use it, jeopardizing a child's life, but this stupid ho's antics called for swift action.

"I want that bitch Raegen Crosby. She murdered my baby's daddy."

Well, now. Somebody had been spreading lies and tales again. Sure, she shot well, but with her hands cuffed behind her back? *I'm not that damn good.*

On the other hand, being called a *bitch* set her teeth ready to grind enamel. "You think you're bad because you're holding a gun? Put the kid down, then come and get me, *heffah*. So I can whip your sorry tail."

She watched the blonde's eyes search the crowd, knowing one person occupied her mind now.

"Quit hiding and come on out, bitch. We'll see who's bad."

"Switch positions," Raegen whispered. Officers—one stout, one thin—blocked her. "It's me she wants." She maneuvered her way around several other people. "What's the matter, little momma? Chicken? Too scared to face me alone? Shows your true color using a defenseless child to protect your yellow self. I'll make sure you never see her again once I get through with you. She won't even recognize your mug after I'm done."

The woman kissed the little girl's cheek, then whispered something in her ear. Sniffling, the child wiped her eyes with the teddy bear. "I will kick your ass from here to kingdom come, bitch."

Raegen suppressed a she-cat hiss.

Threatened, the blonde was too incensed to lose face. The child, however, did mean something to her and she set her down on spindly little legs.

Sheer terror shined in the little girl's glassy eyes. Her small body trembled. Among a gallery of strangers, and unconditionally trusting the one person who, moments ago, held a gun to her head, she clung to her mother's waist.

"Yeah?" Raegen said sassily. Cops were close enough to grab the girl once she distracted the mother. The risks high, she squeezed between Slater, who was poised to drop the woman where she stood, and another detective, whose hand hovered over his weapon. "Don't do it," she told them in a low voice. "Remember the bystanders. Think of the kid." Always protect the children.

"Prove it!" Raegen yelled to the young blonde woman. Crawling on hands and knees behind the main desk, passing by Thaine, she moved closer to her prey. She continued the banter and peeked around the corner. "Get your daughter away from the action and drop the gun."

Eyes big and wide, the woman shook her head.

"She'll remain safe here. Let her go. Nobody else will touch you. *Nobody.*" They knew not to intervene. "It's you and me, but you'll wish somebody got to you first once I lay into your fat ass. You're right. I put that lame devil out of his own damn misery; should've filled him full of hot lead."

The blonde peeled her daughter's arms away and shoved her

aside. Wired, and fueled with unmitigated rage, she readied to box, prepared to avenge her man's death.

Perfect. Almost. Once a single brave soul secured the child. Raegen offered one last stinging bit of repartee to keep the woman's focus on her. "Who the fuck you think you callin' a bitch, bitch?"

Thaine shoved her leg with his foot. Damn him. Two lousy cuss words and he jumped annoyed.

The gun clattered to the floor. All but one cop stayed rooted where they stood. Balls re-inflated, the courageous officer snatched the girl into his arms.

"Mommy!"

Armed spectators instantly parted for the cop racing toward safety. Her mother never blinked, but her face grew stormy; cherry-red eyes narrowed and fixed, teeth bared, her jaw grinding bone.

Raegen got to her feet. She laid the derringer on the main desk in front of Thaine, kept her gaze on the woman. "Hang on to this for a minute, sweetcakes."

Facing her deluded foe now, she signaled her forward with all ten fingers. "You want some of this, Blondie? Come and get it. I got something for your fat behind for holding a gun to your baby's head."

"Enough!"

Shit. The commander's energized voice would ruin a high-powered orgasm. Like others, Raegen swung her gaze toward him.

"Watch out!"

She slammed against the counter on an explosive impact, deflating. Dazed momentarily, Raegen quickly found her equilibrium and her next breath. An elbow to the blonde's chin caught the woman off guard, snapped her head to one side. Rolling on top, Raegen connected again for a sure black and blue shiner. The blonde screamed, cursed, thrashed crazily.

"Get them apart," Vanderbilt shouted.

Cops converged.

"Get your goddamn hands off me. I'm gonna kill this ho." Swinging wildly, Raegan put one cop down. Another backed away after she fattened his lip.

"Raegen!"

She heard Thaine's voice and ignored it. Rabid, she continued pummeling the witch who'd blindsided her, suspecting she'd have bruises for a week. At least, a headache.

Thaine plucked her from the woman's chest as if she weighed no more than an ounce. He manacled her body with his own muscled self. Officers took charge of the blonde, cuffed her.

Panting, Raegen said, "Take her to interrogation."

"Fuck you, bitch." She had the nerve to mouth off when fresh blood dripped from her nose and lip. "They'll get you. Hide and seek. Hide and seek. They'll get you good, Raegen Crosby. Look around you. Watch your back."

She talked riddles. "From who?"

Blondie laughed wickedly, her voice coming deep from hell. "You'll see. Hide and seek. Family mean much to you?" She was too high, her mind addled after kissing Raegen's fist.

"Get this trash out of my sight." *God, please protect the little girl from this nutcase.*

"Get cleaned up," Vanderbilt ordered, pointing at Raegen. "Then I want you, Slater, and Duffy in my office."

Five minutes later, she flinched. "Ouch!"

"Hold still, little bit," Thaine said. He dabbed cotton swabbed with alcohol high on her cheekbone with the softest touch. "You need a Band-Aid."

"Bullshit, hotcakes. No way." *Band-Aid? For a scratch? Please.*

He straightened, hand resting against his belt. "Keep it up, hear? You'll need more than a roll of gauze after I'm done tearing up your behind."

Did this do-gooder ever cuss or do anything dishonorable? Lie to save his butt, cheat to win a bet, or even steal a single grape from the corner grocer? Like her—in some respects—he had accepted fate, had prepared to forfeit his life to protect the innocent. Unlike Thaine, sainthood had passed by Raegen without the slightest sideways glance.

"We got a date with Vanderbilt," she replied in her testiest voice. "He's waiting to chew my . . . to talk."

She signaled to Slater on the way and knocked on the commander's door.

"Enter."

Slater dragged an armchair noisily toward the commander's desk. Following suit, Raegen and Thaine sat on opposite sides of him.

Tall, a slender man of impeccable breeding, Vanderbilt boasted a thick cap of wavy black hair. Habitually, he balanced his clean-shaven cheek against his right fist, rocked in his squeaky, antique chair, and glared his subordinates, one by one, into silence. No need today. Their lips were zipped closed.

Raegen shifted uneasily. The commander had warned her against needless infractions. Instigating fights, mishandling suspects, and, of all things, tardiness had totally jacked with his patience more times than she could count on one hand over the last year. Today, the reprimand just might bust her back to uniform. She glanced at Slater. He'd love to have her job. Dammit, this was just great. All of her hard work chasing down and jailing criminals was shot to shit in ten minutes . . . okay, a year.

"I think it's time we think about safety options," Vanderbilt said. "The situation has grown too dangerous."

What? "I can handle it. We can."

"I agree with the commander," Thaine said.

"Ditto," Slater concurred.

What the fuck was this? A gang rape? "Now, just a damn minute," Raegen demanded and shot to her feet. "I didn't earn my position by *opting* out of any situation to catch criminals. I beat the odds *then,* I'll do it now."

"*Sit* down, Rae," Vanderbilt snapped in that no-nonsense tone of his. "Listen for a change."

Suitably censured, she fell back into her chair, crossed one leg over the other, and swung it like a pendulum.

Ten steaming seconds went by, but the commander didn't move from his position. Chin balanced, chair squeaking obscenely loud, piercing gray eyes on her, he said, "When you've had three attempts on your life in less than twenty-four hours, you and your family become my immediate responsibility."

Big-Mouth Slater had squealed about the torch job when she'd diced him into small pieces for the Simon McDuff screw up, or he'd blabbed because she'd told him "booty's off duty" again. Sainthood had soared past him long before it swooped by her. For all she knew, he'd already broken all ten commandments and committed the seven deadly sins, leaving his career without a rocket booster.

"May I make a suggestion, commander?" Thaine asked.

Too polite, Raegen thought.

What fresh hell saturated his mind anyway? Didn't Thaine remember the law of the land? New kids on the block were like children eons ago: seen and not heard. The commander *always* laid down rules on the first day after academy graduation.

Short of bruising the rookie's ego, Vanderbilt would attach a plunger to sweetcakes' mouth before . . .

Swiveling his gaze toward Thaine, he said, "Talk to me."

6

Raegen complained more than an overactive child relegated to solitary confinement without toys or a listening ear while they unloaded clothes and essentials from her tired Ford Escort.

Since Slater had a wife and kids at home, Thaine volunteered for the first bodyguard tour of duty with another officer. He requested a female. Four-year veteran Charlie Stafford—dyed redhead wearing green contacts and built like a shot-putter—stepped up to the plate.

The last thing he needed was to spend time alone with Raegen. The scent of her was intoxicating, her eyes captivating, and the sound of her voice sexy, except for her language, but she was angry anyway. Mostly at him for what she called "starting shit and filling Vanderbilt's head with the same stinky manure."

"I'm not sleeping with a damn woman," she said crossly. "I sleep alone."

With only two queen beds, the tacky loveseat was barely large enough for a child.

Mumbling, Raegen stripped her bed down to sheets. She checked every threaded inch. "Better not find one damn bug."

Their new digs were a stone's throw from the Interstate in case a fast getaway was necessary. Adjacent rooms were emptied, just in case. Cops cruised this area regularly. Who knew how long the department would, or could, pay expenses? Locating criminals most often took time.

"What idiot chose this raggedy place?" Raegen asked. "I wouldn't board my dog here."

"You don't own a dog," Thaine replied.

She fisted her hands on her hips. "If I did I wouldn't leave him here."

For someone who lived in a cheap apartment complex, she was a piece of work.

By nightfall, she'd surfed through the few measly TV channels at least a hundred times. Listening to *bad* news on the news channels was depressing. Cop dramas and soap operas were trimmed from the same stupid cloth, in her opinion. Who solved vintage crimes in an hour? No sports caught her eye. Then, she switched off the game station because Thaine answered all the questions. Cartoons stayed on longer than any other show.

Admitting boredom, Charlie left to snoop around the premises and surrounding areas.

Thaine decided this was perfect timing to engage Raegen in conversation, to find out what made her so tough, what made her tock when other people ticked. "What do you do in your spare time?"

"I keep busy."

"Doing what? Ever try reading?" To pass the time, he'd brought a mystery thriller, the *Wall Street Journal*'s latest edition, and a television minister's book that had been left unread on his bookshelf. His former girlfriend had suggested he read her father's printed thoughts and persuasions. Except there was something unsettling about a guy spreading the word of God via television, something unethical about a millionaire accepting tithes from the poor, the desperate, and the weak.

"Sure. Menus. In decent restaurants." Raegan said.

The local establishment had failed at getting a single-star rating for food, service, or cleanliness. It still beat their kitchenette's luxury ensemble.

"You mean ones like Mickey Dee's under-twelve choices?" He held up one hand. "Forget I said that. From now on I'm the Invisible Man." Why banter with a woman who insisted on winning every round, right or wrong?

Obviously, the next few days were going to test both their temperaments. Maybe Raegen's partner had better luck taming her attitude. In fact, maybe Slater could give him a few workable pointers.

Thaine opened the minister's book. Raegen turned the television on and upped the volume.

Shortly before ten, Charlie returned. She set the door's two security measures. "I stopped by a couple bars down the street. Nobody's noticed any troublemakers. Should be quiet tonight. Storm making noises in the distance. Do you know they have an old man working here as night-shift clerk? He's deaf. When I asked for sheets, he pointed to a sign that said: Bathrooms are for tenants only."

Obviously, Charlie didn't intend to sleep with Thaine either. She tossed an armful of linens to him, grabbed her duffel bag, and marched into the only bathroom.

"She's into both sexes," Raegen said. "I'm not giving her any reason to think I swing since I always sleep naked." Slowly, methodically, she stripped down to satin skin and climbed into bed under the sheet, embarrassment never entering the equation.

After that teasing dance, what was her reason for not wanting to sleep with him?

Thaine tugged at his ear, drawing on willpower to tamp down the high-energy lust charging through his system. Long night ahead with no way to release the frustration needling his overactive psyche when they'd already set his satin sheets on fire. The feisty woman sure knew how to wring the last trace of love juice from a man. And demand more. Have him wanting more of her.

He kicked off his loafers, draped his shirt over the nearby chair, and shed his trousers down to boxers, then spread linens over his too-small place of rest. He'd have a backache for sure.

Sometime later, thunder dragged Thaine from sleep's erotic dreams. A rustling sound brought him fully awake to the sound of rain pummeling the roof. Since his back faced the beds, he guessed it had to be Raegen closing the bathroom door. She was a light snorer. Charlie's sawing songs included violins.

He squinted at the glowing hands on his watch. One-fifteen. He hadn't slept long, the loveseat a cramped version of his king bed, causing his knees, elbows, and neck to crack with every movement, no matter which direction he turned. Neither woman had respectfully given up their pillows.

Seven minutes rumbled by amid four big thunder bumpers that shook Thaine's bladder. He wondered what kept Raegen tying up the bathroom. It hit him. Her volatile anger, distaste of the accommodations, the bathroom window . . . He rolled off the loveseat.

Nothing worked well in this place, except the lights. Lock set, the door swung open without so much as a click.

"Go away," Raegen said.

"What're you doing?"

"Mattress too soft."

So the tub was better? He would've gladly given her the wooden platform he slept on. Besides, she never complained about his bed. "Why are you shrouded from head to toe?"

"Cold."

The room was hotter than fire to him after the ladies turned down the AC. A suspicious sniffle caught his attention, but the following thunderous explosion shook the floor beneath his feet. The lights flickered.

Pulling the sheet tighter around herself, Raegen said, "Go away." Her voice was one note the good side of trembling.

Thaine sat on the tub's rim. When he tried pulling the sheet back, she yanked it from his hand. For a tough cookie, she possessed fears and vulnerabilities like everyone else. And he'd thought a different mold had been created specifically for her.

"Come here, little bit. I'll keep the demons away until the storm passes," he replied on a chuckle.

She unfolded on the next thunder bumper, and what he saw squashed his ego. Her watery eyes were rimmed in red; Raegen had been crying since the sky opened up.

When he bent over to lift her from the tub, her arms instantly locked around his neck in a stranglehold. "You won't tell anyone, will you?"

Thaine smiled as he carried her to the bed. She felt good in his arms. Tremulous. Vulnerable. Trusting.

"I'll kill you if you do."

Sitting with her in his lap, he placed a chaste kiss on her forehead. "I like living," he whispered, so as not to wake the roomie. And Raegen slept, her deep breathing fanning against his throat in a butterfly caress, her hand pressed against his thumping heart. "As much as I'm falling for you, little bit."

He didn't sleep long, her hands moving over his body, gently seeking. Caressing and arousing and welcoming. She whispered encouraging words and his wordless responses were tumultuous as the weather.

In the end, their lovemaking ebbed like the tides after the storm.

"What made you so afraid of storms, lightning, thunder?"

"It's silly."

"Tell me anyway."

She was silent for long seconds. "When I turned eight, I sneaked out of my bedroom window at midnight on a dare to meet my partners. We weren't doing anything wrong—playing in the cemetery, scaring each other—but we didn't expect rain. A bitch of . . . I mean . . . a terrible storm moved in. Gusting winds. Torrential rains. We split up to go home, only the tree outside my window was swaying. I—" She paused, leaned up on her elbow, and stared at the window. "Did you hear something?"

"If he didn't, I damn sure did." Charlie threw the covers back.

7

"Hard to sleep with you all humpin' like there's no tomorrow. Honey, he must be damn good to drag all that oohin', aahin' and hissin' out of you. Sounded like a porn queen."

"Shut up, Charlie." Thank God for darkness . . . except for the ray of light shining across their bed. Had Charlie watched them making love? If she had, somebody else could've seen them as well.

Charlie peered through the curtain's open sliver. "I don't have my glasses on, but it looks quiet out there."

Even in darkness, Raegen imagined the woman grinned, showing all thirty-two.

"Bedsprings whine. I got good ears, but if somebody had my legs hiked over their biceps, banging that much meat into me, well, doggie-style is old-fashioned, I guess."

"Get dressed," Thaine snapped. "Both of you."

Raegen had laid out her clothes in good order: black T-shirt, stretch jeans, and running shoes. And the bra, that sucker was too tight, too confining, but she stuffed her trusty derringer into cleavage. Constantly reloading the handgun wasn't an option in any tenuous situation, but the derringer had saved her life once.

Two spare clips fit inside her hip pocket. She belted her holster.

Thaine sneaked a peek between the flimsy floral curtains. "Yeah, somebody's out there messing— Car fire!"

"Mine?" Damn it, those were the only wheels she owned.

"Bathroom window. Go."

"I'll cover," Charlie whispered. "Get her out of here. They won't get past this." She came prepared with her personal .45-caliber Ruger.

"No way," Raegen said. Damned if she'd let an officer face her deadly threats. "You go."

"Bullshit," Charlie snapped. "Ass bigger than yours. Window's too small, too high."

"Quit arguing and get going." Thaine dragged her toward the bathroom. "We'll call for backup and swing around the front. Don't do anything crazy."

Crack! The window shattered.

"Bottle," Charlie said.

"Get away from there," Thaine said.

Charlie parted a narrow slice of curtains. "Naw, naw. I see that little fucker." And she opened them wider.

Taking aim, she never saw it coming. Neither of them did. The Molotov cocktail smashed against her forehead. As liquid fire waterfalled down her body, Charlie staggered backward screaming a god-awful sound that raised the hair on the back of Raegen's neck.

"Oh, my God." As Raegan and Thaine started toward her, the second cocktail landed near Charlie's feet, then a third one, torching the curtains and engulfing half the room in seconds. Licked the ceiling in a savage blaze.

Paralyzed, Thaine yelled, "Simon!"

Dear God. This was what he'd meant.

A single shot ended Charlie's screams. Her own bullet? Reflex?

Raegan laid her hand on his arm. "No, baby, that's not Simon." Two consecutive rounds penetrated the inferno's rage, hit the bed, set the unlit bottle aflame. "We gotta go."

Snapping out of the trance, Thaine propelled Raegen into the bathroom.

What could they do when a barrage of gunfire blasted through the window, paper-thin door, and dirty wall? The kitchenette added protection, but bullets splintered wood, ricocheted off metal. One tore through the medicine cabinet, shattering the mirror on impact.

An all-out war had begun, and their guns were no match against any high-powered weapons. The psychos had arrived with combat artillery.

The motel's shabby picnic area was outside the window exit. Reagen hit cement with both feet. Thaine followed.

Sprinting, mud and water sloshed under their shoes. Raegen slipped, went down, scraping her knee painfully, but Thaine hauled her to her feet, kept them moving.

"Car's on the other side of the breezeway. Silver Pontiac," he said. "God help us if they know."

"Toast, buttered with molten lead."

They lucked out. For about three seconds. The bullet's hiss whizzed between them. Ducking, they took cover behind his car.

"Take off. Stay low," Thaine said. "I'll draw their fire."

"No dice, sweetcakes. You stay. I stay." She drew her weapon. "Call for backup. Tell them to get here yesterday."

Approaching sirens blared the next second. Somebody heard the shooting, or a passerby saw the fire. Raegen squeezed her eyes shut, still smelling the stink of gas, smoke, and burning flesh, Charlie's screams echoing in her ears.

"How many do you think?" Thaine asked.

She shook off the disturbing reminders. "Don't know for sure. Several different weapons, though."

Two more bullets cut through the street's hard surface, scattering gravel like BBs. Another blew the car's taillight to smithereens. Raegen took aim. She returned fire in three random directions, avoiding the motel's stuccoed building. Monthly renters. Vacationers. Children. Who knew what curious people were thinking, doing, tempted to look, besides being in the wrong place at the wrong time? Those folks who *lived* in this dumpy area knew to take cover.

Thaine squeezed off three rounds in rapid succession.

Huddled beside him, Raegen held her breath, anticipating the opposition's next move. There was no next move.

Ceasefire. Quiet. Almost.

Patrol cars roared toward their hiding place, sirens blaring, spewing gravel, and effectively running off the snipers, who dissolved into the shadows.

After a three-minute blazing gun battle.

Tolleson wasn't too bad. Safe, but a slow ride from Phoenix in the middle of the night. No matter how much she argued, Thaine had been adamant about the move.

They'd switched cars before they left Phoenix. He'd rented an everyday kind of vehicle since his two-seater hot rod beckoned trouble they didn't need.

The Comfort Suites was better than decent. The place was clean, neat. Free of bullet holes.

They collapsed on the king bed after Raegen pulled back the bedding. She never sat on any motel's filthy comforter.

"Wake me when you're done showering," Thaine said.

"Wake *me* if I'm not out of there in ten minutes. I might be drowning."

He kissed her then, a long meeting of the lips that re-fired an old blaze in her belly. She took the lead, took her usual position on top, and ground her pelvis against his while she kissed and nipped at his chin and throat. Her jeans' scratchy fabric intensified the delicious sensation on her throbbing clit. "Ooh. Want to shower together?"

Hearing no reply, she asked, "Bath? Fine, as long as you shove that big cock inside me. I'm already wet. Forget the bath. Baby, I need you now."

She levered up on her elbows, and her jaw went slack. "He sleeps. The man goes to sleep when I'm hot and bothered after a rough night."

Miffed, and blinking rapidly, she realized something was definitely wrong with this picture. Raegen rolled off Thaine, then the bed. Wasn't this scenario supposed to be reversed, he wanting to get into her panties, if she had some on, and she too tired or headachy?

"Fine."

Slowing the water to a light rain, she lathered her body with the motel's in-house gel brand and showered leisurely, taking maximum time to bad-mouth the lame devil in the other room. She didn't need him anyway, could get her rocks off on her own.

"Son of a bitch thinks he's got a dick made of gold. Well, I got news for him. Plenty of men out there want what I got between my legs. Gold? Hah! Platinum. As soon as I get my ass back to Phoenix, I'm gonna find me a good fuck, turn the son of a bitch inside out, upside down, blur his vision, and lay the motherfucker—" She was so damn mad, she slapped the washcloth against the wall, wishing it was Thaine's face. "Treat me like some tired-ass girlfriend he's been screwing for ten years. I'm nobody's girlfriend. I do what I want, say what I want, when I want. If he doesn't like it, tough. I don't answer to him. We're done anyway. Ought to call Slater, if it wasn't in the middle of the night. He'd give me a good bump, grind, and screech in a pinch.

"Teach that pompous ass to nod out on me. Damn men think they know how to treat women. Bullshit. Too damn young anyway. I don't like rookies and I don't have time to train anybody." She shut the water off, yanked the white towel off the shower rod, dried off. "Fucker can go straight to hell for all I care. He'll never get another piece of tail from me. Never."

She wrapped the terrycloth around her body and snatched the curtain back. And screeched.

He had that folded belt in his hand. Raegen lost her breath and chewed on the hardened piece of skin along a stubby fingernail.

"Stop that."

She tucked her hand behind her back.

"Thought you wanted to shower together. Then I hear all kinds of cussing and fussing. 'Pompous ass.' 'Son of a bitch.' Bad-mouthing somebody's Mother." His voice was too soft, deceptively mild.

"I . . . I—"

Oh, damn. The malicious glint in his eyes suggested he planned to tear her ass up. With nowhere to run, no place to hide, she crowded into the shower stall's corner.

Mommy! her mind screamed. Trembling now, she wished her mother was here. Momma would never let a soul put their hands on her baby girl.

"Come here, Raegen."

Oh, God. She didn't want to move, couldn't, and shook her head.

"I said, come here." He set the belt on the counter. "Don't make me come and get you."

She gulped in air, swallowed. She was no longer dry after toweling off. Sweating liquid bullets, a small creek flowed down her spine.

"As much as you deserve a good spanking I'll wait until I cool off, let you think about the penalty your foul mouth earned."

Enough time to sweet-talk him out of it. *Babycakes?* And use her doe-eyed stare, fluttering lashes, sweet smile.

"You slept with Slater?"

Oh, hell. "Twice," she said suddenly. "Three times."

"I don't want to hear how many! Who else on the force have you let sleep in your bed?"

"No one."

"Not what I heard."

"They're lying."

No man had slept in her bed. *She* hadn't slept in her bed or at the apartment since Richelle's death. Two years.

Men and dating or even her private needs weren't priority. She devoted off-duty time to nieces and nephews. She took the kids shopping for clothes and toys, paid for their tutors, treated them to junk food, and huddled and slept with them on the floor after watching late-night, scary movies. She slept in Richelle's bedroom most often, kept the sanctuary like a shrine, all of her niece's dolls and horse statues in place. Richelle had wanted a real live horse. To this day, Raegen still deposited biweekly funds into a secret savings account, unable to discontinue.

Not one day passed that she didn't think about the beautiful little girl who had tragically died in her arms. The young punks were after Raegen. They missed their mark, claiming a sweet child's life instead.

Thaine's eyes narrowed. "Why would *they* lie, Raegen?"

She'd cleaned up her act after being promoted to detective. As for an office affair, Slater was her only mistake. Until this man showed up. Not that she hadn't been tempted; she'd teased a few sniffing pups. Walked away.

Evidently, lies, tales, and gossip were spreading faster than wildfires in Arizona's bone-dry forests. She was single and black working in a male-dominated profession. Sure, she'd talked smack to keep the network of good old boys in line, but no one could accuse her of dishonesty.

"B-because they wanted to a-and I wouldn't."

"Uh-huh. Right."

Anger reared its nasty head. Yeah, she'd told fibs to save a life, told a big fat one to save his pristine soul.

Raegen stepped out of the tub, clutching the towel tightly, and got in his face. "I don't lie. My mother raised me better."

"Uh-huh," he replied sarcastically. "But, she forgot to teach you common decency. She forgot the training sessions on respecting yourself. You walked into my home expecting to get laid. You took your clothes off, stripped without thought, care, or hint of embarrassment, and willingly, *willingly*, climbed into my bed. Tell me where I'm lying."

Well, that stung all to hell. She bristled righteously. "Pot can't call the kettle black! You wanted me. *You* told me take off my clothes and *you* carried me to *your* bed, then *you* screwed *me* blind. Willingly!" she shouted, stabbing her finger at his chest.

She'd thought he was a gentleman of impeccable breeding, the caring lover and friend. Hah! He was the chief fraud in disguise, and she'd fallen for his scam. Fallen for him, dammit. Fallen hard after one sizzling night.

"What makes you think you're so damn special?" Raegen asked. "What makes you think you're so much better than me? You're just like the next horny bastard hot on a pussy trail. So where the hell do you get off badmouthing me when you and the rest of the pack of sniffing hounds can't keep your dicks one notch below half-mast?

"But, you know what?" She threw one hand in air. "I don't care if you believe me. My biggest mistake ever was sleeping with some sanctimonious asshole. Go ahead, McDuff, tell the world how you fucked my brains out."

She stalked out of the bathroom, slamming the door behind her.

8

Suitably chastised—at worst, castrated—Thaine showered, thinking, absorbing Raegen's blistering rant. Common decency? Where did he get off preaching to her?

Pot can't call the kettle black.

She was right. He'd used the same slogan on his former girlfriend of five years, when Val had slept with a partner of his in retaliation for Thaine's straying and the reason they were no longer a couple. No denying he was a pack member, and he'd screwed up first. Unlike Val, who was haughty and prudish, the "other" woman was as bold as Raegen, exciting, but not nearly as passionate or demanding in bed. On the other hand, there was something altogether different in Raegen neither Val nor his one-night stand possessed. Compassion—and she tried to conceal the emotion with attitude.

She'd witnessed his freakout when Charlie went up in flames, had run her soft hand down his arm in a soothing caress. She'd spoken quietly, compassionately, but firmly, which freed his mind of the bizarre nightmare. He'd had them before, only this time he was wide-awake watching the horrifying sequel.

She had attempted to clean up her language while in his company, Thaine thought, smiling at her accomplishment. Until he'd pushed her hot button with blatant accusations. She'd slept with Slater—her partner, for God's sake; married, no less. They'd have to talk about that particular breach before their relationship moved to the next level.

Toweled off, Thaine wrapped the white terrycloth around his waist and marched out of the bathroom. They needed to set some rules. Now.

She'd dimmed the bedside lamp, but Raegen wasn't in bed. On the desk, divided into two piles, he saw currency. He spread the money out. She'd left exactly half the room cost and half the car rental payment.

"Damn." She'd pulled up stakes and left. He couldn't believe she'd put herself at risk. No way. She had smarts, but she was gone anyway.

Thaine swiped the cash from the desk to the floor as he started for the closet. He sure didn't need or want Reagan's money. He wanted her. Right here. With him.

As he passed by the small table and chairs, he caught sight of a shadowy figure. Raegen, her arms wrapped around the king pillow the same way she'd held on to him during the storm. She chose to sleep elsewhere—the floor of all places, using the comforter as pallet and sheet—after listening to his callous rhetoric, rather than sleep in the same bed with him.

Exhausted after a long night, she didn't wake when he put her in bed, spooned her supple body, and kept her close. "Tomorrow, little bit," Thaine whispered. He yawned hugely. "We'll discuss this jealousy thing that turned me into an idiot."

Raegen rounded the corner and stalked down the hallway toward Vanderbilt's office. One knock; she barged in and tossed her duffel on the chair. "I need a new team member."

The commander kept his eyes on the newspaper he clutched,

reading glasses balanced on the tip of his nose, his ear to the phone. She waited, and Vanderbilt finally hung up without responding to the person on the line. "You're in early for a change, detective. But who, pray tell, are you thinking of replacing and why? This had better be good since you rudely interrupted my conversation."

"McDuff." Because this morning she woke comfortably in his arms, legs entwined with his, their bodies warming each other, breathing him. He had a lot of damn nerve cuddling after spouting off trash. She slipped out of bed undetected, dressed quickly, and caught the first thing smoking back to Phoenix.

Vanderbilt's chair began squeaking that awful sound she was beginning to hate. "Not a chance, Rae. Sit down." When she stayed where she stood, the commander glared her into the chair already in front of his desk. "What's the real problem of the day?"

"Rookies don't work for me. He's too easy-going, then he switches up and tries to take command of things. I can't work with a man like that. Not on a case like this one."

"Rookie," he replied flatly, his hand assuming the position under his chin. The rocking ceased, the screeching quieted. "Let me tell you something about Thaine McDuff. He's worked nine years undercover and as a negotiator. He came here recommended by Denver's commander, who reluctantly passed on a dazzling referral, when Thaine refused a big promotion. Their IA division, their SWAT, and their mayor all wanted him."

What?

"Rookie? Not by my standards. You will continue working with him until I say otherwise. And," Vanderbilt added, irritation filtering through, "his brother is your suspect. Thaine is the one link we need. Simon was released within an hour of the bust you said was unnecessary. He was loose on the streets last night when one of my people died, burned beyond recognition and shot, detective. What the hell went on out there?" His chair snapped forward with a loud bang. "The public's saying an act of terrorism, the media's speculating, and our damn mayor has her girdle in a wad. Mind telling me what happened before she gets here? She's pledging to jump down my throat and I'm planning to dive down yours if I don't get some damn answers."

Said he whose boxers had twisted and wedged. Hell's bells. Someone knocked before she opened her mouth, which gave Raegan the reprieve to gather her thoughts enough to put together an oration about the gun battle.

"Enter," Vanderbilt snapped.

Of all people . . . "Commander." Thaine nodded, then caught her gaze, held it.

Raegen looked away. Too bad he didn't oversleep.

He didn't waste any time. Thaine launched into his dialogue about the shootings, didn't give her one second to say squat on her behalf. "I thought it was safer to get Raegen out of the area," he finished.

Vanderbilt chewed on it for a moment. "I've heard a great deal of praise for you, Thaine, on how you've closed cases. What do you suggest now?"

Raegen slumped back against the chair, rolled her eyes.

"I've got a brother I need to talk with first. He was angry yesterday, but it's unlikely that Simon would take an arson route."

Figures. Blood would always be thicker than water. He'd signed, sealed, and delivered the severing blow to their once-upon-a-time relationship. Turned it into a one-night, forget-you stand. Fine. Who cared? "Slater and I can—"

"You're under the radar," Thaine said.

She rewarded him with a wicked smile, circled the curves of her lips with the tip of her tongue. "I know. Bob and I are tight. He'd be happy to take over guard duty while your loyal self trots around Phoenix."

"That's enough, detective," Vanderbilt said in his deepest commanding tone.

She knew better. The good old boy network considered sniping bitchiness unprofessionally female. She'd earned respect over the years. Now, chances were she'd blown it with the pack's honcho.

The phone rang. While the commander talked, Thaine pinned her with a chilling glare.

"She's right here," Vanderbilt said. "McDuff, too. . . . All right, good. . . . I'll let them know. That was Ballistics. The bullet that killed the suspect came from the same gun dumped down the storm drain."

Raegen expected to see relief tumbling off Thaine's shoulders. Nothing of the sort. He continued the stare down.

Unable to withstand his penetrating gaze, she looked away, plucked an imaginary piece of lint from her jeans, and flicked it into thin air.

"Thaine," Vanderbilt said. "Did you hear what I said? You were not at fault."

"I heard. Let me finish what I started. If I get the slightest inkling Simon is involved in this case," he continued, raising his palms, "I'll cuff and bring him in, charge him with murder, arson, attempted murder, etcetera."

Gulp. If swallowing a foot was possible, she'd scarfed down hers and his.

"I need assurance, sir, that I won't be followed, that I can meet Simon without interference."

Vanderbilt's gaze swung to Raegen, steadied, leveled. "Done. Thirty-six hours, Duffy, then we pick him up."

Whoa. For a split second, she saw something oddly different flash in Thaine's eyes before his gaze veered to the commander's stoic face.

"Rae, talk with Slater. I'm also ordering you to stay in the building until arrangements are in place."

Incarcerated. Why not go the distance, bound and gag her?

When Vanderbilt ended any meeting, the signal was quite plain. He readjusted his reading glasses and spun his chair around to face the window.

"Commander," she said. Raegen waited until she gained his full attention. "Somebody gave up our location."

"We think alike, detective," Thaine interrupted, pissing her off more so when the commander focused on the man. "It's possible we were tailed, or there's a remote possibility that we have a snitch in the building. Don't get me wrong, I'm not pointing fingers. But let's keep this plan under wraps for now. Slater and the three of us. Precautionary. I'll make contact with Simon before the day is out, then I'll be back in time to escort and guard the detective with her partner."

Oh, he was slick with that bit of hell. And, what was with this I'm-king-and-what-I-say-is-most-important kind of shit?

She walked away from him as if he didn't exist in her life, sashaying down the hallway, tight jeans and T-shirt accentuating the sweet curves of a body he'd love to caress again.

Thaine watched Raegen until she disappeared around the corner.

She'd punched his fire-breathing button with sass and bundled crap, accusing him of disloyalty to the badge he carried with pride and using Slater as leverage. She pushed hard, deliberately torqueing his anger, unaware of the jealous streak he was losing control of now.

By noon, he'd left six messages for Simon. He'd caught one glimpse of Raegen. She ignored him.

Three o'clock came and went. Thaine believed his game plan had gone straight to the deepest caverns. Raegen was tucked away in her cubicle and, on occasion, talking quietly with Slater . . . planning? And here Thaine thought he'd get some workable pointers from the detective striding toward him.

"We got a place in Chandler," Slater said.

How hard was it for Raegen to stroll across the room, pass on information? Instead, she sent her married playmate to deliver the news. He was average height, maybe six feet, blue eyes, and dark brown hair, and Raegen had found something worthwhile in the guy to sleep with him. Three times.

"Have you heard from your brother?"

"Not yet, no. He'll call." Soon, he hoped, and checked his watch. Four-ten.

Slater gnashed on a toothpick. "No problem. Take your time. I got my partner covered."

Thaine bet he did. Full-body coverage, apparently. "Appreciate you doing this. I know it's particularly hard when you'd rather spend time with the wife and kids."

Shrugging his wide shoulders, Slater said, "They're used to it. Six-thirty, McDuff. We'll find some way to kill off time until you get there. You play poker?"

And that lousy question very nearly had Thaine coming out of his chair. "I don't gamble." And Slater swaggered away.

Raegen *would* be left alone with her poker buddy for an unspecified amount of time if Simon called late. Growling ominously, Thaine tried his brother's cell again.

This time the voice said, "I'm sorry. The number you have . . ."

"Dammit!"

9

Squeezing his eyes shut, Thaine pinched the bridge of his nose. How the devil was he supposed to find Simon before Vanderbilt let a uniformed squadron loose on him?

There was Slater's weasel. Who believed PeeWee the Snitch? He told as many, if not more, lies as Simon. Thaine didn't have the time or patience to search the entire city, chasing the weasel's false leads.

The chance to find his brother had come to a grinding halt, but the no-go left him available to thwart a strip-poker party.

At Raegen's desk, he said, "Simon shut down his phone. Guess we can leave any time."

"So, you got the Do-Re-Mi," she sang like the "disconnected" recorded song. "Why am I not surprised?"

Do-Re-Mi? "Let me borrow your cell."

"Use your own, Slick."

Slick? "Dammit, Raegen, just give me the phone. I didn't get the music." She handed it over. "When I'm done with Simon, you and I are—Simon, what the hell are you trying to—Son of a bitch. He hung up."

"Give him two minutes. Call back from a different number. Don't sound angry. Give him a reason to talk. Lie if you have to. Oh, pardon me. Let's not taint your pristine slate." Raegen swiveled her chair around.

He spun it back to face him, braced his hands on the chair arms, and loomed over her, inhaling her distinctive scent, his heart racing at breakneck speed being so close to her. "We need to have a conversation."

"We don't have anything to discuss, McDuff. By the time you catch up to your brother, Bobby and me will be settled in the motel enjoying each other's company."

She knew exactly which buttons to mash. Not Thaine or hotcakes or sweetcakes. Not even Duffy. McDuff. He'd gotten used to hearing the pet names she'd given him, especially during their slow promenade when she whispered sensual words, demanding encouragement, jolting him to the highest plateau. No other moment surpassed the split second she'd snapped around him, hot and vicious. Raegen wielded extraordinary magic that sent him tumbling out of control and completely into her clutches—body, mind and soul.

He backed off when Slater waltzed into the cubicle. Thaine erased Simon's number from Raegan's phone.

"Hey, hot stuff," she told Slater. "We can leave anytime. Slick here sounds like he'll be late. No sense in us hanging around after I contact my family. If their cells work in the boonies."

Her family vacation started early for their protection. Raegan was pretty down about not RVing to Yellowstone with everyone else, but this case was important to her. She spent a lot of time with nieces and nephews. Family meant a lot to her, and Thaine understood the connection.

"Are you ready, hon?" she asked Slater.

God damn her. Thaine left before they came to a decision, before Slater's grinning mouth tasted his fist.

He borrowed someone else's cell. "Listen to me, you son of

a bitch. You owe me. They gave me thirty-six fucking hours to make contact. No interference. You've already wasted eight of them with bullshit."

"I don't owe you diddly squat," Simon snapped. "Since when did you start cursing filth, choirboy?"

About ten minutes ago, and it was all Raegen's damn fault. She'd used needling magic to pierce his nose, had already inserted an imaginary ring. She yanked hard.

Thaine vigorously rubbed the flesh between his nostrils. "We have to meet."

"I got nothing to say."

"You'd better find something worthwhile. They plan to pick you up. You can run, but you can't hide, Simon. There won't be any escape. Knowing Vanderbilt, you won't make it out of the city undetected. He'll put everything he's got on the hunt. Talk to me."

Five full seconds went by. "All right, bro. Not by phone. Second priority stop. Hour. Better be alone this time."

Down the hall, Raegen and Slater were talking. Thaine caught her partner's gaze. "No problem," he said. No tail this time.

Inside the designated café, Thaine looked at the wall clock again. The waitress had refilled his coffee cup. He ordered ice cream to look busily relaxed. Simon was way past late. Customers filed in and out, busboys noisily cleared tables, and short-order cooks yelled when somebody wasn't on their job.

Exactly twenty-five minutes from now, his roomies were due to check into the Chandler motel. They'd have a lot of time together before Thaine arrived, plenty of time to knock off . . .

"May I sit here?"

He looked up at the woman. "I'm sorry, the seat is taken." Ten more minutes and he'd give up the booth.

"There's nowhere else to sit. I've been waiting for a place at the counter. You've been sitting here alone for the last fifteen minutes, taking up space." She was a snippy broad with stunning ice-blue eyes, clutching a black purse in one hand and a bible in the other.

In no mood to discuss religion, Thaine signaled the waitress. "Check, please."

"Not until you buy me a piece of homemade pie, bro."

Of all damn disguises. He hadn't recognized Simon. Heavily made up, he passed for a fifty-something white woman. Thaine looked him up and down. If his brother had strolled in here with high heels on his big feet, he'd have disowned the man. "Don't sit next to me."

"Like I want to look like your girlfriend. Good to know I passed. If I can fool you, I can fool anybody." Ladylike, he tugged at each gloved finger until his brown hands were free. He decided against stuffing the pair inside his purse, laid them on the table, kept his hands hidden.

"Until somebody sees those manly mitts and hangs cuffs around your wrists. Carrying unlicensed, concealed weapons is illegal in this state, especially for ex-cons." Thaine had seen the butt of the gun sticking out of the purse.

Simon's gaze traveled around the café, finally settling on Thaine. "A woman needs protection from big, bad wolves. At least these mitts haven't shot anybody in the back.

"He turned twenty-one last week, Thaine. He was a good kid, just easily influenced by a bad crowd. Like the majority of punks running loose in this city, he got caught up in a trade he had no business messing with. We all know money talks and bullshit walks, but Jerome wanted his daughter to have a better life."

Thaine let him blow off steam. The girlfriend's mouth had shut good and tight. Social services gained custody of her daughter and they coaxed Jerome's last name out of the little girl. Sometime soon, Thaine planned to visit Jerome's parents, offer his condolences, and see what they knew about their son's habits.

Shaking his head, Simon continued. "I tried to get him to open his eyes and see the danger in what he was doing. The little fucker thought his friends knew more than me. He jumped stupid one day and I whipped Jerome's narrow ass, then talked about him so bad he bawled like a baby. Thaine, he promised to change. I believed him. Then, Scooby said you shot the boy. He said you were shooting everything. He said he tripped, luckily, hit the pavement and damn near broke his arm. Still in pain, too. How could you shoot Jerome in the back?"

"I did no such thing. The bullet that killed Jerome didn't come from my gun, Simon. It didn't come from any cop's weapon."

"Oh, so now you want to tell me the bullet fell out of the sky, that God struck him down for doing wrong."

His brother was angry now. Simon had strayed from the family tradition on religion ever since the fire nearly took his life. The day following their parent's funeral, he refused to set foot inside a church again. "No, what I'm saying is . . . Who's Scooby? What's his last name?"

"Why? You want to take him out, too? Uh-uh, no way."

"Listen to me. This Scooby guy, how does he know so much about Jerome's death? We haven't released any information. He had to be there."

"Scooby wouldn't shoot his partner." But Simon's face showed a stitch of skepticism.

"Listen to me. The bullet that killed Jerome came from the weapon the second guy tossed down a storm drain. He shot his partner in the back. Not me. Not any cop. I need a name, Simon."

He'd do the right thing. Trouble had followed him through life, including enemies, but Simon had a thing about "other" people being straight-up. Scooby had crossed the line.

"No can do. Can't drop a dime on anybody. You're on your own, bro."

Thaine clenched the napkin. "Fine, but let me tell you something, Simon. If I hear one mention of your name, one hint, you won't have to worry about Vanderbilt's squadron. I'll be your worst nightmare."

"You wore that same damn title twenty-seven years ago."

It was worse than a slap to the face.

His brother was seven at the time and Thaine was nine. They were playing, then a shoving match ensued, the charcoal cooker fell . . . Simon spent weeks in the hospital with burns over forty percent of his small body.

He slid out of the booth's seat. After all these years, Simon still hadn't forgiven him for the accident.

As he started for the café's exit, Simon said, "I'll call later. Need facts."

Thaine grinned. "Don't forget your gloves, ma'am."

Slater finally opened the damn motel door, barefoot, shirt partially unbuttoned. Raegen was nowhere in sight.

"Where is she?" Thaine snapped. Playing cards were scattered on one bed. Sheet and comforter stripped from the other.

"Bathroom."

Son of a bitch. If he broke up their strip poker after-fun, he'd kick some ass.

"Bathing."

"Why?"

"Why?" Slater shrugged. "Sweaty? Ask her."

Thaine clenched both fists. This bastard was cruisin' for a bruisin'.

"Can't get in, though," the detective added. "Door's locked. Been jackin' around in there since we got here." He sat on the bed, gathered the playing cards, shuffled and laid out a solitaire hand.

Apparently, the jerk had tried to enter. Why didn't she allow him inside?

Raegen stepped into the room, dressed in T-shirt and shorts, gun and holster attached to her hip. Why was she wearing shorts at a time like this, showing way too much leg?

Avoiding eye contact, she said, "Thought I heard your voice. How's the brother? Did you nail him?"

Staying silent, he willed her to look at him.

She stuffed clothes inside her bag then looked up. "Well?"

Too much sass. "Not as of yet, no. He'll call later. I suspect we'll meet again tonight. I'm not convinced he's part of these crimes, Raegen, after talking with him. Before you start in, let me explain why."

She sat on the bed, drew her legs beneath her. Thaine spun the desk chair around, straddled the seat. What he had to offer was weak at best when Simon knew both shooters well.

The detectives listened without interrupting.

"I got somebody to run this Scooby dude. If he's in the system, we'll find him." He'd called Smitty.

"If he's not, your brother's time is running short," Raegen concluded.

That was a distinct possibility, and Thaine tugged at his ear.

"I need some grub," Slater said. "Who's game? Chinese or Mexican."

"Your choice, just not too warm." Thaine plucked a hundred-dollar bill from his wallet. "On me."

Raegen handed over a twenty. "I pay my own way. Hot, hot stuff."

Like her damn temperament. Disguising his scowl with a smile, Thaine said, "Suit yourself."

The second Slater closed the door Thaine engaged the lock, set the chain, and spun around to face her. "We're going to have a little chat."

10

He didn't give her the chance to object. "Sit down. I've just about had it, Raegen. You've been screwing with my mind since last night and I don't like it. I don't like it at all!"

Tough. "I'm already sitting, but yelling will get you zero conversation." She narrowed her eyes. "And don't point your finger at me."

He stared long and hard into her eyes. "I'm not the kind of guy—" Thaine started saying.

When he licked his lips, God help her, she wanted to feel them all over her body. Her breasts swelled. Instant dampness soaked her panties. At the station when he'd loomed over her, he was close enough to kiss. She wanted his kiss, wanted him to make love to her. Why couldn't she control her horniness with him around? One touch from Thaine McDuff and she melted into a puddle at his feet. No one had ever made her melt.

"Don't do that, Raegen."

Huh? "Do what?"

"Stare at me like you do. I'm having a hard enough time

trying to explain something and you continue to mess with my head."

"You want me to look at the floor?"

"No, dammit." He turned away. The curtains were closed. He lifted his hand to part them, changed his mind, jammed those talented fingers into his trouser pockets, the same fingers she wanted to rouse her body. "I don't like knowing that you see Slater."

"He's my partner. I have to see him."

His sigh fluttered the curtains. "What I mean is, other times."

"What other times?"

"Off duty, dammit!"

Realization struck hard and fast.

"I'm jealous," Thaine snapped. "I don't like being jealous, don't like this feeling that I'm losing control. I don't ever lose control."

Uh-huh. He'd lost more than that while they'd made love. He'd sacrificed himself in bed, given himself fully, unconditionally, and she'd given back the same enjoyment, the same natural, caring devotion.

"I don't like sharing, either," Thaine said. "Can you understand that?"

She climbed off the bed, moved in behind him.

"Do you?" He spun around.

Lacing her fingers with his, Raegen said, "That depends."

"I will tear into your—"

She kissed him thoroughly, dragged his hand up to her heavy breast, craving his touch, and helped him massage the tenderness. "I need you. Take me to bed."

His lips moved across her cheeks to her ear, delved, sending a bolt of lightning heat through every nerve ending. "Can't. Slater."

Her insides quivering to the power of his swelling cock was too persuasive. "Let him catch us. Let him watch."

"Belt, damn you."

She smiled against his lips. "You weren't upset knowing Charlie saw us."

He lifted her from the floor, swung her around, and pressed her back to the door. He drew her legs around his waist, rocked against her sensitivity.

"Why didn't you let him in?"

"Let who in?" she asked, grinding her hot spot against his hardness.

"Slater. Why didn't you let him in the bathroom?"

"Because. Because I didn't—don't—want him," she admitted. "I wanted you."

He kissed her hard, tongues dueling, hands caressing, his body moving with hers. Torching hers.

"We have time. I need you," she said, panting.

"No."

"Please, babycakes?" She circled her hips. "I want to feel that big cock pounding inside me. I'll make you come, squeeze every drop from your body," she said, kissing every inch of his face. "I'm already wet, soaking. I need some lovin', sweetcakes."

The sound of his zipper buzzed in her ears. He tugged her shorts and panties aside. The scorching head of his beautiful cock pressed insistently at the gateway to her heat. She imagined the heavy veins pulsing with every rapid heartbeat. She'd kissed and licked each one, up to the inflated head, swirling her tongue, sucking, teeth grazing taut skin—until her teasing shattered his control.

Primed, spreading her thighs wider, she readied to accept the bulging head, his cock's girth. He'd fill her completely with slow, tantalizing strokes. She'd plead for more, beg for every thick inch and still want more. All, then she'd change the rules and drive them both toward a feverish pitch. But time ran short.

"If Slater—"

Raegen screeched as Thaine shoved her down his rigid length, impact nearly splitting her in half.

"Sorry. Sorry. Baby, you make me crazy just mentioning his name."

He kissed her softly, held her hips immobile and massaged the cleft between her butt cheeks. Dipping one hand down between them, the gentle, soothing caress eased the ache as usual. His clever fingers began the ritual that always sent her into orbit, toying with her clit, pressing, pinching, and stretching until she purred.

"I won't let him have you. Anyone. I won't let anyone have you."

He was hers now. Hers in every way. Maybe. Still a bit uncertain, her juices flowing, Raegen lifted slowly, sliding easily. She locked her gaze with his in defiant resistance. He forced her down his length again, drew a gasp of pleasure from them both when she clamped tightly around his cock.

"Mine, dammit. Only mine."

And she belonged to him. "Yes. Always."

Doubt glowed in his dark eyes.

To prove she meant the words, she goaded him with her body, rising, barely lowering, rising again, higher this time and nearly released him. She offered her breast to his gifted mouth. Selfishly, Thaine latched on with dedicated finesse, sucking noisily, laving, a nip or bite here and there. She moaned with pleasure as he squeezed the fullness.

"Fuck me," Raegan whispered. "Fuck me hard." She dropped down his length in one smooth motion, and the simple enticement began their journey across the galaxy.

She rode him at maximum velocity, egging him on, demanding he give in to her, insisting he would. Challenging.

He banged her against the door in a wicked rampage, the butt of her gun bumping the metal. "Mine," he muttered over and over again, each pillaging stroke more powerful than the last.

"Always," she agreed. "Always."

There was no going back now. Only forward. Together, they chased their star across the universe. Caught it. Embraced it, embraced each other while Thaine's body quaked on a muffled roar. She ran her hands up and down his back, through his hair, kissed his neck and shoulder, until the final pummeling stroke caught her senses off guard. Vision blurring, she trembled violently on a sob and gave up all she had to give, left nothing in reserve.

She refused to allow him withdrawal, held on tight through the aftermath, each subtle movement tripping another deep and delicious rippling wave.

"I can still feel that snapping thing you do," Thaine whispered, his harsh breath fanning her cheek. "If you don't stop, I'm liable to—Goddammit."

Tightening around his cock, she took whatever he had left. Took it all because he belonged to her now. Weak, her legs slid down his hips as she shimmered through completion.

Bam! Bam! Bam! The door shook against her back.

"Bathroom," Thaine ordered, lifting and setting her on the floor. "Get in there."

He tucked himself away and waited until Raegen was out of sight.

Poised to knock again, Slater asked, "What took you so long? Thought maybe you got nailed."

Thaine raised his eyebrows. Sure enough true.

"Where is she?"

"Bathroom."

Slater grunted. "Guess she doesn't want either one of us."

Thaine grinned.

"Somebody'll nail her," Slater said, "and put her out of her misery."

Mexican food burned from tongue to gut.

At eight-thirty, Thaine's cell vibrated. Smitty had said he'd make contact, but the illuminated number was unrecognizable.

As usual, Simon wouldn't elaborate, except in person. Thaine talked him into meeting somewhere nearby. Half hour.

Thrusting his arms into the sleeves of his jacket, he decided he trusted Raegen. He didn't trust her idiot partner who shuffled cards faster than a trick dealer stacking the deck. On second thought, she was acting too nonchalant for his taste, engaged in a dollar-a-hand poker game, ignoring him, unsympathetic when his gut danced the cha-cha to its own rhythm.

Opening the door got her attention. Slater dealt the hands.

Be good, Thaine mouthed.

When her return came as a silent *I will*, with a sly grin attached, he fingered the belt buckle. Her wink calmed him, but he settled completely on her next declaration. *You and me*.

Always, he said silently, *always*.

"Where to this time?" Slater asked. The cheater held all the aces. "Mesa?"

"Not far from here, didn't want be gone too long. Chandler Park. Are four aces good to keep?"

Laughing, Raegen folded. The million-dollar smile and twinkling eyes did something wild and crazy to Thaine's heart. Stuttering. Bleeping. He closed the door before he snatched her into his arms and made some kind of declaration she wasn't ready to hear yet.

The park was only blocks away. He walked the distance, thinking it was best to scope out the area before Simon arrived.

He wanted to trust his brother, except Simon wore "devious" too well, like some detectives he knew.

Drifting slowly out of the east, an indigo sky blended into pale red, pink, and orange clouds. Soon, the days would grow shorter. Longer nights to spend with Raegen. The gentle breeze blew the sweet scent of lilacs in his direction. He inhaled deeply, feeling pretty damn good about himself and Raegen. Contented. He would feel even better if he closed this case. Thaine picked up the pace, striding toward his destination.

Heart still beating in a romp, he almost missed his phone's vibrations. Smitty's name showed up on the screen.

"What do you have?" Thaine asked.

"Nothing yet."

Damn. "I'm meeting Simon at Chandler Park in a minute, hoping—Hold on." Across the street, his brother swaggered toward him, dressed as himself for a change. He met him halfway.

"You were right," Simon said. "Lamar 'Scooby' Griffin. Girlfriend took the lousy son of a bitch to Chandler Regional."

Thaine raised the phone to his ear, passed on the information. "Pick him up. Make him talk."

"Listen to me, Thaine."

Instead, he shoved the phone into his jacket pocket. "Does Scooby work for you?"

Simon rolled his eyes. "I wouldn't hire that no-good—"

"Who, then?" He got in his face. Simon was of equal height, except Thaine packed more muscle.

"Don't push it, bro. I'm not that little boy anymore." He pulled his trouser pockets inside out. "I ran out of dimes."

Staring off at the small wine-tasting business that he'd ventured into one day, a place he intended to show Raegen on their first date, Thaine contemplated his words, gathering his thoughts. They were brothers. Brothers talked. "Look, I got a thing for her, Simon, and I will *not* let anyone hurt Raegen. You or anyone else. Understand?"

"Booty galore. Pussy galore, too?"

"I'll kill you."

"Hold up." Backing away, Simon chuckled. "I'm saying she's got you pussy whipped. It happens. Makes a man do crazy shit." He went on and on about three women who'd teased his pecker, had his brain thinking love. "Look here. I'll drop a nickel, but you have to keep the pack animals off my back. I'm planning to open a legitimate business with my part of the inheritance."

Their parents' estate was more than they ever expected. Money had burnt a hole in Simon's pockets. Fast cars, fast women, plenty of dope to fly high. He finally came to his senses when jail stared him in the face. Too late. Three years ago, after Simon's release from prison, they sold their grandfather's farm. Few people believed massage parlors were legitimate. Or even adult stores.

"I don't want to know anything about it." Of all times, the vibration nagged him again.

"Whatever," Simon said and snorted. "What you need to do is take a look in your—"

"Hold up. I need to get this." Smitty again. Best scenario, Griffin had given him a name.

"You're not going to like this," the cop said. "Griffin spilled his guts without a fight. He fingered Simon, said he was the kingpin. He said he was *ordered* to take out Jerome for talking too much shit to too many people. Griffin just saw Simon not too long ago. He said Simon told him to see a doctor."

"I don't believe it." His brother was on the verge of giving more info. Was Simon lying again?

"That's not all. Vanderbilt contacted Chandler PD, asking them to work with us on picking him up. They don't have a choice. Look around you. There's no way out."

Over Simon's shoulders, patrol cars lined up at the far end of the park, probably surrounding the area.

If Thaine showed his cards, Simon would bolt and never forgive him. Or trust him again. Thaine needed that nickel's worth of info, the only way he might verify Simon's innocence and prove Griffin lied.

"I need more time, Smitty. Give me ten."

"It's not my call."

Cops were headed in their direction. Then, another person stepped out between two cars. Detective for sure. Plain-clothed. Darkness hid the man's features, but Thaine saw the glint of hardware pressed against his leg. He looked at Simon when the detective raised his gun. This was it. They'd take his brother away again, lock him up, and hide the key. He'd lawyer up and refuse to talk to anyone. Including Thaine.

"Simon—"

Boom! The bullet's impact knocked him forward into Thaine's arms. "Simon!"

He gently lowered his brother to the ground, ignoring the chaos. He loved Simon too much to care.

The same old silly smile spread across Simon's mouth. "Guess the big guy didn't want me to open the teen center. Didn't believe I'd changed."

"Don't talk," Thaine said, barely able to maintain the steadiness in his voice. "Ambulance is on its way."

"Shit burns worse than the fire."

"Sssh. Hang in there. You'll be fine." Through blurred vision, he saw rookie Kimberly Purcell kneel beside them. "He's my b-brother."

"I know," she replied and touched Thaine's arm.

"Was this a setup to take him down? Why? He didn't deserve this. I don't think he's armed." Simon shook his head.

"No, no setup," Kimberly said. "We got Simon's shooter, though. It's Slater's snitch. PeeWee."

"That little butthead," Simon snapped. He levered up to his elbows. "I got in his face today, told him you'd have his number. I think the little bastard meant to get you, but the SOB can't shoot for shit. He shot *me* in the ass. Thinks he can take my brother out, I'm gonna beat the bitch bloody. Help me up."

Chuckling, Thaine and Kimberly pulled Simon to his feet. He'd be okay. And they had their man, too.

"I don't need your help, bro. Got this hot momma right here." Simon would always be Simon.

Limping, he made his way toward his target with Purcell's help. Although officers had handcuffed PeeWee, Simon hauled off and tagged his jaw, knocked him to the ground.

"What the fuck you do that for, man?" PeeWee struggled to his feet.

"You're not smart enough to do anything on your own," Simon snapped. "Who sent you?"

"Go to hell."

Simon struck him again. The snitch staggered backward. "Who? Come in here looking to shoot my brother. I'm gonna make you talk, motherfucker, cause you've lost your damn mind. Nobody messes with my brother." The backhand surely drew blood.

"Help! Help!"

Game, set, and match, Thaine thought. Three officers watched the foray while others kept the gathering bystanders at bay.

Before Simon went too far, Thaine knew he'd have to end the one-sided brawl.

"Shut up, bitch. One more time. Who sent you?" PeeWee didn't answer fast enough and Simon popped him good and hard, sent the snitch sliding across the grass.

"Damn, man." He blubbered worse than a sobbing child needing his mother's comfort. "It's Slater! He runs the show."

Thaine hit the pavement at a dead run.

11

He had his gun out long before he made it to the motel's parking lot. As a twelve-year veteran, Thaine knew it was the worst he could do without a decent plan and no backup. Only one other person knew their location.

From the street, Thaine heard Raegen cursing, then a loud crash came from inside the room.

He exploded through the door, hit the floor, rolled and came up ready to fire. The door slammed shut on its own swinging energy.

"Let her go, Slater."

Raegen's arms were pinned to her sides with one of her partner's beefy appendages. Other than her pulse beating rapidly, she didn't dare move. Slater's .44 Magnum with silencer was pressed against her temple.

No matter how much strength Reagan portrayed in a situation, Thaine avoided looking into the eyes of the woman he cared deeply for. She would never show fear. Witnessing terrified emotion in those golden depths would unravel him, dealing a devastating blow to them both.

"Impressive, McDuff. Just like the cops on TV."

Slater's face looked similar to some of those actors. Raegen had branded the guy: black eye, fat lip, bloodied nose. Thaine wondered if he still had gonads.

"I've never seen a negotiator performing gymnastic routines." Slater grinned, showed teeth. "Let her go? That's it? Aren't you supposed to talk me down?"

Dealing with an agitated convict or even stressed-out, unstable patients was one thing. A cop put the ball in a brand new court. Tonight would test Thaine's expertise. There was no room for error.

"What'd you do to PeeWee?"

Thaine shrugged, keeping his eyes locked with a predator who carried a license to kill.

"This jackass called him when I was in the bathroom," Raegen slipped in.

No fear there, but she closed her mouth when Slater pushed the weapon harder against her skin.

"He nailed Simon, didn't he? Then what? Did you beat the little shit until he talked? Is the stupid fucker still alive?"

"I'm a cop like you, Slater. We took an oath to protect and serve. How long ago did you solemnly swear—"

"Shut the hell up. I don't want to hear that crap."

He should've read Slater's file more carefully, as thoroughly as he'd read Raegen's dossier. Slater had been passed over for promotion. Evidently his pathetic self had failed to make the grade. Or impress Vanderbilt.

"You're a decent cop, Bob. Don't make a mistake now."

"Yeah. Decent, but not good enough. Do you know what it's like to go home every day, knowing your old lady's gearing up to bitch you out because the landlord was nagging her for the rent? Or there's not enough food in the house? Or that the kids need clothes or shoes or lunch money? Huh. Like it was *all* my fault we had a family of six. She's Catholic, not me.

Don't get me wrong. I love Tammy. Love the shit out of my boys, too. She's pregnant again."

Good omen. Family love prevailed in many shaky circumstances. Thaine knew the emotion would ease the tension. He'd never met Slater's wife nor had he seen his boys. "I know taking care of the family is rough."

"Do you? How? You don't have a wife. You don't have kids, but you can buy tailored suits, silk shirts, a bad-ass ride."

"Material junk. You're fortunate to have someone to go home to every day, someone to love and care for." The perfect relationship he'd looked forward to having one day.

"Need dollars. Happiness comes with cold, hard cash. I'm not earning enough ducats from the department to care for my family. They bypassed me again. No promotion. No increase in funds."

"Money doesn't buy happiness, Bob."

"Maybe to you it doesn't. Tammy's happy now. The kids are ecstatic. They don't have to wear hand-me-downs anymore." He grinned. "Kids are the one thing me and Rae have in common. We both love kids. Kind of pulled us together, didn't it, sweets?"

At a quick glance, Thaine saw Slater's thumb caressing her arm. *Bastard.*

"She took my boys to *Waterworld* with her nieces and nephews. She knew I was short on cash." He tightened his arm around her.

Raegen was that kind of woman. Compassionate, a quality that had drawn him to her, kept him within her clutches.

"No more," Slater said.

There was something dire-sounding in that statement.

"Everything was going so well. Then Rae had to stick her nose where it didn't belong. She's good, too, except she was fixated on Simon. Good bait. It worked until you came along, denying Simon was involved, talking trash to Rae, screwing up what I'd worked so hard to get. I'm in deep with the man. Number Two."

"Change it. Get out while you still can, before you ruin your career. You have the chance now. Do it."

"Can't. He knows where I live, knows everything about me and my family. He won't let me walk."

"What about your kids? What do you want them to think when this is over?"

"Funny, my oldest wants to be a cop like his dad."

"Then show what a real cop is, show what you stand for."

"Too late. I'm in too deep. There's no going back."

"You want them to visit you in prison? You want that branded in their mind?"

"No way that will happen. Don't you see? My kids mean everything. You don't mean shit to me."

"Shoot, Thaine," Raegen screamed. "Shoot through me. Kill him."

Thaine flexed his trigger finger.

"He won't take the chance. You know why?" Slater asked. "Quote. Mine. Unquote. Oh, yeah, I was right outside the door. You gave him pussy and refused me. What was it you kept saying? Oh, yeah, booty's off duty." He chuckled. "Well, now you'll both be off duty. I'll take you out, one by one."

"You'll never get away with it," Raegen said.

"Sure, I will. Remember, no one knows our location."

"Vanderbilt does," Thaine put in. Something odd flickered in Slater's eyes. "He'll hunt you down. You won't be able to drag four or five kids around the country hiding out. They'll ask why. What're you going to tell them and your wife? Eventually they'll hear the story about their father and husband who fell from grace, Bob. They'll be ridiculed. Outcasts. They'll hate you for what you put them through for the rest of their lives. Don't let it happen." Thaine remembered Raegen's words. *Lie if you have to.* "Vanderbilt will work with you if you give up. Put the gun down, Bob. It's the best way. The only way."

"Like I said, too late. I'm finished. There's nothing left."

Thaine pressed on since he had Slater's attention. "You're wrong. Give me some names: ringleader, henchman, anybody. We'll get them all. It'll put a plus in your column."

"Can't. They'll take out my family then they'll come after me. No way out." He was sweating now, fearful.

"*Names,* Bob. We can protect your family. We can protect you."

Hand trembling, Slater shook his head hopelessly. "What have I got to lose?"

Take the shot. Slater knew he faced a long prison term for murder. No loving father and husband wanted their family to live in shame.

"Tell my wife I love her. The boys—"

"You tell them."

He cocked the gun.

"Don't do it, Slater. Don't do it. Think of the family." *Take the shot. Take him out,* Thaine chanted silently.

Boom! Boom!

"Raegen!"

12

"Open your eyes, Raegen."

No, she had been in the middle of a luscious dream and the sound of this woman's voice, one she'd heard somewhere before, made her head hurt. Why was this headache so bad?

"Come on, baby. Open your eyes for me."

Ooh, now this sensuous tone wrapped around her like a snug blankie, warm and comfy. She'd rather fall back to sleep, drift into the dream again, snuggle closer to her man. Coax him into making love to her again.

"Raegen, can you hear me?"

She licked her dry lips, swallowed. At least she tried to swallow. Her throat was as dry as parched dirt. "Don't want hear, chickie," she whispered. "Tired. Hurt."

"Dammit, give her something for the pain. I don't want her in pain."

"She's on an automatic drip system, sir."

Drip system? Was she a piece of vegetation, a shrub? Her body didn't seem to be attached. A distant feeling. Numb, except for the damn headache.

"Open your eyes, Raegen."

"Can't. Glued." No amount of effort made her eyelids flutter.

She felt warm fingers curl around hers. Numbness hadn't affected her hand. They were nice hands, smooth, skin softer than her own. Calming. The nerve of this woman. She had big mitts, too. "Bitch, move fucking—"

"Raegen."

And that voice meant business. Why did the very sound of his commanding tone make her nervous, wary, and anxious?

"It's my hand holding yours, little bit."

She felt her arm lift, felt something smooth and soft press against her fingers. His lips? Like the man in her dreams. She must be dreaming still, the reason she couldn't open her eyes. "Tired."

As she drifted into darkness, she heard his fading voice again, trembling this time. "Will she make it?"

She didn't know how long she'd slept, but she was awake now. The headache had subsided to a nagging twinge. Tolerable.

The room they'd put her in was screaming white everywhere. The stench of antiseptics was enough to make her gag. She needed water. Anything. Her throat was way too dry and scratchy.

Then she saw him. His eyes were closed, his head bowed. He held her hand clasped between his, the same soft hands that had caressed her in the dreams.

She started moving her body, making sure everything worked. Achy neck. Sore hand. The needle was attached to a long tube hanging from the half-full IV bag. She wiggled her toes, shifted her legs. All was well and good.

He looked up suddenly. Raegen didn't move, staring. He

was beautiful: thick lashes, sexy lips, brown skin smooth as a baby's behind.

Quietly, he said something she couldn't hear, then kissed her fingers and looked into her eyes again, fluttering her heart. "You're back."

"I didn't know I'd left."

His eyes showed signs of fatigue. Then, a single shimmering diamond slid down his cheek. Raegen caught it with her finger. "Was I in another hospital? You were always in my dreams, always there talking. How could you not be there with me? I heard your voice, heard the pain. Why were you in pain?" She was rambling and glad her own voice was shot, hiding emotional tremors after seeing tears in his eyes. "Sweetcakes, I need a Pepsi."

Laughing and drying his eyes, Thaine said, "I didn't think you remembered me. They said you might have some memory loss."

"I would never forget you. Never." Raegen ran her knuckles over his cheek. "How long have I been stuck in this place?"

"Six of the most horrible days of my life."

She reached up and touched the bandage. "Is there lead in my head? Did the doctor leave it there? Am I bald? I'll kill that man if he shaved my head. I spent way too much money at the beauty shop."

"No, no lead. And you still have hair. Most of it."

"How much is this stay going to cost me? My insurance isn't for shit . . . I mean . . . isn't very good. I bet a fortune. Six days, surgery, doctors, nurses, anesthesia folks, Kleenex. I'm taking everything home because I have to pay for it. Barf bucket, pitchers. Crap, I'll be broke forever. No car. Torched apartment. Hole in my head. Didn't they get enough blood? Can't squeeze it from a turnip."

"Don't worry about anything. It's all taken care of."

"How? They can't touch Richelle's account without my consent, goddammit. I won't let them have it."

"Sssh. Nobody's touching Richelle's savings or any of your money, baby. Don't worry."

For now, she thought, *until they release me from this prison.* Damned credit collectors would crawl over her back within the month.

Thaine toyed with her fingers, kissed each tip, and the monitors hooked up to her body began singing their own tunes.

"I need a kiss right here," Raegen said, tapping on her lips. "You haven't kissed me. Six days."

"Actually, I have many, many times."

"You have? Don't you think I'm ready for a real one while I'm awake?" she asked, grinning.

The door swung open. A doctor and his nurse came storming into the room. Raegen groaned. She didn't need them. She only needed Thaine, but they sent him away.

The doctor went through the discovery ceremony, checking this, that, and the other and asking a drove of questions. *Thirsty,* she told them. The nurse gave her a puny, lemon swizzle stick.

Satisfied with the results of their fifteen minutes of examination, changing the bandage, and taking her temperature, they finally left her in peace.

When Thaine came back, she said, "I need—"

"Forget the Pepsi, doll." He leaned over the bed and laid his lips on hers in a long overdue, sensuous meeting.

Wanting more, Raegen slid her hand behind his head, holding him in place, her tongue dueling with his in a well-deserved ritual. He tasted so, so good. "I need you," she said, drawing his hand to her breast. "We can do a quickie right here. They can watch if—"

"Booty's off duty," Thaine replied and chuckled.

She frowned. "For how long?"

Shrugging, he said, "It's up to the doc."

"Bull . . . baloney. I want out of here."

"We'll go home when they say you can. Your family should be here anytime. Took a while to get in contact. Mom's frantic, everybody is. I'll call again and let them know you're out of danger."

She blinked. Did she hear him correctly? "We? Home?"

"Our home, so I can take care of you."

When he shook his head, Raegen knew he was second-guessing himself. "You did what you had to do, babycakes."

"And Slater's bullet nearly took you away from me. I should've taken him out sooner."

"But, I'm here. In fine shape. Thirsty." It drew a smile. "And horny." Seeing his frown, Raegen sighed. "I know, I know. Booty's off duty."